She was no prostitute...

Even with the hat concealing her hair, and the sunglasses hiding much of her face, and the red lipstick looking dramatic and foreign to her lips, she appealed to him on a bone-deep level.

Trev's continued regard brought a flush to her face, and she turned her head. "The weather's taken quite a turn," she finally remarked. "It's too warm."

"We can roll up the windows and turn on the—" Trev's words broke off and he did a quick double take. She'd shrugged free of her blazer...and she wore no bra.

She settled back onto the seat, smoothed the transparent folds of her dress over her long, lean thighs while her rosy dark nipples strained against the delicate fabric.

The car swerved and veered onto the grassy shoulder. "Why the hell are you dressed like that?" She was naked under that dress!

"What's wrong?" she teased. "Afraid people might think you're with a *naughty* girl?"

Dear Reader,

When I was little, my friends and I frequently played "house" and dolls and other games of make-believe. Even then, my fantasies revolved around romance. Stories like *Cinderella* and *Sleeping Beauty* affected me deeply. Till this day, the idea thrills me that, in a world full of strangers, two people meet and recognize each other as soul mates...and forge an unbreakable bond.

In this story, Trev Montgomery met, loved and lost his soul mate. After seven lonely years, he has vowed to set aside his memories of her, to get on with his life, to open his mind and heart to someone new. The last thing he needs is to meet a woman who reminds him vividly of his late wife—especially considering that this beautiful stranger claims to be a prostitute. If he were honoring his newly sworn vow, he would walk away from this living, breathing reminder of all he'd lost.

But one stolen kiss makes that impossible. One stolen kiss awakens a need and hunger within him that has lain dormant for seven years.

Perhaps the story of *Sleeping Beauty* left more of an impression on me than I'd thought. For our heroine awakens to her prince's kiss, too...much to her dismay.

Hope you feel the wonder of magic and love with every romance you read.

Sincerely,

Donna Sterling

Books by Donna Sterling

HARLEQUIN TEMPTATION

INTIMATE STRANGER
Donna Sterling

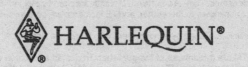

HARLEQUIN®

TORONTO • NEW YORK • LONDON
AMSTERDAM • PARIS • SYDNEY • HAMBURG
STOCKHOLM • ATHENS • TOKYO • MILAN • MADRID
PRAGUE • WARSAW • BUDAPEST • AUCKLAND

I dedicate this book to my editor, Susan Sheppard,
for giving me five wonderful years of
encouragement, support and inspiration.
You make my work a pleasure.

ISBN 0-373-25903-4

INTIMATE STRANGER

Copyright © 2000 by Donna Fejes.

Visit us at www.eHarlequin.com

Printed in U.S.A.

1

STANDING ALONE in the dark on the hotel's pier, the salty tang of the Atlantic misting like ghosts around him, the surf roaring like demons, Trev Montgomery balled his fist around the wedding band he'd just removed. The circle of gold dug painfully into his work-hardened palm.

The ring hadn't left his finger in seven years.

The time had come.

With bleak determination, he drew back his hand and pitched the ring as far as he could. The wind and the sea and the darkness blinded him, deafened him, but he clearly envisioned the glint of gold arcing into the stark black water beyond the whitecaps. Imagined the splash. Felt the cold descent into endlessness.

No sense of liberation rewarded him. No sense of closure. The grief, the anger, the loneliness still rode heavy in his gut.

But the time had come, and he *would* put the past behind him. As of today, he was no longer a married man. He was, officially, a widower. The court had declared Diana dead. A seven-year-long nightmare had drawn to a close. At least, in a legal sense.

It was up to him to draw it to a close in every other sense. He swore to do just that. He would slam the door on the questions that had gnawed relentlessly at him—what had happened to her; how and why she had disappeared without a trace. Logically, he knew she must have been taken and probably killed. Otherwise, she would have come back to him. Emotionally, though, he hadn't been able to give up hope of her return, or cut himself free of their marriage.

He was bone-tired of fruitless hope. He would do whatever it took to turn the page, to begin a new chapter in his life.

Staring blindly into the chill night wind, he told himself that he'd made a good start. He'd left his hometown in southern California—the little suburban valley where he'd met and married Diana. Where they'd lived and loved for four golden months. Where she had disappeared.

This morning, directly after the court had declared Diana dead, he'd left that place of broken dreams, flown to the opposite coast and closed a real-estate deal for the land where he would build the homes he'd designed. He would make his fortune, as well as open his mind and his heart to new people. Eventually, he would heal.

His family and friends back home had been urging him to get on with his life for years now. A few of his female acquaintances had done more than simply urge; they'd insinuated themselves into his personal space with clear intentions of filling the void. He felt an overwhelming compulsion to get away from them, his family and his hometown.

He needed something new. Some*one* new. The time had finally come for his new beginning.

He'd been thinking about building homes in Sunrise, Georgia, from the first time he'd seen it. The scenic lay of the land and the cozy feel of the community would complement his dream homes perfectly. So what if he'd discovered the town when he'd been with Diana, on their honeymoon?

Although the place had retained its beauty and small-town ambience, it had also changed drastically. The luxury hotel where he was now staying hadn't been here then. Exclusive subdivisions were now tucked discreetly into the lush foliage along the rural highways. He'd barely recognized the beach where they'd strolled, now bordered by a golf course rather than wilderness. The seafood shack where they'd stopped for lunch had been replaced by a fashion boutique.

No, the memory of Diana *would not* haunt him here.

Sliding his ringless left hand—a hand that felt naked and bereft—into the pocket of his jeans, he pivoted away from the ocean and strode along the pier toward Sunrise's only high-rise hotel.

Diana was gone. Forever. Ruthlessly, he quelled the grief that always accompanied that thought.

He would begin his new life tonight, without thoughts of her.

The courts had declared her dead. And now he had, too.

JENNIFER HANNAH was breaking one of her own rules—and breaking *any* rule made her nervous. *Don't socialize with co-workers.* Other than the requisite holiday parties, she'd staunchly kept to that principle for the entire seven years she'd been in Sunrise. In fact, she rarely socialized at all. Her social life consisted of noonday friendships with women in her aerobics class, on-line chats with faceless pals and volunteer work with deaf children.

Her job as an account representative for a small but growing company, and her volunteer work, kept her busy enough. Or so she told herself.

But her co-workers had persuaded her to stop by the lounge of the new hotel for a Friday-after-work drink to celebrate the goal they had reached. All the company's temporary workers were placed in offices on long-term secretarial assignments, a fresh crop of promising talent had recently applied, and Jennifer had solicited accounts from businesses in Sunrise, Savannah and Brunswick to keep those new applicants working. Helping Hand Staffing Services was growing by leaps and bounds.

How could she refuse to celebrate the fruits of their teamwork?

As she pushed through the revolving glass doors at the main entrance of the swank hotel, she admitted to herself that she was looking forward to an evening away from her apartment. An evening in the company of friends—or, at least, acquaintances. As busy as she tried to stay, the loneliness always dogged her, especially on Friday and Saturday evenings.

But she wouldn't dwell on her loneliness...or remember the days that had been filled with real friends, genuine laughter and the most heart-thrilling love.

Love. No, she certainly couldn't think about that. Love had been a part of a different life, and someday, when she was strong enough, she would cherish her memories of it. But that time hadn't come yet. The memories only tormented her. Devastated her.

She stopped inside the entrance of the plush lobby to clear her mind, her heart, of the grief pressing in on all sides. *Don't think about a lifetime away from Trev.* The pain of that prospect was still strong enough to destroy her. *Take one moment at a time. Just one moment. Then the next.* She'd gotten through seven years of moments.

Loneliness was, after all, a small price to pay for survival—hers, and possibly his, too.

Collecting herself, she cut through the crowd of people bustling every which way in the massive hotel lobby. Her high heels clicked against the marble floor as she passed by elaborate fountains, tropical foliage, gilded cages with exotic birds, aquariums with colorful fish, glass-bubble elevators that soared upward thirty stories to the top of the domed center. The thought of such cosmopolitan luxury in Sunrise was bittersweet. The hotel afforded the town new employment opportunities. She herself had placed a number of their temps in the offices here. But the hotel also meant commercial growth.

She hated to see Sunrise spoiled by too much "progress." She'd found this quaint little fishing village during her *real* life, and had shared it for a few brief hours with Trev. Couldn't *something* from her past remain the same?

Resolutely quelling the thought, Jennifer headed for the lounge. But then a sign caught her eye: Welcome Montgomery Builders.

Montgomery Builders. How ironic that she'd been thinking of Trev, and then saw a sign bearing his company's name.

That thought stopped her dead in her tracks, and her heart gave a painful little jolt. Montgomery Builders—surely that couldn't be *Trev's* business! No. He worked in California, on the other side of the continent. Not Georgia. He had no reason to come to Georgia. And Montgomery was a fairly common name. There were bound to be dozens of builders in the world with that name.

But the possibility that it *could* be Trev shook her to her soul. What if he was here? What if she actually ran into him? Powerful emotions clashed within her—fear that he would somehow recognize her, and hope—the most blinding, thrilling hope—that she might see him again. Just see him.

No!

That would be breaking the most important rule of all. If "Montgomery Builders" referred to Trev Montgomery, she had to leave, immediately. She couldn't take the chance that she might meet him and that he might see through the changes in her appearance.

But how could he recognize me? And why would he be here?

He had liked the town, she remembered. They'd taken pictures of its scenic spots, and they'd even chosen a site along the beach where they'd build their dream house, if they ever had the money to build it or the desire to leave California.

But they'd only been dreaming. Playing. Talking nonsense, as they so often had.

Trev probably didn't remember their leisurely stop for lunch during their honeymoon road trip down the east coast. Even if he did, he would never work this far away from his home and family.

Paranoia, she told herself. This was just an attack of paranoia, as her relocation inspector had predicted she'd suffer. He'd been right. At the start of her new life, she'd taken a fright more than once, and for less reason than a sign welcoming Montgomery Builders. Paranoia was to be expected when a person was hiding from everyone she'd ever known. In fact, paranoia was one of the most plaguing problems for the surprising number of people in her position.

But what if this wasn't paranoia?

Glancing around at the strangers strolling by her in the massive lobby, Jennifer struggled to think rationally. She would ask the concierge about Montgomery Builders. She needed to know if Trev had come to Sunrise.

If so, she'd have to move away from this town. She'd have to pack up her belongings, find a new home, start all over. She wasn't sure she could do it again. She'd "started over" so many times in her life.

But, oh...to see him again! Even from a distance. Just a glimpse. She'd yearned for so long to see his face, hear his voice. She'd fought the temptation to dial his phone number, just to listen to him say "hello." She never had, of course. She couldn't allow herself even that much leeway.

Her old life could never intersect with her new.

Diana was dead, and Jennifer Hannah knew nothing of Trev Montgomery, or his warm, loving family...or the stirring kisses and passionate lovemaking that still simmered in her blood, in her heart, in the middle of the loneliest nights—

A sudden commotion disrupted her doleful reverie.

"Oh," she cried, throwing out her arms to keep her balance. A leather leash tangled around her ankles, nearly tripping her, as a yapping little Pomeranian darted around her.

"Stop that this instant, Duchess," warbled a prim, white-haired lady who held on to two leashes. "And you, too, Countess. You promised to behave." An identical little dog on an identical leash pranced in the opposite direction, until Jennifer's ankles were wrapped by the two leashes and the dogs scampered in merry circles around her.

The bellman hurried over to tell the woman that pets weren't allowed in the hotel, to which she sharply retorted that these were not her pets, but her *children*. While the two argued, the antics of the frisky little pups and the difficulty of extricating herself from their leashes forced a laugh from Jennifer. When Jennifer had worked her way free of the tangle, the woman apologized to her for "the children's" high spirits—excitement over their vacation, she explained—then snatched the dogs up and stalked out of the hotel under the watchful eye of the irate bellman.

Brushing a few strands of dog hair from her black wool skirt and gray sweater, Jennifer turned toward the concierge desk, still smiling from the misadventure.

And her gaze locked with that of a man who stood across the lobby from her. A tall, tawny-haired man with impressive shoulders beneath a forest-green Henley sweater and a familiar slant to his wide, firm mouth.

The smile froze on Jennifer's lips. The blood drained from her face. Her heart seemed to stop. *Trev.*

It was him! In the flesh. Her husband, her lover. *Her past.* He stared at her with questioning intensity, as if thunderstruck by the sight of her, yet unsure of what he saw. A fierce desire rose in her to cry out his name. Go to him. Throw herself into his arms.

Clusters of people crossed between them, breaking the gaze that had held them both captive. Cold realization then flooded her. She *couldn't* go to him. She had to get away!

He started toward her.

Panic set in, and she did the most foolish thing imaginable. She ran. Blindly. Madly. Through the crowd, down a side hallway, into a maze of back corridors.

"Diana!"

The gruff, frenzied call from a short distance behind her only added to her adrenaline rush. She skidded around a sharp corner, then bolted down a straight-of-way, as fast as she could run in her narrow skirt and high heels.

"Diana, stop!"

How could he have recognized her? Her hair was blond now instead of brown; her eyes were blue instead of green; her nose, chin, mouth and eyelids had been surgically altered. She was twenty-seven, not twenty. She'd gained weight. Grown older. He couldn't possibly recognize her.

But he had.

She turned another corner and saw an obscure exit tucked between vacant conference rooms. Dashing for it, she slammed her hip against the bar that opened the heavy door and pushed through, only to find herself in a gray, concrete stairwell with steps leading both up and down. Seeing only darkness below, she opted for above, hoping to lose him on one of the upper floors rather than brave whatever lay in the dark.

She hurried up the stairs, as the door was flung open behind her.

"Diana!" The shout echoed off the walls, and footsteps clamored behind her.

She reached the door on the next level and shoved against its bar to open it. The door, however, was locked.

Strong hands gripped her shoulders. "What in the hell...?" he growled, whirling her around and pinning her against the smooth, concrete wall. "What in the holy *hell*—?" His angry words broke off and he stared at her, his face only inches from hers—Trev Montgomery, the only man she'd ever loved, the man whose life she could so easily destroy.

His gaze ravaged her face in searing paths, from feature to feature and back again.

She'd forgotten how big he was. How powerfully virile—all strength and sureness and well-honed sinew. His face, deeply tanned from years of outdoor work, had taken on a leaner, harder look, with the angles of his jaw and cheekbones more pronounced. The faint new lines fanning out from the corners of his whiskey-brown eyes and the deepened grooves bracketing his mouth somehow added to his rugged allure. *Dangerous* allure...at least, for her.

"You—you've mistaken me for someone else," she said between ragged breaths, her words nearly inaudible above the thudding of her heart. Careful to speak in the bland, dialect-free voice she had worked so hard to cultivate, she added, "My name's not Diana."

Bewilderment etched a frown across his face. She forced herself to hold her gaze steady, to keep her expression impersonal—not easy when chaotic emotion churned through her. She hadn't expected to ever feel his hands on her again, or inhale his scent, or exchange as much as a single word with him.

Disappointment, bleak and terrible, slowly seeped into his gaze. "You're not her," he whispered. "You're not—" He shut his eyes, and his lips tightened into a thin, white line. The muscles in his strong throat worked slow and hard.

But he didn't let her go or move away from her. It seemed he'd forgotten that he held her—a stranger—pinned against a wall in the stairwell of a hotel. Clearly, he fought a battle within himself, and an ache grew in her chest as she watched him.

She wanted so much to touch him, hold him. Be what he wanted her to be. *Who* he wanted her to be. But she never had been. Not really. And the option of pretending no longer existed.

She should break away from him now, before he had the chance to look more closely, or ask questions. But she couldn't leave him yet. Not quite yet. His pain was so apparent...and she was hurting as much as he.

This would be the last time she'd ever stand this close, or feel his touch. The last time she'd ever see him. Anguish wrung her heart.

"I'm sorry," he finally rasped, opening the golden-brown eyes that had mesmerized her from the very first time they'd connected with hers. "I thought you were...my wife."

His wife. Not *ex-wife*. Her heart gave a gratified pang, even as she wondered at his oversight.

Blinking as if realization of their present circumstances had just dawned, he released his hard grip on her shoulders and eased away. "I didn't mean to scare you. You...you just look so much like her."

"I do?" Surprise had forced the words out of her. She'd taken such pains to change her appearance. How had he detected a similarity?

"And your laugh. That's what first caught my attention. When I heard it, I—" He bit off his words, looking thoroughly disgusted with himself, although his gaze continued to linger on her face. He couldn't seem to help it. "She's been missing for several years."

Missing. What an odd way to put it.

He let out a harsh breath, plowed back a thick lock of his hair with long, tanned fingers and turned away from her, toward the door. More to himself than to her, he said, "I guess I just can't stop looking for her."

A horrifying suspicion gripped her. Hadn't he gotten her letter? She'd explained in it that she wasn't what he'd thought; that their relationship couldn't work; that she would never come back. She'd expected him to divorce her.

The secretary of the U.S. Marshal who had been assigned to her case had sworn to send that letter. Jennifer hadn't been permitted to send it herself. All mail had to go through secured channels. Had the most important letter of her life not been sent?

"What—what happened to your wife?" she asked, knowing she shouldn't converse with him at all.

He stopped near the door and looked back at her, as if debating whether to answer. "I don't know. She left home for an out-of-town writers' conference. Never showed up for it. Never came back."

Jennifer stared at him, horrified. The letter hadn't been sent, obviously.

"She wouldn't have voluntarily left me," he swore with quiet fervor.

A soft, anguished cry rose in her throat, and tears of guilt, regret and loss pushed at the back of her eyes. She *had* voluntarily left him. For his own good. He didn't know that, though. He'd been left to wonder this entire time what had happened to her, to believe that she might come back. *For seven years.*

"I'm...um, sorry," she whispered through a clenched throat. "About your wife."

He stared at her as if she had somehow surprised him. Inwardly she cursed her inability to remain unmoved...and his uncanny ability to perceive her emotions, even when she tried to hide them. He should have taken her apology as a generic expression of sympathy—something anyone might say. And yet, intensity gathered again in his expression.

"I'd better go." She wrenched her gaze away from his and brushed past him toward the stairs. She'd have to return to the lower landing, since the door at this level had been locked.

"Wait a minute." He fisted one hand around the stair railing, blocking her descent with his forearm. He continued to scrutinize her face as he stood unnervingly near. She sensed a new, streetwise cynicism in him—and iron-strong determination. He was, undoubtedly, a man to be reckoned with.

Fear skittered within her. Not of him, but of herself. She'd never been able to refuse him anything. Isn't that why she'd relied on a letter rather than telling him in person about her need to disappear? This new hardened edge he'd acquired somehow evoked a longing within her, making her all the more vulnerable. She wanted to soften that edge. Dispel the cynicism.

"Why did you run?" he demanded.

"R-run?" Had he recognized her after all?

"You saw me, and took off running." He searched her gaze. "Why?"

"I...I..." Her mind drew a blank. What reason could she possibly give for sprinting through a hotel lobby? Desperately she improvised, "I thought you were someone else."

"Who?"

"I don't believe that's any of your business." She heard the slight tremor in her voice and knew that he'd heard it, too. Good. He would never knowingly intimidate a woman. "Now please let me pass."

Amazingly enough, he didn't budge. And his expression didn't soften. That "hard edge" apparently went deeper than she'd thought. "Tell me why you ran."

Diana, the starry-eyed girl she'd once been, would have caved beneath that intensely determined stare. But Jennifer, the world-weary woman she'd become, had acquired a few hard edges of her own. "Do you realize you're holding me *prisoner?*"

A mirthless smile bent his mouth. "I also chased you through a crowded lobby and pinned you against a wall. If you want to accuse me of wrongdoing, there's not much I could do about it now." Before she had time to threaten him, he murmured, "When a woman takes one look at me and makes a mad dash for the exit, I want to know why. Who were you running from, if not from me?"

Why, oh, why had she run? She'd done the exact thing she'd intended not to do—arouse his suspicions. She had to find a way to allay those suspicions, or he could cause terrible trouble. "I thought you were hotel security."

He lifted his brows in surprise. "Why would you run from hotel security?"

The answer—a truly inspired one—came to her from a movie she'd once seen. "I've...um, been asked not to come back here."

"Why?"

She raised her chin. Drew in a deep breath. "If you must know, I'm a working girl. I came to solicit clients." Not too much of a lie. She *had* solicited clients for her firm at this hotel. He didn't need to know that her solicitation consisted of a few visits to the hotel offices to place temporary clerical workers.

His frown deepened. "Are you telling me you're a hooker?" His incredulity couldn't have been more apparent.

"I prefer to call myself a 'professional.'" Realizing that she'd thoroughly dazed him, she took advantage of his momentary lapse and pushed her way past him. Her legs trembled as she descended the stairs and strode toward the door through which she had entered the stairwell.

This door, too, was locked. Was she locked in a stairwell with him, for God's sake?

His footsteps echoed as he descended the stairs behind her. "Problem?"

Reluctantly she released her death grip on the door handle, but she kept her back to him. The less time he spent examining her face, the better. "It's locked. We'll have to check the other levels." She hurried down another flight of stairs, but darkness awaited below.

Darkness had always unnerved her.

Pausing on the landing, she peered down toward the door. A mass of ladders, tools and heavy construction equipment filled the darkened lower landing, barring her way to both the inner and outer door.

"Great," she muttered.

"Good thing there's no fire," he mused from directly behind her. "Maybe they've left one of the doors upstairs unlocked." He turned and led the way up to the level above the one they'd previously tried. Checking the handle, he grimaced and shook his head.

She led the way up the next flight and tried that door. Locked!

"Why would they have a door from the lobby level that opens into a locked stairwell?" she cried, thoroughly frustrated.

"The doors on the upper floors are locked to the outside for security purposes, I'm sure, but the door on ground level should remain open from the inside in case of emergencies." Staring at the mass of heavy equipment below them, he shook his head. "An oversight that needs to be corrected."

"Immediately!" she concurred with heartfelt zeal.

He glanced at her. "Yeah, immediately would be good."

Her breath hitched at the mild amusement glinting in those familiar brown eyes. How often had she dreamed of seeing his gaze lit with just such humor? How often had she longed for the comfort of his large, powerful body, the sweet delirium of his kiss?

She had to get away from him! Abruptly she pivoted to climb another flight of stairs. A sense of futility filled her, though. She could well imagine climbing to all thirty floors—with a double flight leading to each—only to find every door locked.

His hand shot out as she tried to pass him, halting her. "If you don't calm down," he said softly, "you'll hyperventilate before you reach the next floor."

She realized then that she *was* breathing rather heavily—not from exertion, but from panic.

"Sit down." Gently gripping her arms, he seated her on the stairway and settled down beside her. "There's no need to panic. I might have *seemed* like a madman, but I'm really not too far gone. And we won't be trapped here for long."

"How do you know that? With my luck, we'll be here all night."

He reached into the pocket of his jeans and drew out a small cell phone.

Relief forced a slight smile from her. "Maybe my luck's changing. If I have to be trapped in a stairwell with someone, I guess I picked the right guy."

"My luck must be changing, too. I mean, if I have to be trapped in a stairwell with someone—" his stare again took on the intensity that had shaken her "—who better than a beautiful 'professional'?"

Her face warmed. What did he mean by that? Was he coming on to her? Even believing she was a hooker?

"For a professional, you sure do blush easily."

She compressed her lips and glanced away from him, trying to still the pounding of her heart. "Just call for help, will you?"

"Sure. If that's what you want. Hotel security could be here within minutes. That's who would come, you know."

The implications quickly registered, and she glanced at him in dismay. She'd told him that hotel security would know her for a prostitute. She couldn't very well urge him to bring them on...especially since they might recognize her as Jennifer Hannah, the representative from Helping Hand Staffing Services. She'd visited this hotel quite a few times in the past couple of weeks and had chatted with more than one employee in the security office.

She couldn't let Trev know her name or where she worked. She had to break all ties with her past. Just in case he somehow realized her true identity, she would leave no trail for him to follow when she moved. And she needed to use her current employer as a reference during her job search.

The thought of having to start all over in a new town, a new job, filled her with desolation. There was no help for it, though. Trev was in Sunrise, which meant she couldn't stay. The thought of leaving him for a second time made the desolation that much worse.

She shouldn't be with him at all.

He lifted the phone to key in the numbers.

She stopped him by placing her hand over his. "Maybe you can call someone you know, instead of hotel security." She certainly couldn't call anyone *she* knew. The only ones she could think of were co-workers, who'd be sure to give away too much about her. "Do you have friends anywhere nearby?"

"A couple of business associates and their wives came with me from California. They are staying in the hotel, but they're not carrying cell phones. And they drove to Savannah for a night on the town."

Though disappointment tugged at her, she couldn't help digging for more information about him. "You're here on a business trip?"

"For business, yes, but it's more than just a trip. I'll be renting a place here in Sunrise until the house I'm building is ready."

Her heart turned over. He was building a house in Sunrise. "You're moving here...permanently?"

"For a couple of years, at least. My company will be developing a community of homes."

She bet she knew where his personal home would be. They'd picked the site out together. On their honeymoon. Apparently he hadn't forgotten. Apparently he'd been as affected by the place as she.

An almost painful yearning gripped her. How she'd love

to see his home when it was finished. To live there with him, as they'd planned. *Oh, Trev...!*

"What about you?" he asked. "Do you live in Sunrise?"

"Me?" She could barely force words past the ache in her throat. "No. I'm just visiting."

"From where?"

"I travel a lot. Stay on the move."

"But you've been to this hotel in this small town so many times that Security warned you to stay away."

"Yes." She nodded emphatically, hoping the lie didn't sound too improbable. "New hotels like this are very lucrative. You know...lots of traveling businessmen. It's well worth my time to come in from—from the big city," she finished lamely.

Intelligence burned too brightly in his eyes, along with ever-growing curiosity. "I'm Trev Montgomery." He extended his hand for a cordial shake, and she reluctantly complied. She didn't, however, tell him her name, which prompted him to add, "And you are...?"

Resolutely she avoided his scrutiny, allowing her dark blond, shoulder-length hair to fall like a curtain over her face and obstruct his view. "I never give my real name." She twisted her shoulder-strap purse around and clutched it in her lap like a shield. "None of us...professionals give our real names. In our line of work, it's not wise." When he didn't reply, she ventured a sideways glance at him. "Why do you want it, anyway? We should be out of this stairwell soon, one way or another."

"Maybe I'm not ready to let you go."

Warmth and foreboding flushed through her. "Wh-why not?"

"Because you look so damn much like my wife that even now, I can't help staring at you." The fervor in his quiet voice shook her. "If you had a Southern drawl, you'd sound like her, too." He hooked a finger beneath her chin and tipped her face to his. "And you blush just like she does." After a long, hard stare, he quietly amended, "Like she *did*."

She pulled back from his hold and channeled her rioting emotions into blazing indignation. "You can't still believe I'm your wife!"

"No, but I can't believe there's no connection, either. Maybe you're related to her."

"I'm not."

"How do you know?"

"Because I have no family."

"Neither did Diana...or so she thought. But now I'm not so sure she was right about that. You could easily pass for her sister."

Afraid of where his conjectures might lead, she shot to her feet. "You need to get over her," she said in a trembling voice. "If she's been gone for seven years, she isn't coming back."

"Seven years?" Slowly he stood up. "I never told you how many years she's been gone."

Hot dismay flooded her. "Yes, you did. You said she's been missing for seven years."

"I said 'several.'"

"Several?" She swallowed hard. "Oh. I...I misunderstood. My mistake."

He stared at her in a searching, doubting way until her heartbeat pounded in her ears. "But she *has* been gone for seven years."

"Look, mister, I don't know anything about your wife. And I have no family. None."

"And you're a prostitute."

"Yes."

His gaze flickered down the length of her, taking in her conservative gray sweater, narrow black skirt and high heels. "You don't look like one." Lifting one broad shoulder, he qualified that with "Except maybe for the black spiked heels."

"My shoes look like a *hooker's?*"

A wry gleam lit in his eyes. "That upsets you?"

"No!" It did, of course. Shoes were a weakness of hers. She couldn't resist a particularly appealing pair, which she'd considered these to be. "I mean, well, in a way. I...I was trying to blend in with my, um, clientele."

"You don't act like a hooker, either."

She planted a hand on her hip and glared at him. "So, you consider yourself an expert on the subject?" She hadn't meant to sound so tart. But here he was, acting like an authority on prostitutes.

Good Lord...*was* he? They'd been apart for seven years, and she hadn't expected—or wanted—him to remain faithful, but she didn't like to think of him consorting with prostitutes. He'd always been a favorite with women. Half the women in his hometown had been in love with him. He wouldn't need to buy sex.

"Maybe I do consider myself an expert on the subject."

"You've been...*with* hookers?" she asked, trying desperately to mask her shock and disapproval.

His wide, firm mouth slanted, suggesting the start of a rueful smile, though his gaze remained serious and intent. "Now, see there?" He swept the back of his fingers gently down her cheek. "That's the kind of look and tone and question that makes me doubt you're a professional."

His gentleness—and the slow, light sweep of his fingers up the outer curve of her face—was her undoing. Closing her eyes, she rested her shoulders against the wall, savored his touch, and struggled against the urge to give up the fight. To tell him the truth. To hold him again. Love him again.

But she could never, ever do that to him. The truth would only ruin his life. She knew that more certainly now than she had seven years ago. Because back then, she hadn't been sure that he would insist on going with her into hiding. The mere possibility had frightened her into leaving him with only a letter as a goodbye. Now she felt sure that he would have opted to go with her—and leave behind his family, his hometown and the business he'd worked so hard to build.

She couldn't take him away from all that and force him into this dangerous, lonely, fear-riddled life. She couldn't turn him into one of the shadow people.

But, oh, the sensuous stroking of his thumb beside her mouth and the warmth of his nearness evoked a poignant longing within her.

"Why would I lie?" she asked, breathing in the virile scent of his skin and hair.

"I don't know." His thumb slid in a lingering path across her bottom lip, and sensations ricocheted through her. "I don't know who you are or what you're hiding, but I know it's something."

Her eyes opened at that. "No, no...it's nothing. I'm hiding nothing."

His golden-brown gaze connected with hers, probing too deeply. "Then if you *are* a hooker," he said, his breath hot against her face, "how much do you charge for a kiss?"

Desire surged through her at his hoarse question. No other man had ever affected her so strongly. No other man had made her ache for him. "I—I don't...I can't..."

"Put this one on my tab." He tipped her face up and touched his lips lightly to hers. A slow, sensual, wide-eyed greeting. A cautious pronouncement of his intentions. Her lashes dipped at the excruciating sweetness—a sweetness she'd been craving for so long—but her gaze never wavered from his. "And this one." He then slanted his mouth, leaving caution behind, plunging onward in deep, hot exploration.

She clung and flowed and closed her eyes, giving everything she dared. The pleasure lifted her above the pain, and she allowed herself to soar, ever so briefly, above the clouds.

The kiss ended all too soon, leaving her hungry for more. He pressed his slightly abrasive cheek to hers and said in a low, tremulous murmur of awe, "My God, you even taste like her."

The pain returned, more voracious than ever. She had to get away! She moved to pull from his embrace, fearing that if she didn't do so now, she'd never have the strength.

But he only held her tighter. "If you're really a hooker," he whispered against her hair, "come to my room. I'll pay."

Heated yearning coursed through her, along with a profusion of conflicting emotions. He was ready to make love to her, a stranger, a woman he believed to be a prostitute. He was willing to *pay* her. She hated that! And yet, he was willing because he wanted *her*...or rather, the woman he'd once believed her to be. Even that idea tore her in two. She couldn't help cherishing the fact that he still missed her, still wanted her—still remembered the flavor of her kiss—but she wished he'd found peace and happiness.

She'd caused him too much pain.

Didn't she owe him at least a few stolen moments of happiness tonight? Couldn't she allow herself the luxury of one last time with him?

No! Loving him incognito would never bring either of them happiness, even for a moment.

As if sensing her imminent refusal, he groaned, pressed her against the stairwell wall and kissed her again with hot, sweet insistence.

She couldn't break away just yet. She'd been without him for too long. She'd wanted this. She'd wanted *him*...and she would never have another chance. She leaned into him, and her arms came around his neck.

Passion built with stunning swiftness, and when the need grew too great, too frenzied, he broke the kiss and braced his jaw against her temple, his heart thundering with hers, his breathing loud and hard. "I haven't wanted anybody in seven damn years the way I want you."

Anguished love for him burned in her heart. "Because you want *her*."

"Yes," he confessed in a drawn-out whisper, pressing her body harder to his. When she couldn't force a reply through her gridlocked throat, he drew back and peered down at her. Never had she seen such a potent mix of agony and desire. "If you're really a professional, you shouldn't have a problem with that."

But of course, she did. Because she wasn't a professional, and she wasn't the woman he longed for anymore. The pain of all she'd lost, all that could never be, cut her to the quick.

"Stay with me tonight," he said.

"I can't."

He shut his eyes. Buried his face in her hair. Inhaled deeply. Held her tightly. "Why not?"

"Because I can't...*be* the wife you lost."

He went very still. His breathing seemed to stop, as if he struggled to face the truth of that. "If you can't be my wife," he finally replied hoarsely, "then be my whore. And let me pretend whatever the hell I want to."

2

THE SUGGESTION HAD been crude. The need behind it, raw. Desperate. *Be my whore. Let me pretend whatever the hell I want to.*

Wicked desire fired her blood and incited a riot in her heart. But it was his desperation that pushed her beyond caution. Trev Montgomery had never been the needy kind. He'd always been as solid as a rock—for her, for his parentless siblings and his elderly grandmother. He'd been their anchor through every storm. And now he needed *her*...to help him deal with a wound that she herself had inflicted.

How could she refuse him?

How could she refuse herself?

"Only for a little while," Jennifer allowed, surrendering to the heat, ignoring the voice of fear. *You shouldn't be with him.* "I...I can't stay long."

He slid his hands down her arms in a warm, lingering way, then tugged her away from the stairwell wall. "Let's go."

"But we're locked in."

Releasing her, he descended the stairs to the darkened bottom level, pushed aside huge scaffolds, ladders, a compressor and other heavy equipment, and cleared a path to the inside door. He tried the handle. The door opened. He then glanced up to where she stood on the stairs, watching him.

Her lips pursed and one brow arched. "You just now thought of that?"

She looked to Trev like a pretty young schoolteacher de-

manding an explanation from a student for misbehaving—
not like a hooker about to bed a john. She also looked very
much like Diana—albeit seven years older, blonder and
blue-eyed—about to cuff him in the shoulder for some nonsense he'd pulled on her. He would have smiled if possible.
Under the circumstances, it wasn't possible.

His blood coursed in hot, needful currents, and his head
spun. How could a woman look, sound, even *taste*, so much
like Diana, yet not be her?

Or was he finally losing his mind, giving in to the grief,
launching over the edge that had yawned before him for
seven long years? That had to be it. He'd lost his mind. Not
only was he seeing Diana in this woman, but he refused to
believe she was a prostitute. He hadn't expected her to agree
to come to his room. Now that she *had* agreed, he didn't believe she would go through with it. He wouldn't believe it
until she actually exchanged sex for money.

He realized that he'd been silently staring at her for too
long. A troubled look had flickered over her face—a face that
was technically more beautiful than Diana's, with every en-
dearing imperfection of Diana's smoothed away. This
woman had a smaller, straighter nose; a more classically
feminine chin; a cleanly chiseled jawline; a fuller bottom lip.

She descended the stairs and passed by him, treating him
to a subtle whiff of a floral, citrus scent. It brought to mind
the fragrant steam that had lingered in the bathroom after
Diana had bathed. And the hot, sensuous showers he'd
taken with her. The scent of her skin, her hair. *Diana's soap.*

But it had been seven years. Was his mind suggesting similarities that didn't exist?

He followed her past darkened storage rooms and into an
elevator, where he pressed the fifth-floor button and settled
beside her. They didn't speak or touch, but he couldn't stop
staring at her, studying her, absorbing her nearness like a
freezing man absorbs warmth from a flame. And though she

didn't look at him, he sensed her heightened awareness. Hot, intensely sexual awareness.

Giving in to the need to touch, he brushed back the heavy wave of hair that had drifted over her face. The dark blond silk sifted through his fingers, evoking a hauntingly familiar pleasure. Diana's hair had been short, dark and spiky in places, but the silky thickness had felt the same.

"What should I call you?" he asked in a voice thick with need.

Slowly, hesitantly, she raised her gaze to his. "Jen," she whispered. "Call me Jen." An answering need shone in her eyes. Familiarity again stroked him.

His desire surged. His body hardened. He curled his hand around her nape and drew her closer, luxuriating in the satiny feel of her skin. Would she change her mind and leave him before they reached his room? Did he hope she would, or wouldn't?

Conflict tore at him. He wanted her—no doubt about that. He wanted to kiss her, feel her, make love to her. He wanted her with the same physical, almost chemical, intensity that he'd wanted Diana, from the very first time he'd met her. But he didn't want her to make love to him for money.

More proof that he'd lost his mind. Was there any chance in hell that she wasn't a prostitute, but a woman driven beyond her usual ethics by the potent sexual charge between them? Slim chance. Crazy to even hope for. But the hope stubbornly burned along with the desire. If nothing else came from this encounter, he needed at least to know if she was what she'd claimed—a prostitute.

The elevator stopped. The doors swung open. Trev held his breath, wondering if his mystery lady would accompany him the rest of the way to his room, or if she'd utter some excuse and remain on the elevator. Expecting the latter, he slid his hand to the small of her back and urged her into step beside him.

She didn't resist. They walked from the elevator and down the long, red-carpeted corridor to his room. Would she find a reason to leave him at his door?

He hooked his arm around her narrow waist and held her close as he unlocked the door. He felt her stiffen. Sensed her hesitation.

He turned to her, drew her into the shadows of a dim, lamp-lit room. "It's okay," he murmured. As much as he hoped that she wasn't a prostitute, he couldn't bear the thought of her walking away from him. Sexual anticipation drummed in his head and chest and loins with a savage, driving beat. "Nothing to worry about."

He closed the door behind them, and his own assurance echoed mockingly in his ears. *Nothing to worry about.* She had everything to worry about. She was alone in a hotel room with a stranger. A stranger who intended to strip her naked and take utter possession of her body. What woman wouldn't worry?

A well-seasoned prostitute.

But he'd felt her hesitation. Did it mean anything?

He gripped her slender shoulders, the plush cashmere of her dove-gray sweater reminding him of her elegance, her refinement. His muscles tensed from the battle that raged in his chest. God help him, he wanted her, here and now. But if she wasn't a prostitute, he didn't want to hurry her into something she'd regret. Then again, why would she lie? Why should he question her claim?

Never had he been more confused. "If you've...changed your mind," he forced himself to say, "that's okay. We can just have a drink. Talk. Or go out for coffee—"

"I haven't changed my mind."

The ardor in her husky whisper trapped the breath in his lungs. Her gaze stunned him even more. Her smoke-blue eyes blazed with the most arousing desire and tenderness. *Tenderness.* And, oddly enough, sadness. Why? What was she thinking, what was she feeling, that generated such a gaze?

Sympathy, because he grieved for his wife? No. Something deeper, he swore.

Whatever caused it, the look infused him with a profound ache. A profound wanting. He suddenly wasn't sure he could take this any further. Torn in two and feeling desperate, he caressed her face, her hair. Drank in her intensity. Wished she didn't affect him quite so deeply—

"Have you changed *your* mind?" she whispered, searching his gaze, probing ever deeper, closer and closer to the wellspring of pain.

He couldn't answer. His own conflicting emotions choked him. But then she took his face between her hands and gazed at him with such tender longing that low, gravelly words scraped out of his throat before he even realized he was speaking. "I was...alone...for five years. *Five years*. And then, in the past two, I...tried. But sometimes having sex was worse than being alone."

He hated admitting as much. Didn't know why he had, especially to a stranger. He certainly didn't expect her to understand. He himself didn't fully understand. No matter how beautiful the woman or how arousing the activity, he often reached a point before completion when a sense of wrongness dulled the pleasure. A sense of disappointment and loss. He always forced himself to finish, sometimes without climaxing. Even when he *had* climaxed, the sex had left him feeling empty. More alone. Less able to ward off the grief.

Why had he thought this time would be any different? His attraction to this woman *had* to be based on his feelings for Diana. He'd picked her out of a crowd because of their striking similarities. But those similarities would take him only so far. When he ran across the differences—and there were bound to be plenty, even if he didn't consciously recognize them—the disappointment and loss might hit him harder than ever.

He wasn't sure he was ready for that.

She seemed to read his thoughts. A surprising sheen slowly filled her eyes, and her whisper sounded strangled. "Then just hold me." She slid her arms around him and melted against him, submerging him in her vibrant warmth, her lush softness. Her achingly familiar scent. "Hold me."

His arms came around her, pressing her closer. He shut his eyes, buried his face in her hair and gave in to the sweet, overpowering pleasure. The thought flitted through his mind that if she *was* a prostitute, she was very, very good at her job. But that idea bothered him too much, so he shoved it away. If she intended to charge him, he didn't want to know.

Because as he held her, savored her softness and scent, desire coursed through him in stronger currents than before, washing away all caution. He wanted her, even if he had to buy her. Wanted to live the fantasy she'd created with her tender, passionate gazes, touches and whispers. He wanted to feel that tenderness and passion *for her*.

She turned her face into the curve of his neck, and her lips grazed him. His body throbbed in immediate response. She groaned ever so slightly. *Moved* ever so slightly—an almost imperceptible thrusting of her breasts, tilting of her hips. He clenched his teeth, gripped her hips and lifted her against his hardness.

Her groan was louder this time, her movement more pronounced—a definite rocking of her pelvis that sent pleasure shooting through him. "Shut your eyes," she breathed against his ear, "and pretend whatever you want to."

Yes. Yes, he could do that.

Better yet... He reached for the lamp. Plunged the room into darkness. A cry of surprise escaped her, and her arms tightened around his shoulders. As if he'd startled her with the darkness. *She'd* always been afraid of the dark. *She'd* always held him tighter in the dark.

But this wasn't Diana.

Maybe *he'd* been the one to tighten their hold, forcing that startled little cry from her. He didn't have time to think about it now. Didn't *want* to think now. She felt too good in his arms, and the fantasy beckoned with too sweet a promise.

He pulled her down onto the bed with him and lay beside her, face to face, heart to heart. He ran his hands up and down her slender back, beneath her sweater, savoring the softness of her skin, the shapeliness of her shoulders. His hands flowed lower, over her hips and the soft wool of her skirt, around her tight, neat bottom, pressing her body to his.

Mmm. A perfect fit.

His temperature spiked as she answered with slow, sensuous undulations and long, meandering caresses—beneath his shirt, up his back, across his shoulders, down to his hips.

She made him feel so right. So exactly right.

With no effort at all, he found her mouth in the darkness, and deeply, hungrily, kissed her. Ah. The taste and textures he'd been craving.

He let the fantasy flow.

Not that he deliberately pretended she was Diana. He wouldn't do that to himself. But he didn't try to block thoughts of her, either. When sensations conjured up her face, he didn't try to replace it with another. He allowed himself perfect freedom, without his usual regard for fairness toward the woman he held.

The experience seemed surreal—a journey beyond reality. Her kisses alone kept him soaring through time and space, closer and closer to the sun, until the heat became a living thing within him, demanding more sustenance.

He moved to her delicate jaw and throat, delirious with the taste of her. When her sweater got in his way, he lifted it over her head. She liberated him from his shirt. Unbuckled his belt. He unhooked her bra. Tugged it off her. They worked silently, urgently, with unity of purpose, divesting each other of all clothing. No awkwardness, no struggles. Easy, fluid motions...as if they'd danced this dance together a hundred times before...

When he rolled her panties down her long, long legs, and she kicked the wispy silk away, he ran both hands with reverent pleasure up her calves, her thighs, her endlessly pleasing body—then fiercely pulled her against him. Naked, breathing hard, their hearts thundering, they melded together for wild, delving kisses. Possessive caresses. He couldn't get enough of her to appease his growing hunger.

He broke away from her mouth and kissed a steamy path to her breasts, cupping them in his palms. Her nipples puckered and beaded between his lips—from blossom-soft to pebble-hard. Each suckling tug drew a moan from her, rousing him into a fever.

But then a difference intruded on his consciousness. Her breasts felt fuller, he noticed. Heavier in his hands. He realized then that he'd overlooked another difference—her entire body was more voluptuous, every curve rounder. Diana had been leaner. More angular.

He didn't welcome the realization. Didn't want to compare. But the memories were there, ever-present, reminding him of what he'd lost. *Whom* he'd lost.

Her fingers tangled painfully in his hair, distracting him. Her body moved beneath his. Her back arched. Her lush, hard-tipped breasts pushed against his face. A little too rough. Too presumptuous. At least, for a stranger. "Trev," she whispered on a throaty, tormented moan. *"Trev."*

The sound of his name whispered just so reached deep inside his gut. *Trev.*

A demand. A plea. More...she wanted more...wasn't ready for him to stop. He recognized that plea all the way to the core of his heart. He'd heard it many times—when he'd purposely provoked it. He knew how to answer. Knew how to prod her into uttering it again. A simple matter of teasing...and then slow, deliberate fulfillment...until she trembled beneath him with even greater need.

He wanted her trembling. Gasping. Flowing like hot silk around him. Oh, how he wanted that.

Heat rushed through his veins as he set about it. A little rougher than before. A little more demanding. Ah, but she was greedy, taking all he offered and goading him farther with seductive gyrations. He reached between her legs, burrowed through hot, moist curls. Worked his fingers with slow persistence. She bucked and arched with breathy little groans deep in her throat.

So right. So very right.

And while he gloried in the heat, adrift on the feel and scents and sounds of her, she stoked his fire with intimate strokes of her hand. Distracted him elsewhere with the heat of her mouth. Turned the tables on him, threatening his control.

Panting with rapacious need, he reached for his wallet and found a condom. She kept his heart thudding with hot, teasing nips at his ear; lingering kisses down the side of his neck; wicked caresses along his most sensitive areas—and with just the right touch and motion to drive him steadily out of his mind. As if she knew all his "hot buttons" and exactly how to press them.

Hell, yes. She knew.

She drove every thought from his head but one: to take her, *now*, with long, hard thrusts, until he lost himself deep within her. He laid her against the pillows, kissed her with desperate hunger, folded her legs around his hips and pushed into her.

The heat, the tightness, immobilized him. Electrified him. Robbed him of breath. Incredible tightness. Incredible pleasure. Rivers of it, coursing through him. He shut his eyes, gritted his teeth and lunged again. The pleasure intensified. She gasped and moaned his name, and the sounds penetrated his very soul. *So damn right.* He moved to the rhythm of his coursing blood. She slung her hips to meet every thrust.

The urgency grew. Though he couldn't read her face in the dark, he sensed that she needed this as much as he. The knowledge enflamed him all the more. He rose to his knees, gripped the underside of her thighs. Drove solidly into her. She angled her legs higher around his waist and propelled him deeper...and deeper still...ah, *yes*...

Sweat dripped into his eyes, sizzled down his face. The intensity of sensation awed him. He tried to hold back. Tried to make it last. But her cries were building to a crescendo, and her inner muscles began to pump him in strong, rippling contractions. Her climax launched him into one of his own. A stunning, searing catharsis. An endless explosion of heat and lightning and keen sensation. He couldn't see, couldn't breathe. Could only feel...and savor...and ride the white-hot spears of pleasure.

Like an ash floating to the earth after a midair explosion, it took a good long while before his senses filtered back and any semblance of thought formed in his mind. Even then, it was more of a gut-level compulsion than a rational thought, spurring him to lock her tightly in his arms.

More. He had to have more of her.

He couldn't let her get away from him.

NO MORE. She could allow herself no more. She had to get away from him. Never had that realization been harder to face than now, while she lay in his strong, hot, muscular embrace, her body sated from their lovemaking, her every nerve glowing and pulsating from the intensity of her climax.

Holding him, loving him, filled her with too fierce a tenderness. If she stayed for even one more kiss, she'd become hopelessly ensnared in her emotions. She'd look for excuses to stay longer. To sleep with him. Become a part of his life again. Soon she'd be striving with every fiber of her being to become the very center of his life.

Trev Montgomery had always had that effect on her.

But she couldn't give in to those impulses. The danger to her—and him—could not be ignored. She forced herself to remember in torturous detail the fear she'd lived with as a child; the tragedies she'd known; the deaths she'd seen; the threats made against her and everyone she loved. The lies she'd told Trev. The truths she'd concealed. The vows she'd made in exchange for protection.

If she was seen with him, that protection could be withdrawn.

If she was recognized, she could be killed.

If he was known to be her "loved one," he could be killed, too.

Why had she risked coming to his room? She must have been crazy! But as he nibbled at her neck and murmured something low and gruff against her skin, the depth of her reaction reminded her of why she'd abandoned all caution. She simply couldn't resist the man.

That fact frightened her.

She had to leave. Immediately.

And never see him again, or speak to him. Or hear his voice. Or feel his touch. Or taste his kiss. The thought broke her heart all over again. She couldn't think about the incredible love they'd just made, or the loneliness they'd both been suffering for so many years. Or the loneliness she would continue to suffer.

She had to leave. Focusing only on that, she pulled away from him. Or at least, tried to.

He tightened his embrace. "Where you going?"

She closed her eyes and prayed for strength. "Bathroom."

He kissed her ear, then rimmed it lightly with his tongue, provoking showers of hot sensation. "Hurry back."

Slipping out of his embrace—away from the heat and feel and scent of him—she swung her legs over the edge of the bed and sat up. *You must do this. You must leave. And you can't let him stop you.* She turned on the bedside lamp and searched for her clothing, which lay scattered about on the floor.

"You won't be needing your clothes for quite some time yet," he drawled, obviously watching her. "I'm already getting my second wind."

Her throat was too tight to offer a reply. Refusing to meet his gaze, she continued snatching up articles of her clothing on the way to the bathroom.

"Jen?" he called after her, sounding perplexed.

She locked the bathroom door behind her and dressed as quickly as she could, trying not to think about the man waiting in bed for her. If she gave him even a sliver of thought, she'd never be able to leave him.

She had to think about the route she would take to leave the hotel—a side entrance, maybe, to avoid being seen by the co-workers she hadn't met in the lounge as she'd planned, or the hotel employees who might recognize her as she sneaked out of a hotel room. Paranoid she might be, but she didn't welcome questions or suspicions of any kind. Whether she liked it or not, her main goal in life had to be maintaining a low profile.

"Jen, are you getting dressed?" Trev asked from outside the bathroom door.

She fastened her bra, then pulled her sweater over her head. "Yes."

"Why?"

"I, um, have to leave." Hastily she stepped into her skirt and zipped it up.

Blindly, then, she stared into the mirror, until her image

gradually formed and she combed trembling fingers through her tangled hair.

Silence answered her.

She'd have to face him in person, of course, before she could leave the room. *Please, Trev, just let me go. Don't make this harder than it already is.* She smoothed her narrow black skirt, stepped into her high-heeled shoes, and braced herself for the task ahead. She would grab her purse from wherever she'd dropped it, utter a calm "goodbye" and head for the door.

And open that door. Walk through it. Never look back. *God help me.*

"It's early," Trev was saying from just outside the bathroom. "Just past ten. Stay a while longer." In a huskier voice, he added, "We're not finished yet."

A pang of longing pierced her. If only that could be true. "I can't stay."

Again, silence.

Swallowing a sudden rise of tears, she struggled to force a calm she didn't feel. It was imperative that she present an impersonal face to him. Only when she'd sufficiently quelled the threat of tears did she open the bathroom door.

After a few determined strides into the bedroom, she stopped dead at the sight of him.

He stood beside the rumpled bed where they'd just made love, his broad, tawny-haired chest, powerful shoulders and rippling biceps glistening by lamplight as he pulled his faded jeans up and over his lean, bare hips. His hair, cropped in short, thick layers around his somber face, gleamed in sexy disarray. His strong, square, capable hands—now occupied in zipping up his jeans—brought to mind the fires he'd so recently set in her blood.

He was so damn beautiful, she had to choke back tears again.

She'd thought she'd felt a new breadth and hardness to his

chest and shoulders, but she hadn't been able to see him in the dark. He looked, if possible, even better than he had seven years ago. His body, still lean and deeply tanned from his work outdoors, was certainly more muscular. He'd apparently been laboring hard, alongside his construction crews.

How she longed to hold him. Just one more time. A brief hug before she left. She couldn't, of course. Or she'd never go. *Find your purse. Get the hell out of here.*

She spotted her purse on the bedside table behind him. A mild sense of surprise nipped at her. Had she set it there? She didn't believe so. She thought she'd dropped it on the floor near the door.

Regardless of how her handbag had come to be sitting on that bedside table, she had to retrieve it. Stealing herself to venture near him as he reached for his sweater that lay draped over the bed, she held her breath and moved past him. His heated male scent assailed her, went to her head like the finest brandy. She bit down on her cheek in her struggle to remain aloof.

One kiss goodbye. Just one last kiss...

She looped the purse strap over her shoulder, tucked the leather handbag beneath her arm and resolutely headed for the door.

He shifted into her path, still shirtless, shoeless and heart-stoppingly male. "If you have to go, I'll walk you to your car." His voice was gruff and intimate, his gaze direct, as he held his sweater between his hands. "Just give me a minute to finish getting dressed."

Her heart turned over. He was such a caring man. A good, decent, caring man...whom she loved beyond all reason. "Thank you, but that won't be necessary."

"I insist."

Her knees went weak at the intensity again simmering in his keen, amber-eyed stare. The man had a way of letting a woman know he wanted her—even without a touch or a word. She'd never been able to resist his silent beckoning.

One night. Just one full night. The temptation called to her with devastating pull. His gaze lowered to her mouth. She drifted closer, hungering.

But, no! She had to resist.

She jerked back and smothered an anguished cry.

"Tell me what's wrong, Jen," he implored. "What did I say, what did I do—"

"It's nothing like that. It's not you." She squeezed both her hands around the purse strap, feeling sick with frustration and anguish. "You were...everything good. Everything wonderful." She choked on the last word and wrenched her gaze away from him, needing to put an end to the torment.

. He trailed her to the door, pulling his sweater over his head and shoulders as he walked.

She halted with her hand on the doorknob. "No, please, don't follow me." The misery was seeping into her heart, making it difficult to think clearly. She had to stop him from wanting her. It was then that she remembered the role she played. "You don't have to walk me to my car. I won't be leaving the hotel just yet." How she hated the lie she was about to tell! "I...I have another appointment."

He drew his brows together as if he didn't quite understand. "Another appointment?"

Had he forgotten that she was, allegedly, a prostitute? She herself had forgotten for a while. Compressing her lips to stop their trembling, she held his questioning gaze. "Another *client.*" The rest of her words eeked out on a whisper. "He's been waiting."

Incredulity gathered on Trev's face as the meaning of her words sank in. Clearly he didn't believe her. Or rather, didn't *want* to believe her.

For both their sakes, she had to make him believe. "Which reminds me." She swallowed a great swelling in her throat and forced a stiff smile. "You, um, owe me." Her heart thudded so loudly she could barely hear her own words. How much to ask for? Twenty? Fifty? A hundred? Having no idea how much a prostitute would charge, she strove for moderation. "That will be fifty bucks."

He continued to simply stare. Oh, but the quality of that stare gradually changed, and her very heart flinched at the difference. Gone was the heat, the longing, the determination—even the astonishment. It seemed that a shield had lowered to conceal whatever it was he now felt. A cool, hard shield that effectively shut her out.

In the cold. The bitter cold. The pain was too great. She had to leave.

It wasn't until she opened the door and turned to leave that she realized he'd extended his hand. At first, she thought he had reached for her, and some of the pain abated. Impossible though it was, she longed for him to somehow stop her from leaving. A wound gaped in her heart that only he could heal.

But then she realized he wasn't reaching for her. He was merely handing her something. *Money.* Crisp, green bills.

She took them. Crinkling them into her fist, she turned sharply away from him. He didn't stop her, or follow her, or utter a single word. She strode from the room with seriously clouded vision. Step after purposeful step, she kept on until she'd reached a widening in the corridor—the elevator bay. Blindly she punched the down button.

Only when she stood in the elevator safely alone did she allow herself to breathe—a loud, gulping breath, then another. She'd done it. She'd left him again. Slipped out of his life, into the night, to meld with the darkness like a shadow. Which, indeed, she was. A faceless, nameless shadow. A void.

She hoped he hadn't seen the tears.

3

TREV KEPT HIMSELF brutally busy all weekend.

Saturday morning he met with his attorney to tie up details of the land purchase, then worked through lunch with his project foreman. He interviewed subcontractors until late afternoon, when he stopped to tour the property with his landscape consultant. That evening, he dined with business associates at a reception held on their behalf by his real estate agent.

He spent Sunday with the same real estate agent, Melinda Gregory, in search of a house to rent until he'd built his own. Melinda, a buxom brunette with large, dark, bedroom eyes, left no doubt that she'd welcome his personal attention. He gave it serious thought as she drove him back to his hotel that Sunday evening. Why shouldn't he take her up on her unspoken offer? He was officially a single man now, and she was an attractive woman with an earthy sophistication that appealed to him. Best of all, she wasn't a prostitute.

A prostitute.

The thought jarred him with an unpleasant rush—and sent his mind veering down the very path he'd been trying to avoid all weekend. He didn't want to think about prostitutes, or the woman he'd foolishly taken to his bed Friday night.

He had no excuse for his behavior. He'd bought sex. Guilt swamped him at the memory of handing her money. He didn't approve of women selling their bodies or men exploiting them. What the hell had he been thinking, then, when he'd asked her to his room? He hadn't been thinking at all.

He'd been too busy *feeling*, and reacting to her resemblance to Diana. His emotions had blinded him. Duped him.

Despite her claims, he hadn't believed she was a prostitute. He'd gone by his gut reaction that she was, for some unknown reason, lying. He'd actually believed that she had come to his room because of a profound need for him. He'd wanted to understand that need, as well as assuage his own. How could he have been so green?

She'd simply been doing her job.

My God, he'd actually compared her in bed to Diana. The very idea now seemed sacrilegious. As arousing as the sex had been, a bought-and-paid-for coupling couldn't possibly have compared to lovemaking with his wife.

It couldn't possibly.

Yet, for the last two days, he hadn't stopped thinking about it. While he'd signed forms presented by his attorney, the sight of his own hand moving across the paper reminded him of when it had moved along warm, lush curves. While he'd sipped coffee at the meeting table, he'd flashed back to the taste and heat of her mouth, silky and sweet. During his tour of the property, the dark, ash-gold sand of the beach and the smoky-blue of the ocean had brought to mind her hair and eyes.

And now, as Melinda Gregory allowed her dress to ride high on her thighs while she guided her Mercedes along a scenic stretch of highway, he thought about another pair of legs, wickedly long and shapely. Legs he'd folded around his hips while he thrust hard and deep....

He shifted his unseeing gaze away from Melinda. He couldn't keep doing this—operating in a daze, reliving the heat of that illicit lovemaking. His body still felt sexually charged, as if a beast within him had been sleeping for seven years, but was now awake and voraciously hungry. Sex was on his mind, in his blood.

In a way, it felt damn good. He'd been dead to true desire

for too long, and now the vitality was back. Best of all, the object of those thoughts wasn't a ghost from his past, but a real, flesh-and-blood woman.

He suppressed a self-derisive laugh. She was real, all right. A real prostitute.

Maybe he *should* take advantage of Melinda's availability. Maybe a night with her would erase the images and sensations that had imprinted themselves too deeply on his psyche.

When Melinda turned her Mercedes into the parking lot of the luxury hotel, however, Trev thanked her for showing him the rental houses and promised to be in touch. He then retired to his room. Alone.

The frustrating fact was, he didn't want Melinda Gregory.

Shaken by his inner turmoil—and the sensual memories that assailed him when he entered his hotel room—he ordered dinner from room service, poured a double shot of Jack Daniel's and turned on the television. He soon found himself ignoring both the drink and the Sunday night movie.

He'd made love to a beautiful stranger here Friday night, in the very place he now rested. Her hair had fanned across this pillow as she'd writhed beneath him. He could almost smell her scent, feel her body heat. Taste her skin.

Muttering an oath, he took his wallet from his pants pocket, drew out a business card and studied it. Guilt jabbed at him. He'd taken the card from her purse Friday night. When he'd realized she was dressing in the bathroom, preparing to leave, he'd been seized with an urge to somehow hold on to her. Not to let her out of his sight. Impossible, of course. As well as insane. At the very least, though, he had to know her name. Her real name—not the one she'd manufactured on the way to his room. From her driver's license and business cards, he'd been somewhat gratified to learn that she hadn't outright lied.

Jennifer, her name was. Jennifer Hannah, Account Representative, Helping Hand Staffing Services.

He almost snorted. *Helping Hand Staffing Services.* What a name. He was surprised that the card listed an actual street address rather than just a phone number, but he supposed there were hundreds of prostitution rings across the country masquerading as escort, dating or "staffing" agencies.

He hated to think of Jennifer working for one. What had happened in her life to bring her so low? And why, if she needed money that damn much, was she charging only fifty bucks? Even he, a greenhorn when it came to prostitutes, knew that fifty dollars was too inexpensive for a woman of Jen's looks and elegance, especially at a luxury hotel.

Tossing back a swallow of whiskey, he rose from the bed and paced. The money wasn't the only thing that confused him. She was obviously good at her work. She'd had him believing that only desire motivated her. She'd possessed uncanny knowledge of his likes, his needs—how to rile him into a heat greater than any he'd known since Diana. This expertise with a man she'd never met before smacked of vast experience as a prostitute.

But other things made him doubt her experience. Not only the low price she'd asked, but also the emotion that had churned just beneath her surface. At first, he'd read it as sexual need—and an oddly passionate tenderness. When she'd been preparing to leave, her passion had turned to misery. Regret. Possibly even fear. She'd been so upset that she'd almost left without charging him.

Another oddity was the fact that she'd lied. She'd told him that she had another client to see at this hotel. He'd been shocked and appalled to think she would leave his bed to go to another man. After she'd left, he'd wandered out onto the balcony of his room to suck in clearing draughts of cool night air, and calm himself. That's when he'd caught sight of her in the parking lot below, hurrying to her car.

She'd obviously made up that excuse to leave him. She'd been desperate to get away. Why?

As he mulled over the perplexities, only one reasonable explanation came to mind. Talented though she was in the bedroom, she was new to the job. The low price, her initial hesitation, the fear he'd sensed from her. And then the misery. The regret. The lie. The tears that she'd tried so hard to hold back. It all fit.

But if she was new to the job, why had she run when she'd mistaken him for hotel security? She couldn't have been barred from the premises if she'd just begun her solicitations. Then again, an experienced prostitute probably wouldn't have panicked, while a rookie might overreact at attention from hotel authorities.

Could he have been her first john? If so, she hadn't technically been a prostitute until he'd paid her that money. By accepting it, she'd become one.

Regret tore at his insides like claws.

If it hadn't been me, it would have been someone else. That reflection brought no comfort. Perhaps she would have changed her mind with someone else. Had he hurried her into a transaction that she later regretted?

And how potent was her regret? Strong enough to prevent her from pursuing her nighttime career? He sure as hell hoped so. The thought of her selling herself sickened him.

He had to stop thinking about her. Just because he'd slept with her once didn't make her his concern. She'd refused to even tell him her full name. Their interlude together was over.

With his muscles tensed in painful knots, he finished his drink, took a long, hot shower and went to bed. But her image followed him into his dreams, where he transformed from her john into her pimp, selling her on a street corner, pushing her into a mob of leering, pawing men, while she struggled to contain her anguish.

He woke before dawn drenched in sweat. He couldn't stand to think of her selling herself, or the possibility that he had given her a push down this road.

The dream also had brought up another concern. Did she work for a pimp? Though he knew little about the subject, his perception of pimps centered around savage, ruthless men exploiting women as sex slaves. Could the fear he'd sensed in Jen have to do with a pimp?

I have no family, she'd said. Was she alone in the world, and at the mercy of someone evil?

By the time he had shaved and dressed, Trev realized one inescapable truth. He couldn't forget Jennifer Hannah. Even if it were possible, he couldn't turn his back on the anguish he'd sensed in her. He couldn't ignore the tears he'd seen brimming in her eyes.

He had to try to help her.

THE PHONE CALL Jennifer had been waiting for all weekend came early Monday morning. Calling on a secured line from a U.S. Marshal's office, Dan Creighton, her security supervisory inspector, cut to the point. "Why do you want to move, Jennie? I thought you liked Sunrise."

"Oh, I do," Jennifer assured him, knowing that he took personal pride in the progress his charges made toward establishing reasonably happy lives with their new identities. "But I, uh..." She hesitated, wishing she didn't have to lie to this caring, fatherly man. "I saw a woman who went to high school with me back in New Orleans." She'd decided on this falsehood as the safest way to keep Trev's name out of the U.S. Marshals Service's paperwork. She'd gone to extreme lengths from the very start to keep his name out of their files, away from prying eyes and possible information leaks. "I don't remember the woman's name, but—"

"Did she recognize you?" Dan cut in, immediately concerned.

"No. I don't believe she even saw me. She was walking her dog past my apartment complex, though, which makes me believe she lives in the neighborhood. A few days later, I saw her again in the grocery store."

For the next half-hour, they discussed the likelihood of the woman seeing through the alterations in Jennifer's appearance and the need for another name change. They talked about her decision to move and her choice of destinations, which she'd been researching on the Internet all weekend. In the end, Jennifer convinced Dan that her cover had not been blown, which allowed her to keep the name Jennifer Hannah and the job references she valued so highly. She also gave her preference of destinations as St. Paul, Minnesota—far away from her hometown of New Orleans *and* her subsequent home of Southern California. She knew no one in Minnesota.

"Let me do a little research into the players involved in organized crime in the St. Paul area, Jennie," Dan said. "If your enemies aren't active there, I'll put the paperwork through and you can be on your way by the end of the week. Until then, lie low."

Lie low. Her life's motto.

She left for work in a grim frame of mind. She hated the prospect of leaving the town she now considered home, the job she thoroughly enjoyed and the volunteer work with the deaf children whom she'd come to care so much about. But she had no choice. Trev now lived in Sunrise. She couldn't stay.

And she couldn't allow herself to think about him. The pain of leaving him again had grown intolerable since Friday night. She'd made it through the weekend by focusing obsessively on her research for possible destinations.

She could, at least, be thankful that Trev hadn't realized her true identity as Diana. Otherwise, she'd have had to leave town immediately, choose a new name, wait for new identification papers and find a job in a new town—without the benefit of job references.

For all the help the U.S. Marshals Service provided to its protected witnesses—identification documents, job training, money, educational credits equal to those earned—it did not offer false job references. According to Dan, the government balked at supplying references without knowing that the individual would be a trustworthy employee, especially since many protected witnesses had been involved in crime themselves before they'd testified, or had profited from crimes committed by a spouse or parent. There was simply too much liability incurred, Dan had explained, to place people with false credentials into jobs within the private sector.

As a result, Jennifer had struggled with that lack of job references at the start of her life as Jennifer Hannah. To make matters even more difficult, the Program prescribed that she find work in a field other than her previous one. Overnight, she'd gone from being a hairstylist with a lucrative business to an unskilled job applicant without a college degree, or job references. She never wanted to face that uphill battle again. She'd labored too hard for the last seven years to throw away the fruits of her work experience.

Yet, if her cover were blown, she would have to do just that. She could leave no trail for anyone to follow, including previous employers or co-workers. Fervently she thanked God that Trev hadn't recognized her as Diana.

She'd been crazy to risk being with him.

Even so, she savored the memory. She'd savor it for the rest of her life.

Forcing her thoughts away from the topic that could tear her apart, she parked her old sedan outside the small brick building on a quiet corner and focused on the task ahead of her. She would turn in her resignation today. She could give only one week's notice. During that week, she would arrange to work as much as possible from home, via telephone and fax machine. She'd stock up on groceries and all necessities, and remain hidden in her apartment until the time came to move. She would take no chances of running into Trev again.

With her heart weighed down, Jennifer entered the carpeted front office of Helping Hand Staffing Services and forced a pleasant greeting for Marlene, the pretty redheaded receptionist seated behind a rosewood desk. "Jennifer, I'm glad you're here. Phyllis is waiting to see you."

Jennifer thanked her and headed toward the back, where Phyllis, the general manager, occupied a corner suite. Phyllis probably wanted to discuss strategies for attracting new temps, since most of their current workers had been placed in long-term assignments. Jennifer supposed this would be as good a time as any to hand in her resignation.

"Er, Jennifer," Marlene called, following her around the corner. "Just thought you should know..." An oddly curious expression flitted across her face. "A new client stopped by to talk to you. A Mr. Montero."

"Mr. Montero?" Jennifer lifted a brow. She knew no one by that name. "He's a new client?"

"Well, I'm assuming he *will* be a new client, since he came by to hire some help. I understand you've worked for him before. He's in Phyllis's office."

"*I've* worked for him before?" Questions, possibilities and fears pounced on her. "And he's here...now?"

Before she reached any conclusion, the door to the corner office opened and her stout, unadorned, perpetually business-minded boss appeared. "There you are, Jennifer. I thought I'd heard your voice. A prospective client has stopped by, and we've been talking about you." With an insistent gesture, Phyllis ushered her into the tastefully appointed executive suite. "I'm sure you remember Mr. Montero. He says you used to work for him...."

The rest of Phyllis's words faded into an incoherent rumble as Jennifer laid eyes on "Mr. Montero."

Trev.

She stared at him in speechless, breathless astonishment. So great was her surprise that her mind emptied of thought, and everything faded from view except him.

He slowly rose from an armchair until he towered before her—broad-shouldered, tanned and rugged looking. Even in his expensive business attire, he emitted the raw virility of a man who worked with his hands, his muscles and his strong back for a living. A white shirt and dark, open sport coat now clothed the powerful chest that had gleamed by lamplight. Gray trousers concealed his muscular legs and hips. His hair, brushed to a tawny shine, still sprawled with unruly nonchalance, reminding her of when she'd run her fingers through its plush thickness.

Most distracting, though, was his golden-brown gaze fixed on her with a dangerously purposeful gleam. "Hi, Jen." His smile was charmingly crooked and distinctly wry. "Good to see you again."

He extended his hand.

For the first time in her life, she felt as if she might faint. The blood had rushed to her head with such force that she gripped his hand and held on tight for a steadying moment. She couldn't, for the life of her, say a word.

What was he doing here? How had he found her? Had he realized her true identity? But, no. He had called her "Jen." And Phyllis had introduced *him* as "Mr. Montero"—not Montgomery. Had Phyllis and Marlene misunderstood his name?

The warm, hard strength of his grip helped keep Jennifer upright, but did nothing to clear her mind. Physical contact with Trev never failed to flood her with sensation rather than thought. The moment she regained her balance, she withdrew her hand from his and struggled to utter a greeting.

"I was just telling Phyllis," he said in the deep baritone that had warmed her memories for so many wretched years, "how pleased I was with you the last time you, uh, worked for me."

Worked for him. The implication of that concept finally hit her. He had to be referring to Friday night. Good God, what had he told Phyllis?

"I couldn't have been more satisfied." An utterly masculine groove curved beside his half smile.

Her embarrassment flaring, Jennifer shot Phyllis an anxious glance. She hadn't given a thought to the possibility that her staid, conventional boss might learn about Friday night—especially from Trev. Why had he come here? Was he trying to get her fired? If so, why?

"I can honestly say she was the best *help* I've ever...had." Though he addressed Phyllis, his gaze remained on Jennifer, galvanizing her pulse into wild action. "That's why I want her again. No one else will do."

His husky words warmed her blood, even as anxiety battered her. What did he mean by these lightly veiled innuendoes? Did he really intend to hire her as a temp through this agency in hopes that she'd sleep with him again?

"I must admit, I am surprised," Phyllis declared, turning to study her. "I hadn't realized that you'd actually worked in the field, Jennifer. As long as you've been here, you haven't mentioned it."

"Th-that was a long time ago," Jennifer stuttered.

"Seems like only days to me," put in Trev.

She shot him a warning glare. *Please, Trev...just shut up!*

"I know you've said you want to hire Jennifer, Mr. Montero, and that no one else will do, but..." Phyllis settled her generous frame into the chair behind her massive desk and flashed Trev an apologetic smile that softened her rather severe features. "Jennifer is our public relations representative. She solicits new accounts for the agency and acts as the liaison between our clients and our girls. She doesn't actually service the accounts herself."

He stared at Phyllis in clear surprise. After a moment, though, approval replaced the surprise. "I see." He actually looked relieved.

But why should he be relieved? And why didn't he correct the misunderstanding of his name?

"To be perfectly honest," Phyllis said with a laugh, "I wasn't even aware that Jennifer possessed the necessary computer skills, shorthand, or any of the other office applications used in the field."

Trev drew his brows together in a frown and studied Phyllis with a searching stare that brought an uncharacteristic pink to her cheeks. "Office applications?" he repeated blankly.

It was then that understanding dawned in Jennifer. He'd mistaken the agency as a front. He'd somehow discovered she worked here and, believing her to be a prostitute, had assumed that the agency sent her out on "calls."

And he'd come to request her services. Illegal services.

Thus, his use of a false name.

If that realization hadn't been so alarming, she might have burst into hysterical laughter. As it was, she had to stop him from saying another incriminating word. "You're right, Phyllis, I don't type very fast or take shorthand. When I worked for Mr. Montgom—er, Mr. Montero, I acted as his office manager." She prayed he wouldn't contradict her. "But only for a short time, while his permanent manager was on maternity leave."

"Ah." Phyllis nodded and smiled again at Trev. "Now I understand. Jennifer *would* make an excellent manager. She's great at problem solving. Our clients know they can turn to her with anything that comes up. She's always willing to go the extra mile to fill their needs."

Trev narrowed his gaze on Phyllis, as if trying to decide

whether to apply an alternative meaning to her praise. He clearly wasn't sure what product they were selling here.

Jennifer surged forward and caught his arm. "Why don't you come with me, Mr. Montero, and we'll discuss your requirements." She felt her face redden at the offer, knowing how he'd take it, and quickly added, "I'll go through my files and find the perfect secretary for you. Or a word processing specialist, or file clerk...."

Looking pleased at the outcome, Trev smiled at Phyllis on his way past her desk. She fairly beamed back at him. Incredibly enough, it seemed that the stodgy, no-nonsense, middle-aged manager had fallen victim to his effortless charm. Not a good thing. She would believe every word the blasted man uttered.

Jennifer prayed to God he wouldn't utter many more within her hearing.

Gritting her teeth, she maintained her smile while escorting him down the hall and into her own smaller, more cluttered office. She'd barely avoided disaster. Phyllis would have been shocked had she realized the true meaning behind Trev's request for "services." No doubt she would have fired Jennifer. And Jennifer would then be back at square one—with no job references.

The moment she'd locked her office door, Jennifer angrily rounded on Trev. "How did you find me here?"

He settled into a casual, cocked-hipped stance, his hands in his trouser pockets, his gaze amiable. "Your business card. I took one from your purse."

Her purse. Of course. That was how the handbag had moved from the floor of the hotel room onto the bedside table. He'd found it and searched it. Why hadn't she been more careful? "How dare you search my purse, or steal anything from it. You had no right. And then, to come to my place of business, and...and—"

"Request your services?" The hint of amusement in his gorgeous honey-brown eyes only infuriated her more.

Clenching her fists, she seethed. "You could have gotten me fired."

"I realize that now, and I'm sorry. But, come on. *Helping Hand Staffing Services?* How was I to know it's legitimate?"

Though she wouldn't admit it, he had a point. The company's name suddenly sounded provocative. "But it *is* legitimate—unlike the phony name you gave."

"A man has to take precautions."

"Yes, well, you can take your precautions elsewhere, Mr. Montero or Montgomery or whoever you are."

He frowned, looking affronted, surprised and somewhat wounded. "The name's Montgomery. Trev Montgomery. I didn't lie to you about that, or anything else." After a tense moment, his expression cleared. Softly he asked, "Aren't you even a *little* glad to see me?"

She gaped at him. Surely he couldn't have expected a warm welcome. But as memories of Friday night's lovemaking rushed back to her, she realized that he very well might have expected warmth—this tender, passionate lover who had touched her very soul. Struggling to remain aloof, she retorted, "If I'd wanted to see you again, you wouldn't have needed to steal my card. Friday night was business, just business. And that business is over. Now please leave."

He didn't budge. In fact, he dug his heels in for a pointedly longer stay. How well she recognized the determination in his expression! A mule could take "stubborn" lessons from Trev Montgomery. "I want you to have lunch with me, or dinner," he calmly insisted. "Today. So we can talk."

"Talk?" That sounded terribly dangerous. Did he suspect her of being Diana? No, she didn't believe he'd hide a suspicion about something as momentous as his wife's return from the dead. "I'm sorry, but I can't go anywhere with you."

"Why not?"

"I...I'm busy."

"With your second job?" Disapproval added an edge to his voice.

She lofted a brow. His disapproval seemed pretty hypocritical to her. After all, he had come to "hire her services" when he'd believed the agency to be only a front. He had bought sex from her on Friday night. She resisted the urge to throw both of those things in his face. "My activities are none of your business."

"Maybe not, but I want to understand." His quiet words and unwavering stare unnerved her. "If you're for sale, why can't I buy some of your time?"

Her heart tightened. *If you're for sale.* How had she ever trapped herself into such a demeaning role? "My schedule is booked."

"Like it was Friday night?"

"Yes."

"You didn't have another appointment, Jen. I saw you leave the hotel."

Damn. Just her luck. Caught in a lie. But why did he care? What point was he trying to make? "The appointment was at another hotel."

"That's not what you told me." He ambled closer. "And I don't believe it, anyway. I think you went straight home. I think you regretted sleeping with me, and it damn near killed you to take the money."

She bit her lip. She hadn't regretted sleeping with him, but she understood how he'd arrived at that conclusion. He'd clearly sensed her anguish when she'd left him. And it *had* almost killed her to take the money. Why should his uncanny perception of her emotions surprise her? He'd read them from the first time they'd met. Determined to stop him from reading her now, she forced an Arctic chilliness into her voice. "What's your point?"

"You haven't been selling yourself for very long, have you?"

"Maybe I have, maybe I haven't. What difference would it make, anyway?"

He advanced, intently studying her face, forcing her backward a few steps until her backside nudged the desk. "Was I your first john?"

"My first *john!*" The term pricked her with foolish pain. Of course he considered himself her john. And the lovemaking that she would cherish forever had been something tawdry to him. What had she expected? Uncertain of his motivation for asking the question, she hedged. "I don't know if I should be flattered or insulted."

"Just be truthful."

That was one thing she couldn't be. With anybody. Ever. "Did I seem like a rookie to you? Were you dissatisfied with my performance? Have you come for a refund?"

She almost hoped that he had. She hadn't taken the crumpled wad of bills from her skirt pocket yet, though three days had gone by. He'd paid her for sex. She hated the sight of that money. Yet, she couldn't give it away. It was the last thing Trev would ever give her. She would tuck it in with the few mementos she'd been allowed to keep from her former life—*if* he didn't want a refund.

"If I *was* dissatisfied," he said slowly, "would you give me a refund?"

"If that's what it takes to get rid of you."

He searched her face and probed her gaze as if trying to drill a peephole through her facade. "You know damn well I was satisfied," he finally muttered.

A slow welling of warmth rose in her at his intensity.

"And I've never heard of a prostitute offering refunds," he said. "I was your first paying customer, wasn't I? And I hurried you into it. *Pressured* you into it."

She suddenly recognized the emotions that drove him—a

dangerous mix of concern and self-blame. She should have known he'd be concerned about a woman he'd slept with—even a prostitute. That concern would certainly turn to guilt if he felt in any way responsible for her actions. It seemed that he did.

"Do you honestly think you led me astray?" she scoffed, determined to absolve him of all responsibility, to send him on his way before his "knight in shining armor" syndrome compelled him to do something rash.

"I think I made your first venture into prostitution easier for you. Opened the door, so to speak."

"You *did* open the door," she admitted. "But only the one to the stairwell! Rest assured, Mr. Montgomery. You weren't my first john. I've been turning tricks for years." She wished she could toss in a few shockingly graphic details—just to lend her credibility—but at the moment, possible details eluded her. Where, she wondered, had she gone wrong in her role of prostitute? "What made you think you were my first?"

"Your hesitation. Your fear. The tears you tried to hide when you left me." He pressed closer, his voice growing softer, his gaze more intimate. "The passion of your kiss. The tightness of your body. The authenticity of your climax."

Heat blazed in her skin. And not only from embarrassment. With merely a sultry gaze and a few gruffly uttered words, he'd managed to arouse her.

She tore her gaze away from him.

"The way you blush," he continued, running the back of a finger in a leisurely path down the curve of her heated face. "Oh...and the fact that you charged me fifty dollars."

Surprise forced her gaze back to his. Had she overcharged him? "You—you don't think fifty was...fair?"

His mouth bent in a rueful, chiding way, yet something like affectionate indulgence warmed his eyes. "You have to know that you could charge a hell of a lot more."

Oh, my. She'd undercharged him. How to explain that? "I, uh, gave you a discount because, um—" she chewed on her bottom lip "—because I had to leave early." There! That made perfect sense.

"You mean, if you'd stayed the whole night, you would have charged me more?"

"Much more," she confirmed. "Double."

"A hundred dollars."

"Yes."

"For the whole night."

His deadpan tone made her wonder if she should have upped the price another notch or two.

Before she had time to reason it out, he said, "A woman like you could charge five, ten, maybe twenty times that for a whole night."

She blinked in sheer amazement. She *could?* "Maybe that's true wherever you're from, but here in Sunrise—"

"Would you like me to find out the going rate, here in Sunrise?"

Alarm coursed through her. He might start checking into her story! "I don't care what anyone else charges. I do business the way I see fit."

"Why are you doing this business at all?"

"That's none of your concern," she snapped. "So please, just get the hell out of my life."

"That's exactly what I want to help you do," he growled. "Get the 'hell' out of your life...whatever that hell may be."

His fervent concern touched a chord deep in her heart. If only she could run to the shelter of his strong, warm arms and put an end to her misery.

"Let me help you, Jen." He reached out and took firm possession of her shoulders, his gaze serious and compassionate. "I know you're not happy. You can barely hide your anguish. And you can't have been selling yourself for long, or you wouldn't be as...as..." He struggled for a word, then shook his head, looking thoroughly frustrated. "You're new at this business. I know it. I was your first customer. I hope to God your only customer."

The temptation was strong to assure him that he was and always would be her only "customer." But that might add to his sense of guilt, make him feel even more responsible for her—and then she'd never get him to leave.

"You weren't my first customer," she said, feeling desperate, "but everything else you're saying makes sense. You've made me realize that prostitution isn't for me. As of right now, I'm finished with it," she swore, striving to inject passionate sincerity into every word. "I'll never do it again."

He didn't look as gratified as she'd expected. In fact, his expression didn't lighten at all. "You don't mean that. You're only saying it to get rid of me."

"No, no, I do mean it. Prostitution is a terrible profession, and I—"

"If you're serious, let me arrange for you to stay with a good friend of mine for a while. Dr. Jane Parsons. She's a social worker and psychologist in Santa Monica who works with women. She'll help you through the worst of the transition, Jen, so you can make a good start toward a new life."

For the second time that day, Jennifer had to swallow hysterical laughter. The last thing she wanted was a "new life." And since when had he become such good friends with Jane Parsons? Jane had been one of her customers at the hair salon, but at the time, Trev hadn't known her. Despite the fact that she should be glad he'd become close with women in the community, jealousy squeezed her nearly breathless. She had to get rid of the man before her emotions got the best of her! "I can't afford the time away from my day job to go traipsing off to Santa Monica."

"I'll find a professional counselor who can help you here, then."

"Thank you, but my future is none of your affair—so please butt out!"

"Just as I thought. Your biggest concern is to get rid of me, isn't it? Makes me wonder why."

He plied her with a searching gaze that escalated her panic. She was getting herself deeper into danger. She didn't want him dwelling on her desire to escape from him. She needed to put an absolute end to his interest in her. Obviously, the I've-seen-the light tactic wasn't the way. He would probably try to keep tabs on her for the rest of her life.

"Do you know why I want to get rid of you?" she burst out, her voice strident with barely subdued panic. "Because you're delusional, that's why. You're not my first customer, or my fifth, or my twentieth. I've had so many, I've lost count. But for some reason, you think you're special. You think you can take over my life."

"I'm not trying to take over your life. I'm offering to help you. Forget professional counseling, since it obviously makes you uncomfortable. But if you're in a desperate financial bind, I can help you get a better paying job, or arrange for a long-term loan, or—"

"I don't want your help!" she cried, horrified at the feeling that she might, at any moment, break into sobs. "And yes, I *was* lying just to get rid of you. I *enjoy* moonlighting as a hooker. I like the excitement. And the extra cash. Not because I need it desperately, as you seem to think, but just to have more spending money. You know, for designer clothes, and diamonds, and spiffy shoes."

"If all that's true, why are you holding back tears?"

"I'm not," she croaked. Her throat closed completely, and she pushed against his broad, solid chest, shoving free of him. Pacing across the small office to a somewhat safer distance—near the corner where her beanbag koala bears sat hugging on top of her computer—she struggled for control. When she finally regained her voice, she said over her shoulder, "Leave, Mr. Montgomery, or I'll call the police. I'll swear out a restraining order against you, if I must."

Trev didn't reply.

That rather surprised her. He usually had an answer for everything. Could he have finally seen the pointlessness in trying to rescue a woman from herself? Only when she'd gathered her composure reasonably well did she risk another glance at him.

He stood with his legs splayed, his arms crossed, his golden-brown gaze impaling her—the very picture of male obstinacy. "Go right ahead. Call the police. I'm ready when you are."

4

JENNIFER SQUARED OFF with her macho adversary in uneasy silence. What would he do if she did call the police?

It didn't take her long to realize she couldn't risk finding out. Who knew what Trev might say or do. Though she doubted that she could be arrested for prostitution on his word alone—especially since he had been her john—her entire life revolved around the need to avoid raising questions, suspicions or undue notice. The slightest hint that she moonlighted as a prostitute would force her into a harsh spotlight, in the community and here at the agency. Her job references would be at stake, as would the references she'd need to rent another decent apartment. And if worse came to worst, the U.S. Marshals Service might get wind of the problem. Trev could cause endless trouble for her.

Then there was the possibility that he himself would dig into her background...and discover that she hadn't been barred from the hotel, and that she'd been living in Sunrise for *seven years*, the exact amount of time Diana had been missing.

No, she couldn't call the police.

Abandoning her attempt at threatening him, she closed the distance between them with her hands outstretched. "Please, Trev, listen. I know you're feeling guilty for...buying my services. Your conscience is trying to make you atone by placing responsibility for me onto your shoulders. But you're not responsible for the choices I make, and there's nothing you can do to change them."

"Thanks for the psychoanalysis, Jen, but—"

"No, please—" she caught his face gently between her hands "—don't argue. My life is complicated, and I'm asking you, begging you, to leave me alone. Your interference will only cause me trouble." She regarded him in imploring silence, her palms pressed against his smooth-shaven skin, her heart filling with painful tenderness. If only he weren't so good and kind and noble. If only she didn't love him so much.

She shouldn't be with him. Saddened by that knowledge and shaken by her tumultuous feelings for him, she lowered her hands from his face. The loss of physical contact released them both from a stare that had gone on too long, penetrated too deep.

"Answer me one thing, Jen," he said, breaking an oddly poignant silence. "Do the complications in your life involve a pimp?"

She frowned. "A pimp?"

"Do you work for a pimp?"

She supposed she shouldn't be so surprised at the question. It made perfect sense that she would work for one. In fact, as she thought about it, a pimp seemed like an excellent idea. A way to convince Trev that she had formidable protection.

"Actually, I *do* work for a…a very powerful man. He watches over me and handles every problem I run across. He's extremely protective. And that's why it's important for you to leave me alone. I wouldn't want him to think you've become a…problem." She paused to let the implication sink in.

His gaze narrowed. "So that's it. That's who you're afraid of."

"Afraid of?"

"You're not alone anymore, Jen." His eyes blazed, and his

deep, quiet voice vibrated with angry sincerity. "I won't let him hurt you, I swear it."

"No, no, you misunderstood. He'd never hurt me. He's very good to me. We're friends. Close friends."

"And you sell yourself for him."

"Well, uh, yes, but—"

"Then he's not good to you. He's not a friend. He cares about you only as a product. An expendable product—or you wouldn't be afraid of him."

"I'm not afraid of him!"

"You're scared, and miserable, and alone. And this mercenary bastard, whoever he is, is taking advantage of that. He's trapping you into a way of life that can only destroy you. Tell me his name, and what rock he lives under."

The intent behind that demand horrified her. He was ready to hunt down a pimp. Although that pimp was nonexistent, fear gnawed at her stomach. Trev was too headstrong. He thought himself invincible. She'd been right seven years ago to withhold the truth about herself from him. If he knew the real dangers she faced—both then and now—he'd probably try to take on the crime bosses themselves!

And if he *did* interfere with the business of any bonafide pimp, he could attract the notice of the local crime lords—the last thing Jennifer wanted.

Alarm spurred her into anger. "Have you lost your mind? You're willing to do battle with a pimp, a dangerous criminal who, for all you know, could be connected with organized crime. And for what? A woman you don't even know. A working girl who doesn't want your help."

"I have a few powerful contacts of my own. I don't intend to take on any criminal without a solid plan and backup. And now that you've admitted he's 'dangerous,' I'm not about to turn a blind eye and leave you to his mercy."

"He's not dangerous to *me*. But if you stir up trouble, *you'll* be in more danger than you've ever dreamed possible!"

The extent of her anxiety stunned Trev. She was pale, wide-eyed and undeniably shaken. She seemed to believe that her pimp was all-powerful, and that no one could help her. But more surprising was the fact that she was worried about him—the john she hadn't wanted to see again. Grave though the situation was, he couldn't help feeling a little pleased by her concern. "Let me get this straight. You're worried about *me*."

Clearly taken aback, she stared at him in dismayed silence. The hard shell she'd been trying to hide behind had cracked, and her softness was showing. "No, hell no, I'm not worried about you," she blustered. "I just don't want you interfering in my affairs."

"You think I'll get hurt."

She let out a scornful laugh. "Do you really think I care?" Unable to maintain the scorn, though, she soon gave in to earnest passion. "But yes, I do think you'll get hurt if you go slaying dragons in the underworld, with or without a 'solid plan and backup.' You will be hurt...or killed. And nothing will be accomplished. Please, don't get involved, Trev. I am what I am, and you can't change it. And I don't understand why you'd be willing to risk your neck to try."

Trev didn't quite understand that, either. And yet, he'd do whatever it took to help her—more so now than ever. In her office with its work-cluttered desk, a coffee mug with a smirking smiley face, two little stuffed bears hugging on top of her computer monitor, and not one personal photograph anywhere in sight, she somehow seemed more real and more vulnerable than she had at the hotel.

He couldn't bear to think of her working nights on her back or knees.

In the clear light of day, she looked barely older than his

kid sister, who had just turned twenty. Dressed in a demure navy-blue skirt and white blouse with little flowers embroidered around the collar, her dark blond hair braided and draped across one shoulder, her eyes wide with concern—*for him*—his "lady of the evening" seemed utterly sincere, wholesome and adorable. He knew in his gut that she was, at heart, an innocent who had been trapped by desperate circumstances and manipulated by evil men. He couldn't help feeling protective.

He also felt drawn to her in an elemental way—as if he'd known her forever, and she was someone precious to him. Her likeness to Diana probably accounted for that. The sense of familiarity still gripped him by the throat and wouldn't let go. Even the secrets lurking in her eyes reminded him of Diana, who hadn't been without mysteries of her own.

Most provoking, though, was the sexual interest Jen stirred in him. Despite her pragmatic surroundings and demure clothing, despite her determination to send him away, despite his knowledge that she was a prostitute—a woman he should steer clear of—he couldn't stop wanting her.

When he'd first seen her today, he'd felt a wild surge of possessiveness, as if he had every right to pull her into his arms. When she'd cradled his face between her hands, his pulse had revved. And now, as she pleaded with her wide blue eyes, he remembered them darkening with passion, and longed to ignite that passion again. To taste her smooth, lush mouth, just one more time....

Had his memory exaggerated the effect of her kiss, of her lovemaking? Probably. He'd been in a vulnerable state of mind on Friday night, so soon after the legal declaration of Diana's death. Since then, he'd had time to collect his wits. What would it be like to kiss Jen now? If he did, he wouldn't go beyond a kiss. He intended to free her from prostitution, not exploit her further. But a kiss couldn't hurt her—and it just might free *him* from his crazy desire for her.

"Meet me when you get off work this afternoon, Jen," he murmured, his voice sounding huskier than he'd intended.

"Oh, for heaven's sakes, Trev!" Grabbing the lapels of his sport coat, she bunched them in her fists and tried to shake him. "What do I have to do," she cried, enunciating each word with every jerk of her arms, "to get it through your thick skull that I can't see you again?"

He watched her in surprise. Only one other woman had ever grabbed him by the clothing and tried to shake him like that. Diana. He'd always gotten a charge out of it, knowing she was trying to be fierce. The same sweet ferocity shone on Jen's face now—an earnest mix of exasperation, anxiety and determination to be heard.

But she's not Diana. God Almighty, Trev...don't confuse the two! The familiar gesture, the sound of her voice, the scent of her hair and skin—all blended together to boggle his mind. And kick-start his heart.

Unable to stop himself, he reached for her. Hooking a hand around her nape and the other around her slim waist, he drew her nearer, breathing in her scent, relishing the feel of her. "I'm not going to pay you for this one, Jen," he whispered, his gaze dancing with hers. "Understand? I'm not paying."

She didn't back away, or try to evade him, but maintained her fierce hold on his lapels. Her lips parted, her breathing deepened. Her gaze darkened in that oh-so-familiar way.

He kissed her with solemn intent. He needed to taste, to probe, to analyze. But the heat flared with stunning swiftness and seared away all thought, all ability to reason. She was sweetness. Vitality. Life-giving fire. He needed her heat. Had been needing it for days.

Her arms went around his neck, and his hands splayed across her back, seeking the warmth and softness of her skin through the interfering silk of her blouse. Their kiss slanted and deepened, her tongue wrangling with his in the most provocative give-and-take, until sexual need smoldered within him. He longed to explore the very depths of her...every blessed one of them....

She uttered a groan that ended on a cry, and abruptly she broke the kiss.

He reeled from the sudden desertion.

"We can't do this, Trev," she said, her whisper rife with anguish. "You've got to leave. And stay away."

Frowning in frustration, he searched her gaze. "Is that what you really want?"

"Yes. Yes!"

"Damn it, Jen, you're lying again. You don't want me to go, any more than I want to." He felt her body grow tense, and knew that she was struggling to conceal the desire she'd admitted with her kiss. Biting back a curse, he reluctantly loosened his hold on her. "There's only one way that I'll leave."

"What way?"

"Give me what I came for. Three days of your company. Just three short days. If I can't convince you to accept my help in that time, I'll let you go, and never contact you again."

He wasn't sure what emotion leaped into her eyes. Wistfulness? Longing? Fear? "No, I'm sorry. I can't do that." With regret deepening the shadows in her eyes, she backed away from his embrace and leaned against her desk, as if she didn't trust her legs to keep her upright.

He fought the urge to pull her back into his arms and kiss her into submission. "Yes, you can. I'll talk to Phyllis. I'll tell her I need an office manager. Someone who's familiar with the way I run my business. She already believes that you used to work for me."

"She won't let you hire me. I don't work in the field."

"She'll make an exception this time." He intended to pay whatever it would take. "And I *do* need help. Setting up my office, and finishing a couple of projects. We'll work together, and you can get to know me. And, hopefully, to trust me."

Anxiously she studied his face, clearly debating the wisdom of accepting his offer. After an encouragingly long pause, she murmured, "I'm sorry, but I just can't afford the time away from the office."

"Two days, then. We'll need at least two."

She shook her head and made a move to turn away.

He caught her by the shoulders, trapping her against her desk. Persuasion hadn't worked. On to Plan B. "If you turn me down, I'll have to find another way to help you. I can't guarantee you'll like whatever tactics I'm forced to try. But understand this—I *do* intend to find your pimp, and to close down your nighttime operations...if I have to turn the whole town upside-down to do it."

She turned paler, which only strengthened his conviction that she faced terrible danger. The thought made his muscles jump with anger against whoever posed that danger.

"I...I was only kidding when I said I had a pimp. I just wanted to see what you'd say—and maybe intimidate you a little. I don't really have one at all."

"Then you don't have to worry about 'trouble' when I go looking for him."

She bit her lip, so clearly anxious that his heart turned over for her. He didn't enjoy using threats against anyone, least of all a woman, but the fear and anguish he'd sensed in her from the very start called out to him on a level too deep to ignore.

He hadn't been able to keep his wife safe. She'd disappeared without a trace. He'd damn sure do better for Jen—whether she appreciated the effort or not.

"Two days?" she said uncertainly. "If I give you those two days, will you let me go when they're over? Will you forget about me and my...nighttime operations? And stay out of my life for good?"

It was his turn to hesitate. What if two days weren't enough to persuade her to accept his help? Then again, two days were better than none. "I swear it."

Though she seemed slightly relieved, she wasn't convinced. "And you promise that during those two days, you won't try to find my pimp—who doesn't exist!—or dig out any information beyond what I tell you?"

Again, reluctance delayed his response. He itched to find out everything he could about her and the darkness that somehow enslaved her. Realizing he'd lose this opportunity to win her trust if he didn't compromise, he capitulated. "Okay. No digging for information. I promise."

She still didn't look quite satisfied. "You understand that I...I can't be seen around town with you. It could raise too many questions."

He clenched his teeth to keep from responding unwisely. She was afraid her pimp would find out that she was spending too much time with one john, slowing down her productivity. Trev yearned to find the son of a bitch—"who didn't exist"—and strangle him. "We won't be seen around town."

"I assume you also understand that my duties will be only clerical, and that my workday ends at five o'clock."

Silence settled between them.

This was one compromise he wouldn't make. He couldn't let her have the nights free. Not when some powerful evil held her in its grasp, forcing her into the arms of other men. Never had the thought been more repugnant to him than now.

"I won't try to buy your sexual favors, Jen." He meant it as a vow, to himself as well as to her. Nevertheless, he dug his wallet out of his pocket, extricated three hundred-dollar bills and pressed them into her hand, closing her fingers over them. "But I want the nights, too. Three of them. That includes tonight."

SHE DIDN'T have to do it. She didn't have to go with Trev at all.

She could tell Phyllis that a family emergency had arisen out of state that required her immediate departure. She could board a flight this evening—to anywhere—while Dan Creighton dealt with the logistics of her permanent move.

But Trev's protective instincts were now engaged. If she didn't live up to their bargain, he would worry about what had become of her, or believe that his insistence on helping her had caused some major problem. He might very well start digging into her background in an attempt to find her, or at least understand her. His inquiries about Jennifer Hannah might trip off an alarm at the Marshals Service, which would then draw him to their notice.

Jennifer didn't want Trev brought to the notice of the U.S. Marshals. She'd gone to extreme lengths to avoid that very thing. Amazingly enough, she'd succeeded in withholding the fact from them that she'd ever been married or connected to Trev Montgomery in any way.

This had been possible only because she'd married Trev under a false name.

Closing her eyes and sinking down into a hot, fragrant bubble bath after a long day at work, Jennifer tried to calm herself. Oh, what a tangled web she'd woven! But she'd been caught up in a web of secrets and lies for as long as she could remember.

Secrecy came with the territory when one was raised in a family involved with organized crime. Born Carly Palmieri, only daughter of "Big Vick" and his beauty-queen wife, she remembered being told as a child that certain occurrences or late-night visits to their sumptuous New Orleans home weren't to be mentioned. That Daddy's business wasn't to be talked about, and that if strangers ever questioned her, she was to tell Daddy immediately. As she grew older, she heard whispers about illegal bookmaking, and though she hadn't been sure at the time what it meant, she suspected it had something to do with the men who visited her father.

She hadn't paid much attention to her father's activities, though. Her life was filled with friends, cousins, family parties, pretty clothes, expensive shoes, and just about anything else her heart desired—as long as she followed her father's rules and behaved like a nice little Catholic schoolgirl should. She was, after all, Carly Palmieri, her father's pristine princess.

Her ivory tower remained a fairly happy place throughout her teenage years, although her father's strictness began to chafe. He seemed too overprotective—scrutinizing every new friend, forbidding her to venture too far from home. He actually hired a driver to take her to and from school—even after she'd graduated from high school and went on to study cosmetology.

And then one summer day, her uncle was gunned down on the sidewalk outside his house while she and her aunt were chatting in the side courtyard garden. A stray bullet hit her five-year-old cousin, killing him, too. Her aunt never recovered from the drive-by murders of her husband and son.

Neither did Carly. Their bloody slaughter opened her eyes to a terrifying truth. She wasn't safe. None of her loved ones was safe—even the most innocent.

She noticed then that her father himself seemed afraid. He wasn't as loud, happy and self-assured as he used to be. And her beautiful, vivacious mother soon lapsed into illness— from the torturous stress, it was widely believed.

On her deathbed, her mother told her of other violence committed against family members and friends, merely because they'd angered the wrong people. "Leave home,

Carly. Move far away. Cut all ties with everyone you know. Don't let this life touch you or anyone you come to love."

Her mother gave her a wad of cash, some identification papers that bore the name "Diana Kelly," and a false Social Security number. She wouldn't say where or how she'd gotten the documents. "It's better that you don't know. I made certain of one thing, though—no one knows you have them. Not even your father. If anyone asks, say you were born in Chicago. And pay attention to the birth date on the certificate. You're nineteen now, not twenty. Don't tell anyone who you really are, or you'll be endangering yourself and the husband or children you may have someday. Don't tell a soul the truth, Carly. *Promise* me."

She'd solemnly promised—a deathbed vow to her mother.

And after the funeral, at age twenty-turned-nineteen, she'd run away from her father's stifling home to the freedom of California. The newly created Diana Kelly chopped off her long, dark hair in a spiky new style, pierced her ears in several places, tattooed a butterfly beneath her navel and found work near the Santa Monica pier as a hairstylist.

One of her best customers was Trev's slightly eccentric grandmother, whose ears were also pierced in several places. Babs Montgomery, in her loose-fitting blouses and long gauzy skirts, invited her home for lunch one day to discuss their favorite subject—writing. Babs was an aspiring novelist, and Diana was working on a play.

They were deep into a brainstorming session, when Trev came in. He'd steered Babs into an adjoining room and scolded her for bringing strangers home from the pier again. Overhearing them, Diana knew that he was only trying to protect his grandmother. Emotionally, though, Diana was still Big Vick Palmieri's princess, and the implied suspicion against her was more than she could take.

She thanked Babs for lunch, apologized curtly to Trev for

intruding in his home, and stalked out the door. Babs insisted that Trev bring her back.

They had nothing in common, she and Trev. He was a hardworking college graduate with an architecture degree who was struggling to raise his three parentless siblings, keep his wayward grandmother in line and start up his own construction business. Diana was a footloose rebel struggling with a major identity crisis and a hole in her heart where her family used to be. After her sheltered life at home, her sudden freedom had begun to overwhelm her, and the quirky characters that populated her new life often frightened her.

She fell in love with strong, solid, protective Trev Montgomery halfway through his apology. And before she'd even accepted that apology, they'd both been mesmerized by the most irresistible sexual allure....

That was another new facet to her freedom—sex. No man in her past had dared get too carried away with Vick Palmieri's daughter.

She and Trev got carried away. Quickly. Frequently.

He married her two months later, without knowing her real name or her real background. She'd feared from the start that his love for her had been based merely on sex. And, worse yet, on lies. But she'd felt justified in the deceit. She swore the danger from her past wouldn't compromise the safety and happiness of the kind, loving family she'd married into.

After only three months of marriage, though, her illusion of safety was shattered. Her father appeared on the national news. He'd been arrested on racketeering charges and had agreed to testify against a powerful crime boss.

A person didn't grow up in a family like hers without knowing what happened to "rats"...or their families. An alias might suffice to keep her out of harm's way under normal circumstances, but not under these circumstances. The pressure was on to find her—Big Vick Palmieri's only off-spring. His princess. His Achilles' heel.

She knew what she had to do.

She left Trev—safe, uninvolved and unaware—in the happy, normal life he'd always known, with the family who needed him and the business he'd worked so hard to start. She packed a suitcase, told him she was going to a writers' conference for the weekend—and drove directly to FBI headquarters.

Though she'd felt as if her heart had been torn out of her at leaving Trev, she'd known she was lucky to reach sanctuary alive.

At one simple announcement of her name, agents seemed to spring out of nowhere to swarm around her. She was drawn into an inner chamber, frisked for weapons and wires, then flown in a private jet and driven in a windowless van to the "safe house" where her father was being held. He squeezed her in a warm, hard bear hug and sobbed with relief. "The feds promised they wouldn't tell the media that I was going to testify until we'd found you, Carly. It leaked out, anyway. If you hadn't come, I wasn't going to testify. The men I did business with—they're murderers. They've got to be stopped. But they'll come after us, Carly. Both me and you."

Her emotions had been painfully divided. Though she loved her father as much as always, she couldn't help a certain fury at the way he'd ruined both her life and that of her mother. But her issues with her father would have to wait. The U.S. district attorney was anxious to induct them into the Witness Protection Program.

When asked by the authorities about her recent activities, it was surprisingly easy to omit the fact that she'd lived and married under a different name. She told them she'd been bumming around the California beaches for the better part of a year, spending the cash her mother had given her. Intent on securing her father's testimony against the crime boss, the D.A. hurried the paperwork through the system.

Her father insisted that they undergo plastic surgery to alter their appearances. Although the government refused to pay for the surgery, they had doctors on hand to perform it. Her father spared no expense. "Change everything you can."

In a matter of weeks—long, painful weeks of recuperation and then indoctrination into the Program—Carly Palmieri ceased to exist. A cautious, subdued Jennifer Hannah was born. And Diana Kelly Montgomery vanished into thin air—as far as her husband knew.

She hadn't intended for the latter to happen. Ensconced in a small apartment at the Witness Security Safe Site and Orientation Center in Washington, D.C., a heavily guarded compound run by the U.S. Marshals, Jennifer had written a letter to Trev, stating that she wasn't what he'd thought her to be, she wasn't happy with him, and that she would never come back. Brutal, yes, but necessary to set him free. She'd signed the letter with a *D* rather than her name, and didn't mention anything about marriage or divorce, just in case the letter fell into the wrong hands. She assumed Trev would divorce her on the grounds of abandonment.

All mail had to be sent through secured channels, though, and she'd hesitated to give the letter to the U.S. Marshals for fear that they would read it and add Trev's name to their files on her. With the way she'd been raised—unable to trust anyone too much—she couldn't imagine that any agency run by human beings could be impenetrable by organized crime. She was willing to entrust her own life to the U.S. Marshals because she had no better alternative, but she wouldn't trust them with Trev's life. His name would not appear in their paperwork. Thus, she gave the letter to a motherly secretary she'd befriended at the compound. Jennifer explained that she didn't want the Marshals to read it, and asked if the woman would mail it in confidence.

That letter obviously had never been sent. But since no one from the Marshals Service had mentioned her previous association with Trev Montgomery, she assumed that none of the Marshals had read it, either.

As much as she hated the pain she'd caused Trev for the past seven years by not mailing that letter through proper channels, she was fervently glad that she'd kept him out of harm's way. The men who hunted for her and her father would not hesitate to use her husband—or even a former lover, if they believed she cared about him—to draw them into the open.

She'd kept Trev safe so far. She didn't want to risk that safety now by having him probe into the background of one Jennifer Hannah. His inquiries might trip an alarm and draw the attention of the U.S. Marshals...or, if he pursued the prostitution angle and flashed around sketches of her, the underworld.

Both he and she would be better off if Trev forgot Jennifer Hannah's existence.

As risky as two days spent in his company might be, she believed she could use that time to put a definite end to his interest in her. And if his chivalrous concern for her didn't wear thin, he would, at least, honor his promise to forget about her when the two days were over.

Two days. Just two short days. With Trev.

She laid a hand across her racing heart. She hadn't imagined that she'd ever spend another day with him, let alone two. *And three nights.* Nothing stood in the way except her own hesitation. Trev's plan to convince her boss that he needed Jennifer's help had succeeded with incredible ease. Not only had Phyllis agreed to allow Jennifer to help him set up his office, but she actually insisted that Jennifer accept the assignment.

"You're leaving me in a lurch, Jennifer, by quitting on such short notice," Phyllis had said, stunned and upset by Jennifer's announcement that this would be her last week. "The least you could do is help me out with this one last favor. This could be an important opportunity for the agency to get in good with Mr. Montero's firm. Who knows how many temps we can place with him in the next few years?"

Jennifer hated to allow Phyllis's expectations to grow too high. Trev had come to them under the false name of Mr. Montero. He clearly wasn't intending to do business with them in the future. Fortunately, Phyllis expected Jennifer to handle the paperwork involved in the transaction, as she usually did with new accounts, which made the falsehood easier to process.

Although she felt guilty for deceiving Phyllis, Jennifer was relieved that Trev had chosen to stick with his false name. No one could connect Trev Montgomery to Jennifer Hannah, even through an innocuous work assignment.

The proverbial door was open for her to go to him. Spend time with him. Put an end to his dangerous interest in her.

Her heart twisted at that thought. She would have to leave him then...again. But before she left, she intended to ease his mind and convince him that Jennifer Hannah was not "afraid, miserable and alone," as he'd called her, but an experienced prostitute who knew the ropes, thoroughly enjoyed her work and didn't want to be reformed.

That was possible, wasn't it? Surely there had to be prostitutes who enjoyed the job. There'd been a book written by one happy hooker. Jennifer wished she had time to find it and read it.

Unfortunately, Trev expected her to meet him at six o'clock, an hour from now, at a house he'd just rented. No time to find books about happy hookers.

An idea occurred to her, though. She could take a few moments to search the Internet for some X-rated stories to relate about her misadventures. A few particularly lurid ones should convince him of her incorrigibility.

Consumed with sudden purpose, she lurched out of the tub, dried off, shrugged into her robe and snuffed out the caramel-scented candles on the bathroom vanity that she always burned when she most needed to relax. Time for relaxation was over. She had research to do.

She spent the next half-hour on her computer, surfing from site to site, each one more explicit than the last. It certainly seemed *some* people enjoyed leading wicked lives. How hard could it be to persuade Trev that she'd experienced these things, and loved every minute?

Satisfied with the depravity of the scenarios she'd chosen, she switched off her computer and headed for her bedroom to get dressed for the evening. This time, she'd dress to fit her role. No wonder he hadn't believed her to be an experienced prostitute. He'd seen her wearing office clothes. The only office clothes she'd seen on those X-rated sites had been jazzed up with indecently short skirts, tight sweaters or low-cut blouses.

She wouldn't be Ms. Prim 'n' Proper tonight. Before the night was out, he'd be embarrassed to admit that he'd ever thought she wasn't "that kind of girl."

She rifled through her closet for an outfit she could quickly alter into something naughty, then searched her dresser for jewelry she'd bought but rarely worn. She also found a small kit of makeup she'd received as a bonus gift at a cosmetic counter, with shades of lipstick and nail polish she normally wouldn't have chosen. Then, of course, she had to mull over her wide selection of shoes—her one true extravagance— many with the high spiked heels that would perfectly complete a naughty outfit.

Just as she finished assembling a perfectly shocking outfit, the doorbell rang. She froze. Visitors rarely called unexpectedly, and any surprise of that nature unsettled her. Still wearing her long, mauve, terry-cloth bathrobe, she hurried across her living room to the foyer and peered through the peephole.

Trev stood on her doorstep.

Why? Anxiety pulsed in her temples. She was supposed to meet him at his newly rented house, not here! Never would she have agreed to allow him to come here. And how had he known where she lived?

"Open up, Jen," he called, rapping loudly on the door. "It's Trev."

She didn't want to open the door. She wasn't prepared for him to enter her home. But if she didn't answer, he'd only continue knocking and yelling, which would draw too much attention.

Reluctantly, she opened the door and let him in, but blocked him from venturing beyond the foyer. "How did you know where I live, Trev?" she demanded.

"Your driver's license." He smiled at her with that lazy masculine charm that always warmed her from the inside out. "It was in your purse Friday night."

She supposed she should have realized that. Flustered by his unexpected presence and his potent sexual allure, she frowned. "What are you doing here? I thought I was supposed to meet you at your house."

"Slight change in plans."

"You could have telephoned." Though worry buzzed in her chest, she was all too conscious of his physical immensity, the rugged attractiveness of his face and the undeniably sexual appeal of his muscular build, so evident now in the black shirt and tight-fitting black jeans he wore.

"Didn't have your number. Want to give it to me?"

"Actually, no." She had to be careful with him. Had to keep her head on straight, despite the dazed, breathless feeling he inspired.

She suddenly realized that she might have left something

visible in her apartment that would give away her identity as Diana. A patchwork quilt that she'd kept from the trunk of her car lay across her sofa. A picture that she'd sketched of the dog they'd had adorned her bedroom dresser. A manuscript she was currently working on—simply because she couldn't bear to give up writing altogether—sat beside her computer in the living room. Her writing would surely remind him of Diana's.

"Mmm." He inhaled deeply and glanced beyond her with an oddly questioning frown. "What's that smell? Like candy, or cookies."

"Caramel-scented candles." She'd almost forgotten that she'd been burning them earlier. With a rush of dismay, she remembered that she'd burned them frequently at their home...back when they'd been married. "You've...you've probably smelled them before. Plenty of times. They're very popular. A lot of women love caramel-scented candles. Just about everyone I know burns them."

But a troubled, faraway look now clouded his eyes.

"What change of plans did you come to tell me about?" she asked sharply, hoping to distract him. Scents, she knew, could evoke memories quicker than anything. Fearing the power of remembered fragrances, she'd made a point to switch from her usual bath soap. *You even smell like Diana,* he'd said the first time they'd met. And now he'd entered her home and smelled caramel candles. "I'm not ready to go yet. You said to meet you at six o'clock."

Her sharpness jarred him from his reverie. It took him a moment to reply—as if he was struggling to put the past behind him. "Sorry." He shook his head, raked a hand through his light brown hair and cast her an apologetic smile. "I forgot about the tickets I had for tonight. A potential investor made a point to get them for me. I guess I'd better use them."

"What tickets?"

"For a play at a small dinner theater."

"You don't expect me to go with you, do you? I told you I can't be seen—"

"—around town with me," he finished for her. "But this isn't in town. It's a two-hour drive north of here, in some little town that seems to be populated only by artists, writers and theater people. When the investor who gave me the tickets found out I'm finishing a script for a play, he assumed I was interested in theater, and insisted I check this one out."

Jennifer stared at him in surprise. "You're writing a play?" She couldn't have understood him correctly. Trev had never been overly interested in writing, or in the theater. *She'd* been the one writing a play.

"It's my wife's project. My *late* wife's," he amended with sadness roughening his voice. "It meant a lot to her. It's almost completed. All but the last act. My grandmother is a writer, and I tried to get her to finish it. I'd like to have it published and produced in Diana's memory. Unfortunately—" he let out a slight laugh "—my grandmother refuses to believe that Diana isn't coming back. So, uh, I'm going to try my hand at writing. Guess I ought to watch at least *one* play before I get started."

Jennifer compressed her lips to keep them from trembling. He intended to finish her play and have it produced. Could he possibly understand how much that effort meant to her? She'd worked for years on that play—night after night, as well as any moment she could steal from her busy days. And when she'd met Trev's grandmother, they'd plotted out more twists and turns in the story. They'd cherished such grand hopes.

And Babs believed she was coming back.

Trev had clearly decided she wasn't. He'd called her his "late wife."

Jennifer tried to utter something nonchalant, but no sound came out. It was good that he'd laid Diana's ghost to rest. And it was touching that Babs refused to. How she'd love to lay her head on Babs's shoulder for a good, long cry…then sit down over cups of her herbal tea for one of their brainstorming sessions.

"Anyway, I have these dinner theater tickets for this evening. What do you say? There shouldn't be much of a crowd on a Monday night. And in case you're concerned about being recognized by stoolies who might report back to your, uh, nonexistent business associate—" he underscored the sarcasm with a wry twist of his mouth "—I brought you these." He held up a pair of women's large, round sunglasses and a small-brimmed straw hat. "You can wear them until we're out of town."

Struggling to think objectively, Jennifer slowly took the glasses and hat from him. She hadn't intended to go anywhere with him except his home. But she doubted that anyone from the U.S. Marshals Service was anywhere near Sunrise at the moment. And she'd had no reason to believe that she'd been spotted by her enemies. Although she wouldn't want to be seen publicly in Trev's company—purely for caution's sake—the only real threat to her cover was the man standing in front of her.

And she'd already decided to spend the next two days with him. Perhaps it would be better to spend the first evening in a small, dimly lit theater where they'd be occupied by a play, rather than at his home, just the two of them, with plenty of time for conversation…and long searching stares.

"Okay." She nodded decisively, hoping she wasn't making a mistake by venturing out with him. "I'll go to the dinner theater with you."

He smiled, looking somewhat amused—maybe at the extreme gravity of her reply. She'd better lighten up, she decided, or he'd have more reason to believe that she was troubled. "Good. You won't regret it," he murmured. His gaze wandered from her face to her wet, tangled hair, then down the length of her robed figure. "Go get dressed." Was she imagining the subtle huskiness now in his voice, the sensual warmth in his stare? Maybe so, but a responsive heat still flared within her. "We'll have to leave in the next twenty minutes or so to make it in time."

"Fine." She'd barely been with him a few moments, and already her thoughts had turned to the sensual. *Not a good start.* She had a role to play, and though that role had everything to do with sex, she couldn't let herself become personally involved with him again. She was too emotionally vulnerable. "You can wait in the car while I get dressed."

"In the car?" He aimed a curious glance beyond her, toward the small, tidy living room, only half visible from the paneled foyer where they stood. "Why can't I wait in here?"

"No, I'm sorry." She steeled herself to deliver the explanation. "I, um, never allow johns into my home. It's a matter of principle."

Other than a slight furrowing of his brows, his expression didn't change. "But I'm not here as a john. I'm here as your temporary employer. And, I hope, a friend."

"That's sweet of you, Trev. But you *are* a john. That's all you'll ever be to me. And I can't have you in my home."

The silence that fell between them could only be called oppressive. The warm, sensual light extinguished in his gaze, breaking her heart a little more. Excruciating as that statement had been to make, she couldn't allow herself to regret it. She had only two days to convince him that prostitution was her life's calling—her chosen profession—and that she'd allow nothing to interfere with it.

"Then I guess I'll wait in the car," he said.

She nodded.

He turned and reached for the doorknob, then glanced back at her. "You *do* intend to honor our agreement, don't you? To spend two days and three nights with me...in *my* home?"

She didn't miss the barbed point behind the softly spoken

question. He would welcome her in his home even though she wouldn't have him in hers. Her rudeness clearly hadn't shaken his resolve.

"Only because you insist."

"Do you have a suitcase I can carry for you?"

"No, thank you. Just an overnight bag, and it's light."

He inclined his head briefly in response and exited her apartment with stiff, economical movements and an uncharacteristic soberness to his expression.

Her heart ached. He didn't deserve such treatment. He deserved a woman who would cherish him forever—and make sweet, passionate love to him every chance she got. She hoped he'd find that woman soon.

But not too soon. Not until she herself was far enough away that the torment wouldn't kill her.

5

HE KNEW he had no right to be angry. She hadn't wanted his company to begin with. He'd used every ploy he could think of to pressure her into spending the next two days with him. Why should he expect to be welcomed into her home?

He didn't blame her for drawing a line between her personal and "professional" lives. He was glad, *damn* glad, that she didn't bring johns home with her. And he couldn't deny that he *had* been her john—as recently as three nights ago. No reason for her to view him in any other light.

But as he sat waiting for her in the luxury sedan he'd rented, parked on the quiet street outside her garden-style quadruplex, his jaw clenching and his fingers drumming against the steering wheel, he couldn't help feeling as if she'd slapped him.

You're a john. That's all you'll ever be to me. Why should that bother him? He didn't want a personal relationship with her. He just wanted to help her out of a dangerous situation.

Yeah, right. That's all you want.

Memories resurfaced of Friday night's lovemaking. And the kiss he'd stolen earlier today. And the sight of her just now, wearing a robe—*only* a robe, he was sure—with her hair damp and loose around her shoulders, her skin flushed and dewy-fresh from her recent bath...more sensitive to his touch, he'd bet...

He shut his eyes, ground his teeth. Okay, so maybe he wanted more than just to help her, but he wouldn't allow himself anything beyond friendship. The issue was moot, anyway. She seemed resolved to avoid any relationship with him at all.

He should be glad.

But he wasn't. He was angry—with her, for not appreciating his offer of help, and with himself, for wanting her. For caring too much about her. What madness had come over him? She was a prostitute, and she didn't want his help. He was asking for trouble. Possibly big trouble.

No matter what she said, though, he sensed fear and anguish in her as clearly as if she'd begged aloud for help. He couldn't turn his back on that.

How can you be so sure of what she's feeling? You don't know her.

In some remote, analytical portion of his brain, he knew it was only reasonable to attribute his beliefs about her to the fact that she resembled Diana. He was probably endowing Jen with Diana's sensibilities instead of perceiving her as her own person. He had to admit that the more he saw of her, the more she reminded him of Diana. Not only in looks, but in her mannerisms, the timbre of her voice, the way she reacted to him. The way *he* reacted to *her.*

And when he'd walked into her home, its fragrance had evoked the past with stunning clarity. It had taken him a few moments to identify the fragrance: the mouth-watering scent of warm caramel and the pleasantly acrid smell of burnt candlewick.

He didn't doubt that many women lit caramel-scented candles in their homes. For all he knew, those candles were all the rage. Was it such a mind-blowing coincidence that Jen burned them? Probably not. But it didn't help him to know that even her home reminded him so poignantly of Diana.

He ran both hands through his hair and let out a long, harsh breath. He'd lost all perspective where Jen was concerned. All he knew for sure was that he'd vowed to put Diana behind him, to start his life over, without thoughts of her. Then he'd met a woman who reminded him of her, had made love to that woman, and had suddenly found himself teetering on the edge of obsession.

He had to put a stop to it. He had to set aside his preconceived image of Jen and see her for what she really was. Since he wasn't sure that he could trust his gut instincts in regard to her, he would ignore them. He would base his understanding on what she said and did—not on his belief that he could read her soul, and breach her maddening facade.

Perhaps there was no facade. Perhaps she was exactly as she claimed. In which case, he was making a damn fool of himself.

Tense with self-directed anger, he frowned at his watch and scowled at the doorway of her apartment. Thirty-four minutes had gone by. She was fourteen minutes late. Would she change her mind about going with him?

Breathing in deeply to restore his equanimity, he focused on the serenity of the partially wooded landscape and the surprising heat of the September day—hot compared to the last few days, and far more humid than Southern California at this time of year. A sweet aroma wafted from the honeysuckle vines that clung to the mailbox posts. The lazy buzz of bees sounded from the colorful begonia beds bordering the walkway to her apartment.

Just as his tension began to ease, her apartment door opened, and she stepped out onto the cedar-railed porch. She was wearing the hat he'd given her, its small brim dipped low in the front to shadow her face. Only a few dark blond tendrils had escaped to trail down her neck. The large, round sunglasses he'd given her concealed her eyes. And dark red lipstick gleamed on her mouth.

The lipstick was something of a surprise. Her lips had been a smooth, natural, pearly-pink color. The dark red, along with the hat and sunglasses, gave her a glamorous, mysterious look.

Not until she'd finished locking her door and descending the three short steps from the shrubbery-surrounded porch did Trev see the rest of her. The beige blazer was long and slim, more like a tunic, ending mid-thigh. Beneath it, a sheer, gauzy skirt of beige with large red poppies swayed around her legs. A *very* sheer skirt. The bright afternoon sunlight rendered the fabric virtually transparent, clearly illuminating her mile-long legs. Strappy high-heel sandals only emphasized the curvaceousness of those legs. The vampy high-heeled shoes were red, too, like the poppies on her skirt and her glossy lipstick.

Trev swallowed against a suddenly dry throat. Gleaming lips and long curvy legs in high spiked heels had a way of doing that to him. And there was something purposely sexual about the sway of her hips as she walked—

"Sorry I took so long. I decided to pack an extra bag, after all."

The amiable greeting drew his gaze away from the enticing movement of her hips, and he realized she carried a small suitcase in one hand and an overnight bag in the other. Glad to see that she still intended to stay with him, he climbed from the car, took the bags from her and tossed them into the back seat. He then escorted her around to the passenger door and opened it for her.

She no longer smelled like Diana. An exotic perfume drifted to him as she crossed his path to climb into the car. Alluring though the fragrance was, he wasn't sure he liked the change.

She settled into the leather passenger seat, and he noticed another change. She was wearing more jewelry than he'd previously seen her wear. Several delicate gold chains of varying lengths shimmered around her neck, and large golden hoops dangled from her earlobes.

She'd painted her long, oval nails differently, too. Red. Siren red.

Uneasiness stole over him as he strode around the car to the driver's seat. Although she looked good—elegant, really, in a flashy kind of way—he couldn't shake the feeling that this style wasn't her.

But how could he know that? He couldn't. He had to keep in mind that the woman was a stranger, and this was his opportunity to get to know her—*if* he wasn't blinded by preconceived notions. Though she'd dressed much more conservatively the other two times he'd seen her, maybe this *was* her preferred style.

They drove in silence, until he turned out of her neighborhood and onto a rural highway.

"What play are we going to see?" she asked.

"An original work by a local playwright. A murder mystery."

"Oh, good. I love mysteries."

He smiled as he drove, glad to know at least that much about her. "Have you seen or read many of them?"

"I've read hundreds."

"You haven't, by any chance, written any, have you?"

"Written any? No. No, never!"

He angled her a glance. He'd only been making conversation, but the casual question seemed to have upset her. Her denial had been too fervent. She could have added, *I swear I haven't!* and the effect would have been the same.

And now, though half her face was hidden by the sunglasses, she looked flustered by his silent regard. "I...I know why you asked the question, Trev. Because your wife was a writer. But I'm not. Like I told you when we first met—I can't *be* the wife you lost."

Anger stirred in him. "Don't you think I know that?"

"No, I don't think you do. I think you expect me to act just like her. I think that's one of the reasons you can't accept me for what I am—a working girl."

He gripped the wheel harder and stared straight ahead.

She was probably right, but he still felt wrongly accused. "I was only going to say that if you liked mysteries—or had any experience in writing—maybe you could help me decide on an ending for the play I'm trying to finish. My wife left a pile of notes, but I haven't been able to make much sense of them. A connoisseur of mysteries might help me figure out 'who done it.'"

She didn't immediately reply, and when he glanced at her again, she was nibbling her bottom lip. "You mean, you don't even know who the murderer is, and you're going to write the last act?" Now she sounded appalled.

"I've read the play three times, and each time I come up with a different villain. It could be *any* of the characters. How am I supposed to figure out which one she meant it to be?"

She stared at him for a moment. Then, to his endless surprise, she burst into laughter. Genuine, unreserved laughter. The sound delighted him. And shook him. She sounded too much like Diana. Something akin to pain pierced his chest.

"That is the sign of a good mystery," she said, her voice lively from laughter and inexplicably smug. "Then again, if you don't read mysteries, you might be missing the clues that would tell a connoisseur exactly 'who done it.'" She gazed at him again, and he wished the sunglasses weren't hiding her eyes. Her smile had softened in a way that warmed him. "You do need help. And I do enjoy mysteries. Did you bring the script with you from California?"

"Yes. It's in one of the boxes that we'll unpack tomorrow. Since you're officially working for me for the next two days, maybe that can be one of your projects. You know, to read it."

She nodded. "Okay. I'll take a look at it."

"Thanks."

He stopped the car at a red light, and they exchanged companionable smiles. But when the smiles ended, he couldn't look away. She was simply too beautiful. Even with the hat concealing her hair, and the sunglasses hiding much of her face, and the red lipstick looking dramatic and foreign to her lips, she appealed to him on a bone-deep level.

His continued regard brought a flush to her face, and she turned her head. The lighthearted moment was broken, and frustration filled him. He'd caught a glimpse of the real her, but then she'd slammed the door again. Why?

The traffic light changed, and he guided the car onto an expressway heading north. They drove in silence for a good many miles, each lost in private musings.

"The weather's taken quite a turn," she finally remarked. "It's warmer than I'd expected. Too warm."

"We can roll up the windows and turn on the—" His words broke off, and he nearly wrenched his neck in a quick double take. She'd shrugged out of her blazer and now wore a sleeveless dress, the bodice the same gauzy, billowy fabric as the skirt. Beige with red poppies...and sheer. Very sheer.

And she wore no bra.

The car swerved and veered onto the grassy shoulder of the highway, nearly jolting them both from their seats. She grabbed the handgrip above her door, as Trev fought with the wheel to get the car back onto the pavement. When he'd regained firm control, he demanded, "Why the hell are you dressed like that?"

"Like what?"

"You know damn well, 'like what.'"

Releasing the handgrip, she settled back onto the seat, smoothed the transparent folds of the dress over her long, lean thighs and lounged in a sultry pose, her hat riding low over her face, her dark glasses hiding her eyes...while her rosy-dark nipples strained against the delicate fabric, each proud crest as visible as if she wore the sheerest negligee.

She was *naked* under that dress. Or almost naked—she was, at least, wearing panties. Lacy panties cut high at her hips. Red, yet.

"Better watch the road, Trev, honey, or we'll end up on the median."

He scowled, forced his gaze away from her and fixed it on the expressway. Thank God there wasn't any traffic immediately surrounding them, or they'd have been in a wreck by now. "What are you trying to do—get us killed?"

"What's wrong?" she taunted. "Afraid people might think you're with a *naughty girl?*"

"Oh, they'll definitely know that." He allowed himself one more all-encompassing stare. "Is this exhibition meant as a personal invitation, or are you trying to make some kind of point?"

"I'm not sure what you mean. Since I'm away from the office and the neighborhood where I live, I didn't see any reason to be...you know, inhibited." She smiled—a slow, sleek curving of her glossy red mouth. "I have to admit, Trev...it gives me a thrill to turn men on. And on the more practical side, dressing 'for show' provides me with a great networking opportunity."

Networking? Had she said *networking?* He had no idea what she meant. Or maybe he simply hadn't focused on her explanation. She'd shifted in her seat to face him, drawing his attention again to her lush, supple, barely veiled body. He couldn't help responding. His blood rushed; his body hardened. *He wanted her.* He wanted to lay her down on the seat and fill his hands and mouth with her. Feel her beneath him. Push deep, deep into her....

"I watch for men who seem interested, then slip them my number, along with my rates."

That remark cut through his preoccupation, and his anger rebounded, stronger than ever. His teeth locked; his pulse roared in his ears. She was baiting him. Deliberately. And he knew why—to make him realize that he couldn't change her. To make him see her as a prostitute, a willing whore, instead of a victim of desperate circumstances.

Maybe she was right. Maybe this was just what he needed—a strong, harsh dose of reality. How far would she go to convince him?

He had to know.

He let his gaze sweep over her breasts, and noticed a slight blush rise into her face. What the hell was that blush about, if she was so brazen? "Dressed as you are, you won't be disappointed. You'll get plenty of notice from interested men."

"I...I hope that won't bother you."

"You know it will." He leveled her a hard stare. "It'll bother me, Jen, because I want you to get out of the business. For your own sake, not mine."

She averted her head and lifted her chin.

He returned his eyes to the road, although his insides roiled with unreasonable anger, doubt and, worst of all, desire. She didn't look much at all like Diana at the moment, but he still felt a profound connection with her. A damn idiotic, dangerous way to feel about a prostitute.

"I guess you might not understand," she said, "the way I feel about men. There's just nothing as exciting as doing something illicit with a stranger."

Did she really believe that? His first impulse was to rule out that possibility and consider the statement a blatant attempt to convince him she was beyond saving. But he'd sworn not to trust his gut instinct, and to see her for what she really was—not what he wanted her to be.

"Like the other night," she continued. "Last Tuesday. I was working a hotel lobby in Brunswick, and I caught this man's eye. We—"

"We're far enough away from Sunrise now, and no one's here to recognize you. Take off the hat and sunglasses."

"The hat and sunglasses?"

"Yes. Please. They're distracting." And he wanted to read her eyes as she told her tales. "Besides, it's starting to get dark. Soon you won't be able to see."

With a graceful shrug, she took off the hat, causing a few more silky strands from a casual twist of her thick, shiny hair to curl down her neck. She then removed the sunglasses and tucked them into her small beige purse. Her face was exotically made up, he noticed, with thick mascara and bold strokes of kohl that emphasized the size and color of her smoke-blue eyes. Despite the excessive makeup, she was undeniably striking. She belonged on a stage, or the silver screen.

But not on a street corner, which was clearly the effect she'd been aiming for.

"So, what were you saying about last Tuesday night?" he prompted, bracing himself for whatever she was about to tell.

"Oh, yes. Tuesday. Well, I caught the eye of this one businessman, and on the way up to his room, he stopped the elevator, and we…we did it right there, between the eleventh and twelfth floors. He had to be careful to keep his finger on the stop button the entire time. It was *sooo* exciting." She shook her head as if fondly remembering. "Times like that really make the job worthwhile."

He almost snorted. *Worthwhile.* She couldn't be serious. But since he wasn't sure, he replied, "You don't have to be a professional to do things like that. Just find yourself an adventurous boyfriend."

"You mean…give sex away for *free*? Why would I want to do that? There's big money to be made. Take Wednesday night, for example. I got a call from a member of the…well, of a visiting sports team. What a time we had, just me and the guys. Those professional ballplayers really know their moves! And afterward, I walked away with a tidy bundle of cash. What could be better?"

Trev managed to refrain from replying. He didn't want to antagonize her. If she was trying to shock him, she'd be sorely disappointed. Because for the life of him, he couldn't bring himself to believe a word she'd said.

She narrowed her gaze on him as if she sensed his disbelief, then went on to relate in graphic detail a scene that could have come straight out of a porno flick.

She *did* succeed in surprising him. He hadn't expected to hear her describe those actions, especially not in such explicit terms. By the time she'd finished, he had no reason left to doubt her expertise regarding orgies.

So then, why did he? Why did he suspect that those details had, indeed, come right out of a porno flick? Was this what a shrink would call "denial"? He honestly didn't know, and the doubt revived his self-directed anger. Hadn't he sworn to disregard his gut instincts? What the hell was he doing, then, discounting everything she said?

"I hope I'm not boring you," she murmured. "Once I get started talking shop, I—"

"No, please. Talk all you'd like. I find it...enlightening."

Jennifer glanced at him doubtfully. She'd been hoping that he would find it exactly that—enlightening. Was he starting to believe the worst about her? His tone was light, and she sensed skepticism, but the tautness of his jaw and the stiffness of his broad shoulders alerted her to an undercurrent of strong emotion. She hoped it was anger—at himself, for getting so ridiculously involved in the affairs of a prostitute. She hoped she had convinced him to wash his hands of her.

In spite of her best intentions, though, that prospect tore at her heart. Once she succeeded, she would have to leave him. She wished so very much that there wasn't a need to deceive him, or to leave him—but the need was too real to forget.

Determined to finish the job of ruining herself in his eyes, she regaled him with another lewd story she'd found on the Internet. She'd been embarrassed at first to tell him such things. What little remained of the sheltered schoolgirl in her had cringed at every lurid word. But the awkwardness had faded, and she now held back none of the seamy details.

"A cherry lollipop?" Trev drawled when she'd finished. "You danced on an air-hockey table to the tune of 'Cherry Pie,' and the groom-to-be actually did that to you...with a lollipop?"

"Actually, he just held the stick in his mouth, and I...well, I've already explained that part of the performance to you."

His lips tightened. With disgust, she hoped. After a moment, though, he murmured without lifting his gaze from the road, "I read that one, too."

"Pardon me?"

"It's from the Internet. I found a printout of it in my kid brother's room, and grounded him for a week. The cherry lollipop, the air-hockey table...even the cheerleader skirt and pom-pom that supposedly made up your costume. It was all there."

"Are you saying I'm lying?" she cried, anxiety lending too much vehemence to the question. She really couldn't afford to have him catch her in these lies. The whole point of her naughty dress and erotic tales was to discourage his interest in her—not to stir up his suspicions.

"I'm saying you took that scenario off the Internet," he maintained.

"Okay, maybe I did. That's what gave me the idea. And it was a big hit at that bachelor party, believe me."

"The guy just happened to have an air-hockey table."

"Yes!"

"Last Thursday. The night after you did the Baltimore Orioles."

"I didn't say what team it was!"

"But it *was* a professional ball team, you said. Visiting...Sunrise?"

Was that so unlikely? He seemed to think so. "Savannah," she corrected. "I told you I sometimes work in Savannah."

"Ah. So it was one of the many fine professional ball teams who hang out in Savannah."

She glared at him, angry and frustrated by his scorn. "They were there for a charity promotion." Surely *that* was possible! "Why would I lie about any of this?"

"I don't know, Jen." He glanced at her then. "Why would you?" His gaze simmered with dark, serious emotion.

Her heart nearly beat its way out of her chest. How could a single gaze set her pulse to pounding and her thoughts to whirling, and make her want to hit him and kiss him at the same time?

While she struggled with her careening emotions, he stopped the car and turned off the ignition. Glancing around, she realized with surprise that they'd arrived at their destination. The surrounding parking lot was crowded with cars, but only a few late stragglers like themselves could be seen making their way toward the huge, warehouse-like building. A small neon sign above the entrance proclaimed it to be The Georgia Seaside Dinner Theater.

"Ready?" Trev asked her, pocketing his keys.

Stiffly she nodded, striving to regroup after his refusal to believe her. The man could be infuriatingly hardheaded when he wanted to be. Snatching her blazer from the seat beside her, she edged forward on the seat to shrug into it.

He caught hold of the jacket. "You won't need this. The night's still warm."

Her gaze shifted to him in surprise. Why in heaven's name would he discourage her from wearing the blazer? Her dress was much too sheer to go anywhere without one. "Well, yes, the night's still warm, but the air-conditioning inside will probably be too chilly."

"I'll carry the blazer for you." He tugged the jacket away from her and threw it over his arm. "If you get cold while we're inside, I'll help you into it." Without waiting for her reply, he climbed out of the car, locked his door and ambled around to her side.

Suddenly she understood exactly what he was doing—calling her bluff. It would take a brazen woman indeed to strut into a public place dressed as she was. The blazer had been the perfect answer—instant cover, when and where she needed it. She'd never intended for anyone other than Trev to see her in this transparent dress, which she usually wore with a substantial set of undergarments. She'd been sure that he would insist on her wearing the blazer...or, at the very least, not protesting when she did.

He opened her door and offered his hand to help her out.

She sat rigidly in the passenger seat, highly aware of a young couple walking a short distance away in the well-lit parking lot. "Don't be silly, Trev. There's no need for you to carry my jacket."

"I insist."

She gazed at him in growing dismay. She had to have it! As he very well knew, damn him. "I need my jacket," she insisted between clenched teeth. "I'm already cold."

His gaze swept across her breasts, and the hint of a smile curled his mouth. "No, darlin', you're not."

She crossed her arms over her breasts and scowled at him. Didn't he think he was clever? "If I walk in like this, they'll turn us away. Believe me, it's happened to me before."

"Then how did you intend to put your 'networking' plan into action?"

"Discreetly...and only when I'm ready."

"This should be interesting."

"You probably won't even be aware that I'm doing it."

Something serious flashed in his eyes. "Oh, I'll be aware."

"What are you going to do, watch me every minute?"

"While you're dressed like that? Probably. How the hell can I help it?"

She didn't believe he meant it as a compliment. And she

didn't believe he meant to give in. Panic sparked within her. She wouldn't, *couldn't*, enter that theater without her blazer. "Go in without me. Enjoy the play. I'm sure I'll find *plenty* to keep me occupied out here in the parking lot."

Muttering a curse beneath his breath, he tossed the blazer to her.

Relieved to have it, but resentful that he'd shaken her so, she donned the blazer and followed him across the parking lot. He clearly wasn't pleased, striding ahead of her with his mighty shoulders squared and his hands deep in his pockets. But when he reached the theater, he held the door for her, then slid an arm around her waist and pulled her against him. She felt the tension in his iron-strong arm and the warm, hard musculature of his body.

"Do whatever you want, Jen," he murmured against her hair, as they waited for the hostess's attention. "But if any guy makes a disrespectful move toward the woman I'm with, I'll have to demand an apology—and beat him to a bloody pulp if he doesn't give it."

The thought alarmed her. What if someone *did* make a disrespectful move toward her? The blazer covered her sufficiently all the way to mid-thigh, but from there down, her skirt was very sheer. Would some loudmouth jerk make an issue of it, and provoke Trev into a fight? She hadn't seen that side of him before, and didn't want to. Her alarm angered her. "That's another reason you shouldn't be with a prostitute," she furiously whispered to him.

"That's another reason you shouldn't *be* a prostitute," he whispered back. "Men tend to lose their heads around loose women. But then, I'm not sure how 'loose' you really are. You talk the talk, but I haven't seen you walk the walk."

"I slept with you for money, didn't I?"

"I believe that's *all* you've done. And I know damn well you'd have rather died than walk into this place without your blazer."

"I didn't want us to be turned away at the door. And if you're so set on defending my honor against the first guy who looks at me, why did you *want* me to walk in without my blazer?"

"I didn't. I just wanted to see if you would."

"Don't challenge me, Trev. You might not like what I'll do."

"I'm not challenging you. But if you're going to canvass for new customers, don't do it behind my back."

"What good would it do to look for new customers, when you're ready to beat 'em to a bloody pulp?"

"Damn good point."

Their heated, whispered exchange was interrupted by a cheery greeting from the hostess, an aging flower-child with long frizzy hair, a peace sign embroidered on her faded jeans and Greenpeace buttons on her Grateful Dead T-shirt. They followed her into a fairly crowded dining room arranged around a raised stage. The red velvet curtains hadn't yet opened; the diners busied themselves with their meals and quiet conversation. The hostess led Trev and Jennifer to a table in the back row.

Trev leaned in close to the hostess and spoke in a pleasant undertone. She glanced at an upper tier of tables, all unoccupied, then shook her head with clear regret. "Sorry, man. I know it's a bummer, but the balcony's closed on weekdays."

He spoke to her again, his voice low, his tone persuasive. After a moment's hesitation, she cast him a conspiratorial glance and led them up a side stairway to the dimly lit balcony. "How can I risk bad karma by saying no to a honeymooning couple? Especially since you drove all that way to be with us."

She seated them in the very last booth of the vacant balcony—a relatively private compartment shaped in a *U*, with high-backed cushioned seats, lush green plants on either side and red-checked linen adorning the table. The table itself was anchored to the solid wooden railing of the balcony, allowing them a bird's-eye view of the dining room and stage.

Jennifer slid into the horseshoe-shaped seat, scooting to the middle. Trev slid in beside her—much closer than was necessary.

The hostess smiled and set menus before them. "I'll send a server right up. You'll need to order soon. We like to have everyone served by the time the lights go down, so we don't disrupt the audience during the show. Enjoy!" With one last beaming smile, she hurried back downstairs.

Jennifer turned to Trev with a raised brow. "Honeymooning couple? You're sure to burn in hell for that one."

He settled his arm along the curved top of her seat, casually against her shoulders, making her all the more aware of his nearness. And his fresh, masculine soap scent. And the alluring warmth of his muscled thigh against hers.

"Whatever works," he said. She saw no humor in his stare—only dark, hot determination. "I wanted to be alone with you."

The gruffness of his voice made her blood rush. Was she imagining the intimacy in his tone, his words? Unsure of how to read him after their angry confrontation—and ready to make peace with him, to enjoy what they could of the evening, since her time with him *was* so precious—she earnestly assured him, "You don't have to worry about me attracting the wrong kind of attention. I've decided to take the night off and relax."

"Relax?" He frowned and brushed a stray tendril from her face. The featherlight touch of his fingers against her temple sent warmth tingling down her face, neck and shoulder—all the way to the pit of her stomach. "You, the insatiable sex queen...not on the prowl? And here I thought you craved excitement."

The faintest, silkiest thread of sarcasm in his voice set her teeth on edge. Why did he persist in his obstinate refusal to believe in her depravity? "I do," she swore. "It makes me feel alive "

His gaze lingered on her eyes, her hair, her mouth. "Then prove it to me. Make a believer of me, Jen. As soon as the lights go down."

6

SHE DIDN'T IMMEDIATELY reply to his challenge. She turned to the menu as a diversion, and when their jovial, auburn-haired waitress with a rural Georgia twang announced the specials of the evening, Jennifer took her time ordering. She then fell silent, while they waited to be served. Avoiding Trev's gaze by peering down at the bustling dining room, she hoped he would think she was deliberately keeping him in suspense, rather than guess the truth—that she was utterly torn on how to respond.

What exactly had he meant by his challenge? Should she take him up on it, or think of a reason not to?

He didn't show any signs of anxiously awaiting her answer. And he didn't seem bothered by her silence. By the time the food arrived, she'd figured out why. He considered her lack of a reply an answer in itself. That answer was clearly the one he'd been expecting.

He thought he'd called her bluff again.

What she wouldn't give to shock that knowing look right off his too-handsome face! He was so cocksure that she hadn't done all those lurid things she'd described. It made no difference that he was right. She was a stranger to him, damn it. She'd slept with him for money. He had no grounds whatsoever to think she wasn't wildly promiscuous.

She speared a forkful of Caesar salad and crunched down on a crouton in annoyance. Irking her, too, was the fact that he seemed willing to engage in illicit sex in a public place, where they could easily be caught. Maybe even arrested.

What was he thinking? Or...was he that sure she'd turn him down?

She simmered with resentment. He'd called her bluff one too many times. She couldn't allow him to do it again. What exactly did he have in mind, anyway? Her blood drummed at the possibilities. Wild, wicked possibilities. The erotic stories she'd told had opened a Pandora's box of possibilities. How far would Trev go?

She could have the answer soon. Very soon.

When the lights went down.

Warmth suffused her at that thought, and she took a deep swallow of her chilled peach wine. He had to be bluffing. He wouldn't dare do anything too risky in a public place. He'd always been thrillingly bold in their lovemaking, yes, but in the privacy of their home, or a hotel room or sometimes his car while parked in a secluded place. The Trev she'd known had been staunchly honorable, responsible and well-respected in the community—and a stickler for decent behavior from his brothers and sister under his care. He would do nothing that could ruin their family name.

Perhaps she should call *his* bluff.

Then again, she hadn't expected him to buy sex from a prostitute. Stealing a glance at him while he sliced off a bite of his T-bone steak, she had to admit that he wasn't the same man she'd married. He was somehow harder on the inside. Tougher. More cynical. And she was no longer the woman he loved. They really were, for all intents and purposes, strangers.

What would he do if she took him up on his challenge?

She set her fork aside, unable to eat another bite. As if taking his cue from her, he pushed aside the remainder of his steak and lounged back in his seat, nursing a glass of burgundy and watching her. His silent regard and palpable nearness heightened her tension.

To escape his gaze, she peered down from their booth on

the balcony at the crowded dining room below, where servers cleared away dishes from the tables and replenished drinks. The music had grown louder. Spotlights illuminated the red velvet curtains on stage.

The lights would soon go down.

Her pulse drummed in her throat. She had dressed for the role of wanton. She had studied for it, had told outrageous lies to convey the image of hopeless promiscuity.

Prove it to me, Jen. Make a believer out of me.

Obstinate man! He really did deserve to be put in his place.

"Almost show time," he remarked, very near to her ear, a slight but self-satisfied smile in his voice.

Oh, yes...he was certain that he had her pegged. She simply had to disabuse him of that notion. Keeping her gaze trained on the room below, she tipped her head close to his so he could catch a sultry whisper. "So, what did you have in mind for...Act One?"

Silence answered her, as if she'd surprised him. But then she felt his touch at her nape—a slow, downward sweep of his fingers, and his voice, when he spoke, sounded husky and languid. "Like I told you before, I'm no playwright. I thought we'd make up the script as we went along." Her neck tingled from his light caress, and her cheek warmed from his breath. "Of course, I'd value any of your expert input."

Only someone who knew Trev well would discern the wryness in that statement. She knew him well enough. She also knew the exact moves that would drive that wryness from his mind, along with all rational thought. With very little effort, she could light a match to his kindling. Fan his fire. Bring him to his knees.

Oh, my, Jennifer. What are you thinking? You're letting yourself get carried away. It was true—and the very idea thrilled her. She'd been excruciatingly good for too long. For seven years, she'd lived in a prison of caution and fear, analyzing the wisdom of every move. She longed to break free, just this once, for a brief taste of wildness. With Trev—the only man she'd ever wanted. The only man she'd ever loved.

"I don't know, Trev." Summoning her most sultry look, she turned a vampish gaze to him. "You're such a clean-cut, upstanding citizen. I wouldn't want to shock you."

"*Shock* me?" He let out a small, disbelieving laugh. "Shock *me?*"

She tilted her head judiciously and searched his face, as if contemplating the effect she might have on him. She really was beginning to enjoy the game. "You seemed upset by the confidences I shared with you earlier. You refused even to believe them. It's sweet, really. I'd hate to ruin that school-boy innocence of yours."

He stared at her in clear surprise.

She mentally marked a point in her favor.

But then he threw back his head and laughed. Not just a short, dry bark, or even a casual chuckle, but a deep, hardy laugh of genuine amusement. The sound of it embraced her like a heartfelt hug. It had been so long since she'd heard that particular laugh. And even though a sense of loss touched her, gladness buoyed her far above it—the pure, simple gladness of having elicited that laugh from him.

And when his laughter wound down, he wrapped his arm around her and tugged her closer, his smile warm, his gaze playing appreciatively over her face. "Don't let my innocence stop you, Jen. Please. Go ahead and, uh, shock me."

His gaze left no doubt that he was enjoying her. That he'd rather be with her than anyone else. That he saw into her very soul and found only delight. Ridiculous, of course, that she should read so much into a simple gaze. Ridiculous, how that gaze could make her fall in love all over again.

Wanting to prolong the moment, to savor it and tuck it away in her heart, she ran her fingertip across his smiling lips. "But how can I be sure that when I overwhelm you with my wickedness, you won't moan too loud and get us caught?"

Amusement still glinted in his gaze, but with the sweep of her finger across his mouth, sensuality also swirled into those amber eyes. "It's a definite risk. But then, isn't risk part of the excitement that makes you 'feel alive'?"

He'd always been good at turning her own words against her. And she'd always rallied to the challenge. "Without a doubt." Luxuriating in the freedom to touch him, tease him, she ran her hand through his thick, maple-brown hair, her fingertips lightly skimming his scalp, exactly the way he most enjoyed. "There's just something about living on the edge that turns me on."

Even while she talked nonsense, though, she couldn't help wondering what the most wanton woman could possibly do in a restaurant booth, where a waitress could stroll by at any minute.

Before any solid ideas presented themselves, the lights began to slowly dim. She'd expected as much, of course. Knew that darkness would claim the entire massive room. The onset of it jolted her, anyway. Darkness had a way of wrapping a hand around her vital organs and squeezing.

Blackness soon blocked her view of the dining room below, leaving a frightening black hole between her and the spotlights blazing across the red stage curtains. Pressing close to Trev, she sought his warmth and solid presence. Without hesitation, he drew her into his arms. Gradually her eyes adjusted, helped by the faint, hazy glow of tiny floor lights that bordered the staircase and the walkway behind them. It was enough to calm her.

Wondering what he'd thought of her sudden move into his arms, she lifted her head from his chest and peered up at him. He stared back at her with potent heat, and need, and clear, strong reluctance to let her go. His gaze alone stirred embers in her blood, drugged her with sensuality, pushed her ever closer to recklessness.

She barely noticed that in the room below, the stage curtains had swept open, or that the audience responded with applause. She wanted to feel his hands on her. Wanted to taste his kiss.

As if reading her mind, he swept his hand up and down her back, beneath her blazer, where his heat radiated through the sheer fabric of her dress. His stirring caress pressed her body harder against his, and after a long, hot-eyed stare, he slanted his mouth over hers and led her into a deep, rousing kiss.

But the kiss was too moving, inciting too great a need within her. Too great a vulnerability. When he kissed her like this, she was his. Entirely his. He filled up her soul completely. As much as she wanted such oneness with him, her survival instinct wouldn't allow it, and she pulled away in alarm.

With long, hard breaths and converging brows, he searched her face for an explanation.

She knew she had to collect her wits and keep in mind the game they were playing. What self-respecting wanton would shy away from a mere kiss? Forcing a smile, she tapped a finger against his chest and strove for lightness. "*I'm* writing the script here, not you."

He frowned as if he'd forgotten the nonsense they'd been talking and needed a moment to make sense of her retort. In the room below them, actors' voices rang out from a homey living room on stage, and a chuckle rose from the audience. Neither Trev nor Jennifer paid the tableau on stage more than a passing glance.

"Pardon me for ad-libbing," Trev finally replied. "Open the curtains whenever you're ready, Jen. I'm dying to see the performance."

Though spoken in a voice hoarse with desire, the words

were clearly a taunt. She was glad. She could handle a taunt much easier than she could hold herself aloof when he kissed her. She decided then and there to make quick work of this challenge, to consider it a job that needed to be done. Or, at best, recreational sex. Not intimacy. Not an expression of what she felt for him. She would, in fact, become the shallow-hearted wanton she pretended to be.

She knew the moves he couldn't resist—the ones that would speed him along to a quick, hard climax. If both she and he were reasonably discreet, the high-backed booth, the solid wooden railing of the balcony, and the table with its overhanging linen would provide enough cover. No one would see anything more than a couple cuddling.

"If you're really ready for the show to begin," she murmured in his ear, settling against his shoulder again, "think of this as a drumroll." Reaching into his lap, she brushed her fingers over the column of his arousal, hard and broad beneath the black denim of his jeans. She felt his reaction in the sudden tautness of his body. Lightly she scraped her nails up the length of his erection, surprising a harsh breath from him. Before she'd even reached the top, she felt it swelling beneath her fingers, until it strained behind the zipper of his jeans.

His breathing grew openmouthed and erratic, and his hand moved in restless paths along her back, sending hot, sensual sparks through her. Determined to maintain strict control and build his anticipation beyond bearing, she tried her best to ignore his touch while she slowly unsnapped his jeans.

"And now, at long last," she said, her own pulse roaring in her ears, "the curtain opens, center stage." She pulled his zipper slowly down the tight, imposing swell until she'd freed his erection within the softer, giving confines of his white cotton briefs.

"Jen." He tightened his arm around her and pressed his

jaw to her temple. "If this makes you uncomfortable, just say so. You don't have to—"

"Uncomfortable? Me?" She drew back to gaze into his face, visibly taut with suppressed need while his erection continued to burgeon beneath her hand. The tip now protruded an impressive distance above the waistband of his briefs. Slowly, teasingly, she pushed the elastic band and soft white cotton down, down, until it bunched near the thick, pulsating base. "The excitement has just begun. The actors are about to enter the stage."

"Actors?"

She held up her index finger. "The star of our show."

He narrowed his gaze at it, as if he didn't quite grasp her meaning.

Inserting her finger into her mouth, she leisurely sucked on it, then drew it out, wet and gleaming. With deliberate slowness, she reached below the tabletop again. "Don't you feel the plot already thickening?"

"Oh, yeah," he breathed.

She smoothed her slick fingertip across the bare, velvety tip of his erection. At the initial contact, every muscle in his body clenched. She then brushed a soothing kiss across his granite-hard jaw...and circled the swollen head of his arousal with her finger, sweeping lower now and then across the sensitive ridges. "What do you think of the choreography so far?"

He muttered something unintelligible, and as she shifted to grip him with her palm, he grabbed her hand and tightly held it.

Surprised, she raised her face to his in silent question.

"You said you wanted excitement," he said in a strained whisper. "Where's the excitement in a one-act play?"

"That depends entirely on the power of the climax."

"Oh, I'll agree with you there." He released her hand and shifted his large, lean body lower into the cushioned seat, pulling her down with him, into his arms, until she reclined against him at an angle in the *U*-shaped booth, eye-level with the tabletop. "I think we need a larger supporting cast, don't you?"

"Supporting—?"

He held up two fingers. Two long, tan, virile fingers, held straight and stiff and close together. As he slid them into his mouth, his smoky gaze fixed intently on her, and warmth leaped in her loins. He then drew his fingers out, where they glistened wickedly in the meager light. "Co-stars," he whispered.

Reaction flared low in her womb.

"Trev, w-wait." She could barely force the words from her throat. He was pushing this game too far. It was one thing for her to slip a discreet hand beneath the table—which was all she'd really have to do to bring him to climax, and all she'd be willing to do in a public place—but quite another for him to try anything of the kind. She couldn't possibly put herself into such a vulnerable position. "You...you don't have to...I mean, I really don't—"

"You 'really don't'...what?"

The expectant demand in his prompting reminded her that if she backed down, he would win the dare. As she searched her mind for a plausible excuse to sidestep the challenge, he drew her back into the game with a kiss—a hot, persuasive melding of mouths, lulling her into distraction, until she wrapped her arms around his neck and gave in to irresistible passion. The kiss grew steadily more urgent, more blatantly sexual.

Dark excitement gripped her. She never had been able to resist his kisses...or his stirringly intimate touches.

His hand wended beneath her dress, along her inner thigh. She didn't stop him. Couldn't bear to stop him. In fact, she hooked her leg around his beneath the table, granting him easier access. With a hoarse murmur of male appreciation, he stroked between her legs with the backs of his fingers, up and down in slow, light passes along the silk of her panties, until a tortured moan escaped her.

He exhaled in a hot torrent against her neck. "Shh."

While she fought to swallow another moan, his fingers slid beneath the silk crotch of her panties to glide in teasing paths. Fires lit in her blood. Her back arched. Her hips moved. And with a needful groan of his own, he thrust his fingers inside her. Deep. Deeper, in a pumping motion, while his thumb remained outside to stroke, circle and pull.

Heat coursed through her with dizzying force as pleasure radiated and tension coiled. She was losing control, she knew. Her body writhed of its own volition, and she couldn't stop the sounds from rising in her throat. With every rhythmic slide of his fingers, her need heightened.

And she realized that he watched her face, his gaze golden and hot, his jaw clenched, his breathing hard.

"Trev," she whispered frantically, digging her fingers into the hard brawn of his shoulders. "Stop. We've got to stop."

He paused, but didn't withdraw. "Why?" he asked in a low, drawn-out rasp that brought to mind steamy nights of the most provocative lovemaking. "Tell me why, Jen."

"Because I...we..." She could barely speak between pants of breath, thunderous heartbeats and maddening moves of his thumb. Edging ever closer to climax, she stifled a gasp and caught his wrist in desperation.

They stared at each other in hot, tense silence, while somewhere below them an audience applauded.

Slowly he withdrew his fingers from the throbbing, intimate center of her, the movement itself engendering another small crisis of sensation. "You didn't answer me," he whispered. "Why stop?"

She knew what he was after, of course. He wanted her to admit that she wasn't comfortable misbehaving like this.

That she'd lied about all those edgy encounters she'd described in explicit detail. That she wasn't so brazen, after all.

"If you're afraid of being caught," he said, running his hand in a slow, seductive path down her thigh, "or you're embarrassed to do something like this in a public place, just say so."

Though his touch played havoc with her senses, she managed to murmur, "I didn't say I was afraid or embarrassed. But...but—" she searched for a leg to stand on "—why should I be the only one getting all the action? Like you said before, how exciting can a one-act play be?"

"Pretty damn exciting." His hand ventured upward again while he leaned in close to her, nipped at her earlobe and whispered into her ear, "It doesn't bore me at all, Jen, to be inside you. To feel your heat, your tightness. To make you come while I hold you and watch you."

She groaned in helpless arousal, trapped his advancing hand between her thighs before he could completely undo her, and prevented him from saying another stirring word by kissing him into silence. The kiss only made things worse, though, pushing them both farther along into heady recklessness. His hands surged across the thin fabric of her dress, beneath her blazer, where he caressed her breasts and worked her nipples into hard, aching peaks.

Lightning spears of sensation spiked down to sizzle within her feminine core. How easy it would be to surrender to passion!

A roar of laughter from the audience brought her back to her senses. This was no place to indulge in passion. Though only their heads could be seen by anyone in the room below, neither he nor she had been watching out for waitresses or anyone else who might climb the stairway. Shaken by her lapse, she broke from his kiss, caught his hands at her breasts and laced her fingers through his to hold him securely captive.

"You're an exciting man, Trev Montgomery," she said in a shaky, breathy murmur. "I don't need the risk factor to liven things up with you. What do you say we go find ourselves a bed?" The idea sounded nothing less than brilliant to her.

He drew back slightly, his jaw clenched, and stared at her. Ah, the turmoil in that stare! Temptation reigned, strong and hot, but resistance held its ground. He hadn't proved his point, and that point seemed to have become something of an obsession with him.

"What's wrong, Jen?" A crooked smile deepened the groove beside his mouth, but didn't lighten the intensity of his gaze. "Chicken?"

Never had the man annoyed her more! But then, they'd always been good at pushing each other's buttons. Pulling her hands away from his, she glared at him. "No, I'm not 'chicken.' But I'm not stupid, either. Why do you think I haven't been arrested, like most of the other working girls I know? Because I'm cautious."

"Like, doing johns on elevators?"

"He kept his finger on the close button!"

"Why don't you just admit you didn't do any of those things—that you *wouldn't* do any of those things—and if you've ever sold yourself to anyone but me, you despised every minute of it."

Oh, this would never do. He was climbing up onto his white steed again, decked out in shining armor, ready to charge to her rescue whether she wanted him to or not. "Find us an elevator," she challenged, "and we'll see who calls it quits first."

"I don't intend to hold an elevator button while I have you in my arms." His gaze burned into hers. "I've got better things to do with my fingers."

A traitorous wave of heat flushed through her at that thought, and she averted her head, unsure if the darkness would prevent him from noticing the flush. He might read it as embarrassment, which would go a long way toward proving his case. Not that he would stop at that. He clearly intended to force an admission from her that she wasn't as uninhibited as she'd let on.

He caught her chin and tipped her face to his. "Come on, Jen. You know we don't need an elevator. The waitress said she wouldn't bother us during the show, and no one from the ground floor can see what's going on beneath this table. It's dark. We're alone. And we've got everything we need, right here. You and me—" he reached into his back pocket and tossed a small foil pack on the table "—and necessities."

She gaped at the packet. A condom. Did he really think they could engage in an activity that required a condom— here and now?

"Careful. You're looking a little shocked. Not at all like the gal who danced on the air-hockey table to the tune of 'Cherry Pie.'"

Jennifer met his gaze and realized that the bluff had come down to this moment. She could refuse him, and let him believe that he had found the limit to her sexual daring—which he would take to mean she'd lied about her other illicit activities. Or she could play along and find the limit to his sexual daring. Just because he'd initiated a little hanky-panky under a dimly lit, secluded table didn't mean he would actually engage in intercourse at a booth in a restaurant full of people. She didn't believe he would.

"While I suit up," he murmured, retrieving the foil packet from the table and plying her with a deliberately suggestive gaze, "why don't you take off those pretty red panties of yours? Unless you'd rather wait for my help."

No one but Trev Montgomery had the power to so arouse her ire and her keen sensuality at the same time.

Feeling hot, charged, and so brilliantly alive that she swore pure adrenaline pumped through her veins, she reached both hands beneath her skirt and hooked her fingers into the lacy side bands of her panties. With a few discreet wriggles and tugs, she worked the flimsy silk down her legs, slipped off her strappy high heels and bent to retrieve her underwear from around her ankles. She then sat up and flourished the panties for his private viewing like a red silk victory flag. She barely refrained from proclaiming, *Check, and checkmate.*

A slight smile curled his mouth, but his eyes grew darker and hotter as his gaze flickered down her body, reminding her that she sat naked beneath her sheer dress, rendered decent only by a thigh-length blazer. And he'd already touched her intimately; her blood still rushed from his bold ministrations beneath her skirt.

He took the panties from her, tossed them onto the seat beside him, crinkled up the empty foil packet and dropped it into an ashtray. Realizing the implication of that empty packet, Jennifer glanced toward his lower body. The tails of his black shirt and shadows of the tablecloth prevented her from seeing much. Had he put the condom on? Did he really intend to make use of it?

He slid his arm around her waist and drew her nearer. Her pulse quickened. Her blood rushed. Surely he'd call a stop to this craziness. But the heat in his stare and the set of his jaw suddenly gave her doubts. "Draw your legs up beneath you," he uttered tersely.

Surprised by the instruction, she curled her legs beneath her on the cushioned seat.

"Now put your arms around my neck."

Again she obeyed, raising up on her knees to comply. Nearly eye-level with him, she searched his gaze for signs that he would soon give up the game—cry uncle—but the heat pulsating between them was so intense that she soon lost sight of her purpose.

"Swing your knee across my lap," he ordered, sounding gruff and breathless.

Thoroughly breathless herself, she slid her knee across his

muscle-hard thighs to position it on the other side of him. As she straddled his lap, his strong, large hands splayed across her hips and guided her into place. He then tugged at her skirt and blazer to demurely cover her—at least, as far as any potential onlooker could see.

She, however, remained hotly aware of their partial nudity—locked against him in the tight confines between the seat and table, her pliant curves molding to his well-honed muscles, her bare femininity cradling his hard, broad, pulsing erection. Sexual need, for so long denied, now flamed within her. Dizzy, she tightened her arms around his strong neck and inhaled the virile, provocative scent of his hair and skin—the fragrance she always associated with lovemaking.

"Now kiss me," he murmured, his shining gaze shifting with hers, "and we'll get down to business."

Business. The word had never stirred her before. It did now. With a surge of carnal desire, she closed her eyes and angled her mouth across his.

But as their lips touched, he groaned, stiffened and pulled back from her. Her lashes fluttered open in surprise. Was he backing down, calling it quits, throwing in the towel? She wasn't sure if she was glad at that prospect, or keenly, blindly, madly disappointed.

"The only way this isn't going to happen, Jen," he growled, clearly frustrated by her obstinacy in going this far, yet undeniably aroused, and so sinfully handsome it almost hurt to look at him, "is if you tell me you want to stop."

She pointedly didn't say a word.

With a fierce rush of breath and a gaze that threatened to consume her, he slid lower into the seat, wedged a hand between their bodies and touched her. Probed her. Entered her. She gasped at the initial intrusion, arched her back, dug her fingers into the sinew of his shoulders.

He rose again to face her, eye to eye, locking her into close visual contact—a ruthless thing for him to do at a time like this, when her emotions ran so high and her resistance so low. But she couldn't, for the life of her, look away. With slow, subtle gyrations, he drove his immense hardness into her.

THE SHOCK OF SENSATION rendered them both still and silent, their eyes wide, their breathing suspended.

Trev knew then that he had well and truly lost his mind. He was making love in public, and to a woman he'd sworn not to touch. Worse, though, was the emotion pulsing through him. He was savagely elated to be inside her again. What she'd done or hadn't done paled in importance. Not even their surroundings mattered.

The very intensity of the reaction set off alarms in his head. "What are you doing to me, Jen?" His voice sounded hoarse and desperate to his own ears. "I want you too damn much." As he said it, he pushed deeper into her tight, welcoming heat.

She arched and uttered a cry.

Digging his fingers through her upswept hair, he pulled her to him. "Shh."

Nodding frantically, she pressed her face to his neck, but her body writhed, and her internal muscles clenched him. He thought he might die of the pleasure.

Through a heated, sensual haze, he heard her tremulous whisper. "You want me only because of *her*. Diana."

The words made no sense. Or maybe he just couldn't think beyond the blinding desire. He rocked into her again, keeping the motion as minimal as possible. The move, though slight, sent shockwaves of sensation through him. When he was able to speak again, he swore, "Diana has nothing to do with me wanting you." And he realized it was true. He hadn't been thinking of Diana at all. Only Jen.

"No. Shh. It's okay." She caught his face between her palms and kissed him—once, twice…then slower and deeper...courting the flames within him until they leaped and smoldered, and his hardness surged inside her.

He fought to contain the intensity streaming from his loins and the dizzying heat rushing to his head. He had to remember where they were, and the risk of being caught. He realized then how impossible it would be to hide what they were doing if someone climbed those stairs. Her face was too expressive, her movements too sensuous.

He longed to lay her down or brace her against a wall, and drive wildly into her, again and again.

And he wanted to make sure she knew with every thrust that he was making love to *her*, no one else. His memories of Diana were too precious to evoke, and his need for Jen possessed him too completely. But he could no longer speak to tell her anything. It took all his effort to restrict his movements, stifle his groans. She undulated with tiny, secret moves, fanning his inner fire, and the strain soon grew too great to endure.

And from the increasing urgency of her breathy gasps, he knew she was nearing completion. So was he. Just one good, jarring thrust would shove them both over the edge. Unable to hold back a moment longer, he gritted his teeth, splayed his hands around her hips and braced her for the impact.

But then a movement beyond them suddenly hooked his attention. A movement on the stairway. Auburn hair. White blouse. *Someone was climbing the stairs.*

Drawing in a deep, gasping breath, he fought to pull back on his raging need for release. "Jen." Breaking out into a sweat at the tremendous effort, he hoarsely whispered, "Someone's coming."

"Coming," she breathed, dazed with passion, hot and fluid in his arms, her hips circling, circling. "Ohhh...yes..."

He jerked his arms tighter around her, desperate to get her attention, and to stop her gyrations before she and he both lost control. "Not us. A waitress."

"A waitress?" The perplexity in her whisper and gaze soon gave way to wide-eyed awareness. "A waitress!"

"Shh." Struggling to normalize his chaotic breathing and contain the fire in his loins, he squinted through the heat and peered beyond her. Dread gathered in his chest. "She has people with her."

Jen stared at him in dawning horror. "Oh, my God! Do you think they saw us from downstairs? Do they look like they know? Are they coming for us?"

He shushed her with a warning squeeze, and subdued voices reached them from the far end of the balcony. The waitress assured the older couple who trailed her that they'd see the stage much better from here.

Jen went stiff and silent in his arms. She barely breathed, in fact. Her face was burrowed into the side of his neck in clear mortification.

The waitress, meanwhile, seated the silver-haired, dignified guests at the U-shaped booth nearest the stairway, a fair distance from them, but far too close for comfort. When they'd settled in to watch the play, the waitress turned toward Trev and Jen with a smile.

Trev attempted an answering smile over Jen's shoulder—not easy when the urgency still pulsed inside him, and her hold around his neck nearly cut off his air supply.

"Can I get y'all anything?" the waitress asked as she approached.

"No, no." He held up a hand to stop her from ambling any closer, suddenly conscious of the red silk panties on the seat and the empty condom packet in the ashtray...and, of course, Jen straddling his lap, intimately joined with him. "We're good."

The waitress stopped a few feet away from their booth, and her glance flickered over Jen. Or, rather, over Jen's back. "Everything okay, hon?" she asked Trev in concern.

"Oh...yes." Did she hear the unevenness of his tone, the

sexual rasp of his voice? "My wife just gets...emotional...during shows like this."

The waitress blinked in bewilderment, and the audience, damn them, murmured again with laughter. The play was obviously a comedy.

"The, uh, lead actor reminds her of...of someone she lost," he added.

Her mouth formed a silent *Oh*, and she nodded in sympathetic understanding. "Are you sure I can't bring her a glass of water, or more wine?"

Trev shook his head and muttered thanks.

The waitress urged him to wave if they wanted anything. "I'll be watching out for y'all from downstairs, hear?" Mercifully, then, she left them.

To watch out for them from downstairs. Trev shut his eyes and leaned his head against Jen's. No one said that sex in public would be easy.

"Do you think she knew?" came a pained whisper in his ear.

"I don't think so."

"Did she...see my...panties?" Abject humiliation vibrated in every syllable.

"No. She was too far away."

"Are you sure?"

"Positive."

She let out a torrent of breath against his collarbone, but her relief was short-lived. "I can't believe you got me into this," she seethed. "What are we going to do? How can I get off you if people are sitting right there?"

"They're not all that close. And the booths are high-backed. Shouldn't be too hard. At least, not while the place is still dark."

She sucked in a panicked breath. "Do you think they'll have an intermission, and turn up the lights? It can't be time for that yet, can it? Do you think more people will move up here? Oh, my God, Trev," she wailed in quiet misery, pressing her face to his, "we're bound to be caught!"

He ran a hand over her silky, disheveled hair and hoped she'd calm down before she hyperventilated. "No, we won't be caught. The waitress is gone. We're okay."

Her choppy, frenzied breathing gradually slowed, and as he held her, a sense of warm satisfaction grew in him. His mystery lady might "feel alive" while "living on the edge," but not too close to that edge. And if she was upset by the thought of the waitress seeing her panties on the seat, he knew damn well she hadn't pranced around on that air-hockey table, or gang-banged the Baltimore Orioles.

But in his heart, he'd known that, anyway. He'd just wanted her to admit it.

Now he wanted only to make love to her. Soon, and repeatedly. He wished they were already home, their clothes off, her body sprawled beneath his. He longed to watch her face, her eyes, while he thrust deep and she gripped him in the throes of climax.

Enflamed again by serious need, he tilted her back for a kiss—hot, intricate, and not the least bit subdued by their brush with disaster. She soon lost her stiffness, melded against him and moaned in renewed passion. Nothing could have pleased him more. She was just as needy as he.

"Let's go home," he murmured urgently, "and get naked."

She nodded with a gaze that promised endless hours of lovemaking.

It occurred to him then that he'd been intimate with her twice, but hadn't yet seen her naked. The first night they'd made love in the dark; this evening, in public view. "Tonight we'll keep the lights on," he swore, more to himself than to her.

"Lights on?" A small frown etched lines between her brows.

"I want to see you. To know you."

Something about that mission statement brought a flicker of alarm to her gaze. "I—I've always preferred the dark. So much more...intimate. The glare of lights would only ruin the mood."

He stared at her incredulously. Was she too shy to let him see her naked, or to make love in the light? His lady of the evening, his wild Madam X...the temptress who, even now, remained intimately joined with him in public?

No way. Shyness couldn't be the reason. So then, why did she want the lights off?

He'd make it a point to find out—and to change her mind. *Tonight.*

7

TREV DIDN'T INTEND to make a big deal out of her insistence that making love in a lighted room would "ruin the mood." He simply planned to take her to bed, with the lights off, and at some time during the long, hot night of lovemaking, switch on the bedside lamp. By that time, she'd either be too passionately involved to remember her bizarre protest, or he'd discover her reason for it. Either way, he swore, by morning, she'd never again hesitate to get naked with him, even in broad daylight.

He held this plan firmly in mind while he suffered through their physical separation at the restaurant booth—a discreet shifting that took mere seconds. The struggle to zip up his jeans was much more of an ordeal, considering the state he'd been left in. Jen, meanwhile, slipped back into her panties, restored her hair to its shiny, casual twist and finished her glass of peach wine. Trev tossed money onto the table for the bill, then hurried her out of the darkened theater, his blood still coursing from their sexual game.

The prospect of a two-hour drive seemed unendurable.

Jen didn't make things any easier. No sooner had he settled behind the wheel of his car than she slid her arm around him, ran her fingers through his hair and whispered, "What's the big rush? Or should I say...where's the fire?"

While he drove the car out of the crowded parking lot, she proceeded to fan that fire into a blaze by nibbling his neck, stroking his chest and thighs, and wriggling her panties down her long, curvaceous legs—a sight he wished he could see more clearly than the darkened car allowed.

Before he even reached the expressway, he veered the car off the road into the first secluded spot he found, and in the dark, cramped quarters of the front seat, he made love to her. There wasn't any finesse involved—just hot, explosive need. Never had he taken a woman with such savagery. Never had a woman responded with such passionate force of her own.

To be fair, he had to admit they wore each other out.

He regenerated completely during the drive home, though, his mind ablaze with erotic ideas for the night ahead. She, meanwhile, curled up in the passenger seat and fell asleep. At least, he believed she'd fallen asleep.

But when they reached the furnished beach house he'd rented, he wondered if she'd been pretending. Because as soon as he pulled into the driveway and killed the engine, she sat up, mumbled something about finding a bathroom, and tore into the house. Before he knew it, she'd found the guest bedroom, grabbed her suitcases from where he'd set them and vanished behind a locked door.

"Jen," he called. "Come to my bed, or I'll come to yours."

"Sorry. Too tired."

Her reply stunned him. He understood why she was tired, of course, but not why she refused to come to his bed. "We'll sleep for a while," he promised. "Until you get your second wind."

Nothing he said persuaded her. He spent the night alone—a whole night, when he could have been holding her, at the very least. Sleeping with her. It startled him, how much he wanted that.

During long hours of frustrated speculation, he'd mulled over a number of possible reasons she hadn't slept with him. By morning, he'd discounted all but one. She'd been ready to make love to him all night long, he swore—until he'd mentioned keeping the lights on. Only then had reservations entered her gaze. She'd insisted that the light would "ruin the mood," and that the dark was more "intimate."

Had she suspected that he'd planned to show her differently? Had she deliberately provoked their passion in the darkened car to avoid making love at home, in the light?

Alone at the kitchen table the next morning, he pushed aside his half-eaten breakfast and stared through a bay window at the sunshine glinting off the blue-gray ocean. The woman was driving him crazy. Why the hell had she flaunted herself in a see-through dress, tried to convince him she was shameless, carried on with him in public, and then balked at getting naked with him in the privacy of his bedroom? If he accomplished anything at all today, he would at least find an answer to that question.

But then, she presented so many damn questions.

"Is that *bacon* I smell?" The soft, incredulous question sounded from the arched doorway of the kitchen.

"Yes, ma'am. Bacon it is." The mere sound of her voice, the mere knowledge of her presence, mildly aroused him. Annoyed with himself for reacting like one of Pavlov's dogs, he shifted his gaze to her, and his breath stopped somewhere between his lungs and throat.

In sleek-fitting jeans and a white eyelet blouse that tied at her waist, her thick ash-blond hair flowing to her shoulders in silky disarray, her face innocent of makeup and a sleepy morning smile lighting her eyes, she was simply too beautiful to bear. At least, without touching her. Pulling her into his lap. Kissing the very breath out of her.

He wrapped both hands tightly around his coffee cup to keep from reaching for her. She'd stunned him last night with a rejection; he wouldn't risk starting the day with one, too. By the time he reached for her, she would want him. He'd see to it.

Moving closer to the table where he sat, she peered in

amazement at the platter of bacon, eggs and toast. "Does this mean you cooked?"

He quirked a brow at her. "Why so surprised?"

A wry sparkle played in her eyes, and she opened her mouth to utter some irreverent quip, he was sure. But then she stopped, as if she'd caught herself just in time. She actually looked shaken. "You—you just don't seem like the type of guy who cooks, that's all."

He studied her curiously. Had she thought she would offend him with whatever she'd been about to say? He wondered what it had been. He wondered if he'd ever find answers to his questions about her. Any of them.

"So...do you enjoy cooking?" she asked, clearly trying to normalize the conversation.

He decided to help her out. Lull her into relaxing her guard. And then do whatever it took to uncover her true thoughts and feelings about him—as well as the other maddening secrets he knew damn well she kept. He'd somehow come to consider that a top priority.

"I can't honestly say that I *enjoy* cooking." He settled back in his chair in a deliberately nonchalant pose. "I learned out of necessity when my grandmother gave it up. With my sister away at college, that left only my brothers and me to man the kitchen. I might not be a master chef, but, trust me, I was the least of three evils." He smiled and gestured toward the bacon and eggs that hadn't turned out too bad. "Grab a plate and help yourself. Might need to warm it in the microwave. The coffee's on the counter behind you. If you'd rather make some fresh, go ahead. I've been up quite a while." He paused and watched the subtle sway of her shapely hips as she sauntered to the cabinet for a cup. "Guess I had too much pent-up energy to sleep."

If she felt the gentle barb of that comment, she didn't show it as she poured herself a cup of coffee, sat in a chair diagonal from him at the square oak table and helped herself to a small sampling of everything he'd made. "Why did your grandmother stop cooking?"

So, she intended to avoid the issue of where she'd slept, and why he *hadn't* slept. Not for long, she wouldn't. Allowing her only a temporary reprieve from the topic that dominated his thoughts, he smoothly replied, "Arthritis."

"Oh, that's too bad." She looked genuinely dismayed. "She must have hated that." The soft, sad words had barely left her mouth before she hurriedly added, "I mean, I—I don't know *how* your grandmother feels about cooking, of course, but I'd imagine that anyone would hate... well...being disabled in any way."

Trev narrowed his gaze. Was she acting unusually skittish this morning? Walking on proverbial eggshells around him? "Yeah, I guess most people wouldn't be too glad of it."

Her lips pursed briefly at his mild sarcasm, but she avoided any other acknowledgment by digging her fork into the small mound of scrambled eggs on her plate and focusing on her breakfast. After a brief silence, she asked, "Who's cooking for your grandmother now?"

"Her younger sister moved in. I'm hoping the company might cheer her up."

"Cheer her up? She hasn't been...happy?"

"Not since Diana disappeared." A shard of grief pierced him at the mention of her, inflicting enough pain to make him realize how much of a respite he'd found with Jen—and to remind him that in seven hellish years, only this woman seemed to wield the magic to ease his abject loneliness. How could he possibly let her go? But then, how could he not?

Forcing his focus away from troublesome questions and back to the conversation, he explained, "My grandmother's had a hard time accepting Diana's disappearance. You see, she'd been the one to suggest that Diana attend the writers' conference—the trip she never returned from."

Pausing with the fork halfway to her mouth, Jen stared at

him with such a troubled expression that he found himself wanting to reassure her that his grandmother would eventually get over her irrational sense of guilt. But he had his doubts that she would—especially if she never accepted the fact Diana wasn't coming back.

"I'm so sorry that you and your family have gone through such torment."

Something about the anguished sincerity in her voice touched him more deeply than had any other offer of sympathy. Clearing his throat to ease a sudden tightness there, he gruffly replied, "Thank you." The moment dragged on too long, though. He couldn't bear to have the sadness intrude on their time together. Leveling her a deliberately stern glance, he said, "That comment about 'torment'—you weren't referring to my cooking, were you?"

Her brows jutted up in surprise. "Of course not!"

"I'll admit, the bacon might be a little on the well-done side, and the eggs a little undercooked—but the toast, if I must say so myself, is a true culinary masterpiece."

The hint of a smile seeped back into her eyes, and his heart hailed its return like a long-lost friend. "Oh, come on, Trev. It's all cooked to perfection. If I didn't know better, I'd say you're fishing for compliments."

"Good thing you know better."

They shared a smile, then. And his gaze lingered on her mouth. And her gaze drifted to his. He wanted so damn much to kiss her.

An almost imperceptible flush rose into her face, and she abruptly bent her attention to her breakfast. After finishing the eggs and distractedly nibbling the bacon and toast, she said with a rather forced casualness, "I have a feeling you won't have to cook much for very long if you don't want to. Within a month, you'll have half the women in Sunrise lined up at your door, ready to ease your burden."

Trev sipped his coffee and studied her. Was she merely

making conversation to avoid the sensual tension that had gripped them, or did she want to know if he intended to date? Or was this her way of telling him that she wasn't mistaking their relationship for anything meaningful?

Whatever she'd meant, the comment bothered him. It touched on topics he wasn't ready to deal with. Like, what would happen between them when their two days and three nights were over.

Hell, he wasn't sure what was happening between them *now*. He only knew that he wanted to kiss her, and sleep with her tonight. Make her want him so much that she wouldn't think twice about getting naked with him in broad daylight. Wanted to stare deeply into her eyes while they made love, and maybe find that window to her soul.

When he didn't reply to her remark about the women lining up at his door, she ventured a glance at him. Something about his stare soon brought another wash of color to her face and an inescapable awareness between them.

"Why didn't you sleep with me last night, Jen?"

She swallowed the food she'd been chewing—with an effort, it seemed—and set down her fork. "I didn't realize you assumed it was part of the arrangement."

"You and I both know it wasn't. All I expected from our time together was the chance for you to get to know me, and to trust me. And, hopefully, confide in me." Bracing his elbow on the table, he took her hand in his and rubbed his thumb in kneading circles across the tender heart of her palm. "But after last night, I thought you might not be opposed to sharing my bed."

She didn't pull her hand back, as he half expected. In fact, her gaze grew soft and smoky in a way that warmed his blood. "I can't honestly say I'm opposed," she murmured, sounding inexplicably wistful, "but I don't see the sense in us getting too...involved."

"Are you saying that just by sleeping together, we'll be 'involved'?"

She didn't answer, but stared at him with powerful secrets milling somewhere inside her. Her thumb, meanwhile, swept in compulsive arcs across his hand, while his thumb massaged her palm. Their hands, at least, had broken through the stalemate to embrace and caress...and press for a more profound closeness.

"Whether you want to acknowledge the fact or not, Trev," she finally whispered, "I am what I am. There's no room in my life for a relationship."

"Did I say I want a 'relationship'?"

"Do you?"

His hand fully possessed hers, then, in a tight, palm-to-palm hold, while their gazes meshed, shifted and probed. "Yes," he vehemently whispered. "For now, I do. For the days you'll be with me. And it doesn't matter what you are, or what you've done. Unless you're ready to open up to me, Jen, and tell me the whole God-honest truth, I don't want to hear about your so-called 'professional' life. Not another word about it. For the next two days and nights, you have no past or future. Just the present, here and now, with me."

Jennifer bit her bottom lip to stop it from trembling. He couldn't know how wonderful that sounded to her. Because she *had* no past—none that she could claim—and she would never be sure of her future. But she could have these two days. That's all she'd ever have with him. What could it hurt to sleep with him? It was too late to prevent emotional involvement. She already loved him to distraction.

But he'd said he wanted to make love with the lights on— to see her. *Know* her. She interpreted that to mean that he would closely scrutinize, in a very deliberate way. That prospect made her nervous. He might see too much.

No, she couldn't risk that. And then there was the matter of her contact lenses. Such a silly, practical concern when compared to the enormity of spending precious, intimate time with Trev. She couldn't overlook details, though. Her eyes were too sensitive to keep her contact lenses in for days at a time. She had to remove them when she slept, at least for a few hours. And when she removed them, her eyes were no longer blue, but green.

Green, like Diana's.

But perhaps one night of wearing her contact lenses wouldn't hurt....

Ah, temptation was too powerful when she was with Trev! From the tousled mass of his tawny hair that lured her fingers to delve through it, to the solid, muscled contours of his powerful body, so clearly delineated in a faded green T-shirt and tight jeans, to the seductive warmth and keen intelligence that burned behind his amber eyes. *She wanted him.*

Abruptly she drew her hand from his, gathered the plates and silverware from the table and strode to the sink. "Since you cooked, I'll do dishes," she said breathlessly, feeling shaken by her unwise desire for him. "And then I'll be happy to get to work helping you unpack. After all, you *are* paying Helping Hand a hefty fee for my help. You did say you wanted to set up your office, didn't you?"

She sensed his growing frustration with her. He was wise enough not to press her on the issue of their intimacy, though.

"I do have a few crates that need to be unpacked," he admitted, "for my office *and* house."

She soon found refuge in washing the dishes, and then in unpacking the crates he'd shipped from home.

Because the house he'd leased was fully furnished and only a temporary residence until his own home was built, he hadn't brought much. The office he intended to set up in place of a family room was also temporary, where he would keep his files and do his paperwork until he'd rented commercial office space. The crates, therefore, weren't all that numerous, and while Trev moved a desk and filing cabinets into place and dealt with occasional phone calls, Jennifer focused on unpacking boxes and putting things away.

She hadn't expected the task to stir up her emotions.

Many of the kitchen utensils, pot holders, bowls and pans were ones that she herself had bought when she'd been a blissful newlywed enamored of building a nest for her mate. She also unwrapped blankets and quilts that had once adorned beds in their home. And while she unpacked a box of Trev's clothing, memories nearly strangled her—memories of handling his clothes, putting them into his dresser, arranging them in closets. These duties were far too personal, too wifely, for her to manage easily.

The worst, however, was when she came upon a box of photographs and found a large, framed portrait of his three siblings. Gazing at the familiar faces, she felt pressure building behind her eyes and in her throat.

Trev happened to saunter by her in the living room at that moment, and noticed the photo in her hands. "My sister and brothers," he informed her, reaching beyond her to open another box. "But that was years ago."

Yes, years ago. Around the time that she'd known them. Lived with them. Loved them. Mischievous, towheaded Sammy had been eight. Sweet, shy Veronica had been trembling on the brink of womanhood at thirteen. And Christopher, so touchingly determined to persevere despite his disability, had been a bright, lanky, eighteen-year-old who had openly adored her. They'd lost their parents in an automobile accident three years before she'd met them. She'd wanted to help Trev fill the void in their lives. She understood too well how it felt to lose family.

Without offering a comment about the photo, Jennifer set it blindly aside, only to find another. This one was a relatively recent photo of Babs, his grandmother. How old she looked! Her hair, which she'd always worn in a fashionably shaggy style, was no longer a feisty salt-and-pepper, but entirely gray, and cut blunt and short. She wore no earrings, multiple or otherwise. The gentle wrinkles around her eyes and mouth had deepened into grooves, and the *joie de vivre* no longer sparkled in the light brown eyes that so resembled Trev's. Jennifer ached to think that she herself had caused the anguish that had taken that sparkle from someone she loved.

Too choked up to subject herself to another photograph, she set the one of Babs back in the box, intending to turn away—when the photo beside it snagged her attention.

Her wedding photo. In hazy, golden candlelight, a much younger Trev and a blazingly happy Diana smiled at each other with ardent devotion. They'd thought they had forever. And Trev had thought he'd known her. Neither of those beliefs had been true. The tragedy of it broke her heart, for at least the millionth time.

Trev glanced at her, then followed her gaze to the photo lying in the box. He paused in his work and stared at it with unreadable eyes.

Unable to bear any reaction he might have, she quickly gathered all the photos she'd unpacked and stacked them in her arms. "Where do you want these?" She fixed her gaze on a far wall rather than risking a glance at him.

"On top of my dresser, I guess."

She nodded and headed toward his bedroom.

Before she'd exited the office, though, he called, "Except that last one. Of...Diana and me."

Her heart gave a pang, and she stopped in the doorway, waiting for him to say more.

"Put it in the box at the back of my closet," he quietly directed.

A box in the back of my closet. Where he would never see it. She turned to him in pained surprise. "You—you don't want it on your dresser, with the others?"

He shook his head, his mouth a firm, purposeful line. "I'm going to put Diana behind me, Jen, and move on with my life."

An invisible hand clamped around her throat, preventing her from uttering a sound. Not that she'd know what to say, anyway. She had no good reason to feel as if he'd ripped out a part of her heart. Any woman with feelings for him would consider that statement good news…unless, of course, that woman was Diana. Which she wasn't. She was Jennifer, and she *wanted* him to move on with his life—just as she would move on with hers.

She whirled away from him and hurried to his bedroom.

"Jen?" he called, sounding concerned and bewildered.

He'd obviously noticed her distress. How in God's name to explain? Sympathy, she supposed. She would let him think that she'd merely been reacting to his heart-rending situation.

When she reached the master bedroom, she set the photographs on the dresser, retaining only the wedding photo to take to the closet.

He appeared in the doorway of the bedroom. "Jen, do you think I'm wrong for trying to start over, for assuming Diana won't come back?" He searched her face as he met her near the closet. "Do you consider me a married man? Is that why you're afraid to get involved with me?"

"No! No, of course not." She hugged the wedding photo to her breast, her arms crossed protectively over it, as if he might decide at any moment to toss it in the trash. A ridiculous reaction, she knew. She loosened her hold on it and managed to choke out, "Seven years *is* a terribly long time. No one could possibly blame you for wanting to start over."

"I should have told you this before. I'm legally single. Last week, the court declared Diana dead."

"Dead?" Again, she stared at him in stricken silence. She hadn't known! But, of course, it made sense. He needed closure. He needed to be free to get on with his life. She hadn't wanted anything less for him. But when she'd left, she'd assumed he would receive her goodbye letter, and that he'd divorce her for abandonment. Now, of course, she'd discovered that he hadn't received the letter *or* divorced her—but she hadn't realized until now that he'd petitioned the court to have her declared legally dead.

"Jen, tell me what you're thinking." He reached to take her face between his hands, his scrutiny intense.

She backed away, afraid she'd fall apart at his touch. "I...I just feel bad for you. I know it couldn't have been easy, having her declared...declared—" The word stuck in her throat.

"It was the hardest thing I've ever done. But I can't base my life on the slim hope that she'll come back. I don't believe she will. If she were alive, she'd have come back to me by now."

And in a very real way, it was true. Diana no longer existed. Jen couldn't forget that...or allow herself any hopeless fantasies of taking her place.

She forced a painful smile and handed him the photo. "Here, you put this away. Now that the filing cabinets are in place, I'll go unpack the crates of files."

He nodded, and she turned to leave the bedroom. But on her way out, she noticed through the dresser mirror that he didn't head for the closet, after all. He gazed at the photo, then carefully settled it into the drawer of the nightstand beside his bed.

Jennifer wasn't sure if she was glad or not. She'd never been more emotionally confused in her life.

They spent the rest of that morning setting up his office. Around one, they broke for lunch. Jennifer made sandwiches, and they ate outside on the sunny back deck that overlooked a private beach and a tranquil cove of the glimmering blue-gray sea.

While they ate and sipped iced tea, Trev described his

plans for the development he would build, and the house he'd designed for himself. Jennifer tried to remain emotionally detached as she murmured praise of his plans. Many of the features he'd installed had been ideas they'd dreamed up together, long ago. The community would be lovely, she knew, and his house an elegant, comfortable work of art. With a bittersweet welling of pride in him, she realized he'd made a success of his business despite the trauma of his personal life.

She tried to forget the fact that she would never actually see the development, or his house. She'd be long gone by then.

The moment they'd finished eating, she rose from her chair to get back to work, desperately needing the distraction. He followed her into the house, to the newly assembled office, where he retrieved something from a crate.

"You said you wouldn't mind taking a look at this." He handed her an old leather portfolio that she instantly recognized—the rough draft of her play. "I'd like to hear your opinion on who the murderer is. The text might be a little hard to read, with sections crossed out and arrows pointing to handwritten inserts, but you should be able to follow most of it."

"I'd love to read it." Reverently she cradled the portfolio in her hands, beleaguered again by emotion. She'd spent so many hours creating the characters, clues and plot twists— and nursing dreams of making a living with her writing. She couldn't afford those dreams now. Successful writers sometimes found themselves in the public spotlight, which she had to avoid at all costs.

Writing was just another part of herself that she'd left behind.

"Feel free to go down to the beach, or find a comfortable place anywhere in the house to read," Trev invited. "I have calls to make and errands to run. When I get back, I'll bring dinner. And a bottle of wine. We can kick back, relax. Discuss your findings. See how good of a sleuth you really are."

The suggestion sounded soothingly cozy. And he'd stoked her curiosity, along with her artistic interest in how he'd responded to her writing. Had he grasped the clues she'd woven through the story? Had he fallen for the red herrings? Which character did *he* believe committed the murder? He'd said he wasn't sure, but she couldn't wait to hear his theories.

"White wine," she insisted with a smile. "Something on the sweet side. And chilled. None of that warm, dry, red stuff you were drinking last night."

"Burgundy. It's called burgundy, and if you'd share one bottle with me, I'd make a believer out of you."

"A bottle of that, and who knows what I'd be believing?"

"I wouldn't mind finding out." Their nonsensical banter had, as usual, taken on sensual overtones, imbuing his voice with a stirring huskiness and immersing them in a smiling yet lingering gaze...drawing them physically closer... conjuring thoughts of a long, hot, intricate kiss—

The doorbell rang, jarring them out of a blood-warming trance.

Trev frowned in clear annoyance at the interruption and cast a glance through a side window. His expression immediately cleared. "That's my car," he said in surprise. "Christopher must be here. I wasn't expecting him until Friday."

"Christopher?" she repeated, thoroughly stunned. She hadn't expected to meet anyone else from her past. Especially not one of his family members. Her emotions had already risen too close to the surface. The very thought of seeing Christopher again swelled them closer to overflowing.

"My brother," he reminded her, as she trailed him to the living room.

"Oh, yes. I believe you did mention him." She hoped she sounded suitably detached. In truth, she was both afraid of being recognized and thrilled at the prospect of seeing him again. She'd missed his smile, and his teasing. Even his occasional bouts of touchingly boyish social angst.

She'd thought of him often over the years, especially when she volunteered at schools for the deaf. He'd been the one who had taught her sign language. He'd been so pleased when she'd mastered the basics. She'd often wished he could see her now, completely fluent and teaching others.

The irony was almost too much to bear. Now that she'd learned to communicate with him, she'd have nothing of consequence to say. She'd be only a stranger to him. No reason to even let him know that she knew sign language at all. Her knowledge of it might provoke too many questions from Trev, anyway.

"He drove across country to bring my car," Trev explained, reaching to open the door. "And, I hope, my dog." He then uttered in a slightly dry tone, "I wouldn't doubt he brought along his new girlfriend, too."

Curiosity again distracted Jennifer from her precarious emotional state. He clearly disapproved of something about Christopher's girlfriend. She wondered what. She also wondered what Christopher looked like now, at age twenty-five. Had the years treated him well? Had he found a way to thrive socially, despite his deafness? She hoped so. Surely the fact that he had a girlfriend was a good sign.

Trev opened the door, and a joyous bark sounded. A black-and-tan German shepherd then bounded into the living room and pounced on Trev with the zesty, tail-wagging enthusiasm of a dog reunited with its master. Trev laughed and roughhoused with the huge dog, uttering gruff words of welcome.

Jennifer stood back and watched, her heart lodged solidly in her throat. She'd have recognized him anywhere, even though he'd filled out by a good fifteen pounds. *Caesar*. He'd been *her* dog, for the first year of his life. Her father had given him to her for protection. He'd even sent the dog to obedience school to learn defensive moves.

But she'd left home before Caesar had learned much. He'd been only a big, playful puppy when she'd headed for California—her only companion on that rather frightening road trip. Her watchdog, her family, her friend. Ultimately she'd had to leave Caesar with Trev, of course. She should have known Trev would still have him.

As Trev stood up to peer out the door—presumably at Christopher—Caesar noticed her presence, perked up his ears in curiosity and trotted toward her. She murmured a soft but heartfelt hello, stretched out her hand for him to sniff—

And all hell broke loose. At least, it seemed so to her.

With a long, mewling whine and explosive barks, Caesar leaped up onto her, fully outstretched, his paws hitting her shoulders before all of his awesome weight slammed into her, knocking her backwards over a footstool. As she hit the floor, he pounced and pranced, his tail furiously wagging while he licked her face, yelped and whined in a canine frenzy that could only mean, *At last! You're back! Hallelujah! Where you been? Yippee-kayee! Momma's home!*

"Caesar," came Trev's fierce rebuke, "Caesar, heel! Get back, damn it. What the hell...? Caesar!" He loomed over them, tugging on the dog's collar, shouting commands that Caesar blissfully ignored.

Jennifer, meanwhile, both laughed and cried—out of irrepressible sentiment rather than fear—rolling defensively this way and that, shoving Caesar out of her face with one hand and burying her fingers in his fur with the other. Vaguely, she knew that Trev and someone else hovered over them, and before long, the slobbering, misty-eyed beast whom she loved so much was pulled off her.

Trev gripped Caesar's collar and held him while the dog strained and whined. The other man clipped a heavy chain to his collar, opened the living room door, and together they forced the loudly protesting dog to the outside.

The tall, slender, handsome young man with coppery hair and her old pal Christopher's vivid blue eyes slipped outside to deal with Caesar, while Trev extended a hand to Jennifer.

"I'm sorry, Jen. God, I don't know what got into him." He looked shaken and somewhat pale beneath his tan as he helped her to her feet. "Are you okay?"

"Yes, I'm fine." She wiped moisture from beneath her eyes with the back of her hand, sniffled and smiled, feeling rather shaky herself. But when all was said and done, it was nice to be remembered—and welcomed back with such warm enthusiasm.

"Are you sure you're not hurt?" Trev searched her face with concern, dashed a wet trail from her cheek and ran a quick visual check of her body. Finding no broken bones or lacerations, he let out a long breath and pulled her to him in a hug. "When I first saw him lunge, I thought he was attacking."

"He wasn't."

Trev held her tightly against him until his own heartbeat slowed to normal. "I figured that out soon enough." Which had been a damn good thing. Caesar in attack mode could probably rip out a person's throat in the blink of an eye. As much as he loved that dog, he'd have killed him, if necessary, to save Jen.

"He was just being friendly," she said, her voice muffled against his chest.

"Friendly? He was exuberant. Any happier, and he'd have been doing cartwheels." He loosened his hold on her and gazed at her in wonder. *She hadn't been afraid.* An unfamiliar dog the size of Caesar knocked her to the ground in a frenzy, and she hadn't panicked.

She'd been laughing. And crying a little, but not in fear. Why *had* she been crying?

And why had Caesar reacted like that? Bewilderment churned with vague, undefined anxiety in Trev's gut. The only time the dog came close to behaving that way was when Trev returned from long trips....

An almost eerie sensation slid over him, like the shadow of a passing cloud.

"It was probably my sandals," Jen theorized, stepping away from him to brush dog hair off her jeans. "I was visiting my neighbor yesterday before you came for me. She has a female shepherd, and I believe she was in heat. Caesar probably picked up her scent from my sandals."

"Yeah." He forced a smile. "Maybe that's it." But he knew that a female dog hadn't been the cause of Caesar's excitement. Caesar had been neutered years ago, and he wouldn't find a female in heat particularly exciting.

No, it seemed to Trev that Caesar had recognized Jen, and was ecstatic to see her. As if she were a long-lost friend.

Actually, more than just a friend. Way more.

Like, a long-lost mistress.

8

WHAT THE HELL was he thinking? The suspicion gripping him like a vise was so bizarre, so out-of-the-blue, that Trev could barely bring himself to put it into words, even in his own mind.

He'd have to be crazy to jump to the conclusion that anything covert had played a part in Caesar's reaction to Jen. He'd have to be crazy to think that Caesar had been welcoming home his long-lost mistress...and that Jen might actually be Diana.

Intermittent waves of hot and cold rushed through him. *She couldn't be.*

No. She couldn't be.

It was easier to believe that Caesar had *mistaken* her for Diana, as Trev had. He remembered his gut reaction when he'd first heard the sound of Jen's laughter, and when he'd caught sight of her in the hotel lobby. Though her hair was blond instead of dark, familiarity had been immediate. Bone-deep. Absolute.

He'd been wrong, though. At closer look, many differences became obvious. She wasn't Diana.

But as he studied her now, he realized that most of those differences were superficial. Hair color and style. Body weight. Age. Eye color, which could be altered with contact lenses. And the changes in her facial structure could have been engineered with cosmetic surgery.

God Almighty, why was he even *considering* this?

The whole idea was ludicrous. Did he really think there

was a possibility that Diana had voluntarily left him, undergone cosmetic surgery and was living as someone else? It made no sense.

But then, neither had her disappearance.

Nor Caesar's reaction to her. The dog couldn't have mistaken her for Diana, as Trev had, on the basis of sight or even sound. Dogs identified by smell. And smells, to a dog, were so distinctive that a man could be tracked by the mere path he'd walked.

Another psychogenic chill swept through Trev. Caesar wouldn't have mistaken one person for another.

Which meant he must have had another reason for pouncing in exuberance on Jen. Something she'd said or done. A scent that clung to her—maybe from the portfolio that held Diana's play, which Jen had been carrying earlier.

Or maybe Caesar's reaction had nothing at all to do with Diana. Maybe he'd reacted to Trev's admittedly explosive feelings about Jen. Dogs often sensed extreme emotional reactions in their masters, didn't they? Fear or distrust on the part of an owner could easily raise a dog's shackles. Who was to say that a positive emotion wouldn't register on some level, too?

And he wouldn't deny feeling something positive and wild and strong for Jen. Too strong, maybe.

He gazed at her now in near desperation. *She couldn't possibly be Diana.* Just the fact that he'd conceived the idea made him wonder if his sexual need for her had pushed him beyond the limits of reason, into obsession. Delusional obsession. She'd said as much to him, when he'd confronted her yesterday morning in her office. *You're delusional.* Was he?

"Trev." Jen's soft voice cut through a blinding haze of ludicrous, half-formed suspicions and alarming self-doubt. He blinked rapidly, struggling to reorient himself, and focused on her face. Her beautiful, vitally familiar face. "I'm assuming this is your brother Christopher," she prompted with a rather tense, questioning smile.

Trev realized then that Christopher stood before them, his hands in the roomy pockets of his fashionably wide jeans, his amiable blue-eyed gaze lingering on Jen in clear curiosity.

"Uh, yes," Trev said, spurring himself with an effort to function as a rational human being. "Jen, this is Christopher. He's hearing impaired, but he reads lips amazingly well, even when you don't want him to. Christopher, meet Jen, a...a *friend* of mine." As he said it, he realized how wrong it felt to call her "a friend." She was already much more vital to him than that. He felt as if she *belonged* to him.

That couldn't be a sane reaction to a woman he'd known for only five days. And yet, he'd felt the same with Diana, from the first time they'd spoken. Had he fallen in love with Jen, in the same instantaneous, soul-possessing way? Or were his feelings for her based on her similarities to Diana, and therefore just another symptom of obsession?

But there was another possibility, too.

His muscles clenched, and he broke out into a light sweat at the thought. Maybe he perceived clues on a subliminal basis, and his feelings for her stemmed from fact—the fact that she *did* belong to him. *The fact that she was his wife.*

Chaotic emotions clashed and warred with his common sense, and he gritted his teeth to retain at least a semblance of sanity. He couldn't allow himself to get so carried away, with nothing but vague suppositions to go on. He had to ground himself in reality. But he was no longer sure what that reality was, or if he'd lost touch with it altogether.

Ignoring his inner havoc, he focused with keen determination on Christopher and Jen. She'd uttered a polite greeting and extended her hand. Christopher had responded with a courteous shake and a smile.

"I can tell you're brothers," she was saying now, her voice soft, warm and a little raspy, her eyes shining. "There's a strong family resemblance. You have the same smile." She swallowed, pressed her lips firmly together, then curved them into a smile. With an effort, it seemed.

Was it his imagination, or was she struggling to repress some strong emotion...regarding Christopher? It had to be his imagination. She was a perfect stranger to him, and had no reason to get misty-eyed and all choked up.

But then, she'd shed tears when Caesar had rushed to her. And now that he thought about it, those tears *had* looked suspiciously sentimental.

Swallowing a curse, Trev turned away from her, angry with himself for allowing these wild speculations to color his perception of her. He couldn't go on this way. Determinedly, he channeled his attention to Christopher. "Thanks for bringing my car." He clasped him in a brief, back-patting hug. "When I rented one at the airport, they were out of all-terrain vehicles. I've been itching to get back in the woods on my new property and explore."

Christopher replied in sign language, *I figured as much.*

"You're here early. I didn't expect you until Friday."

Yes, I changed my plans, Christopher said with expressive movements of his hands. *Yvonne came with me. She's in the car.*

Trev glanced through the living room window, toward the pretty brunette who sat in the passenger seat of his all-terrain vehicle. His disapproval of their relationship hadn't deterred Christopher from pursuing it, and Trev saw no use in re-hashing the arguments now. "Tell her to come in."

I have something to tell you first.

The taut, wary look on his brother's face warned him of trouble. Though Christopher's silent part of the conversation was undoubtedly lost on Jen, Trev considered taking him to another room where they could talk in private. Before he acted on the impulse, though, Christopher signed, *We're flying to the Virgin Islands this evening.*

Trev lifted a brow in surprise. Maybe privacy wouldn't be

necessary, after all. He wasn't yet accustomed to the higher life-style his brother enjoyed, now that he'd come into his money, but Trev certainly didn't object to him taking an island vacation. He'd prefer that Christopher go without Yvonne, of course, but since she was already with him—

To get married, Christopher signed.

Trev stared at him, stunned. He'd known his brother had lost his head over the woman, but he hadn't expected this. "Don't do it, Chris. Don't rush things."

Anger sparked in Christopher's eyes. *I'm not a kid anymore. You can't run my life. Whether you like Yvonne or not, I love her. We're not changing our plans.*

Flushing with anger, Trev responded in sign language, *You'll regret it.*

Christopher's jaw hardened. *Give me the keys to the car you rented. I'll return it to the airport for you. It'll save me from calling a cab.*

Nothing infuriated him more about Christopher than his refusal to listen to reason. They'd been butting heads like this since their parents died, and Trev had taken over raising Christopher when the boy was fifteen. Emphatically Trev signed, *You're not going anywhere until we talk this out. She'll only break your heart...along with your bank account, if you let her.*

Christopher's face grew ruddy and he glared. *I'll have Yvonne call a cab.* Stiffly he drew a cell phone from his shirt pocket, pivoted on his heels and stalked outside.

Trev clenched his jaw and fought the impulse to drag him back into the house.

"What's going on, Trev?" Jen asked, sounding dismayed and concerned.

"My brother's about to make the mistake of his life."

"Is this about...his girlfriend?"

"Technically, his fiancée."

"You don't like her?"

"Whether I like her or not is irrelevant. She's lived next door for two years, and in all that time, barely said a word to any of us. Last month, Christopher came into money—a trust fund set up from a lawsuit my parents settled years ago. It was over the medical error that left him deaf as an infant. Now that he's driving a Ferrari and wearing ridiculously expensive clothes, Yvonne is suddenly in love with him." Trev tried to tamp down on his frustration, but couldn't. It was fueled by fierce protectiveness. "The money can never make up for his loss, but it's *his*, damn it. I won't have a gold digger bleed it out of him—and then break his heart when it's gone."

Jen studied him in a silence for a moment, then mused aloud, "You believe his disability makes him more emotionally vulnerable, don't you?"

He compressed his lips in annoyance. He should have known better than to try to explain. He'd never been good at expressing his feelings—especially about Christopher. "His disability has nothing to do with this."

"I think it does. I think you're afraid that—"

"Please, Jen, don't psychoanalyze me now. I don't want my brother taken advantage of. Period." Realizing that he'd been too curt—with everyone—but unable to think beyond his worry over Christopher's future, Trev strode to his newly created office and shut the door.

He'd call the cab company and cancel the cab Christopher had probably ordered. After he'd given Christopher time to cool down, he would try to talk to his brother again. If worse came to worst, he'd give him the key for the rental car. As angry as he was, he wouldn't repay Christopher's favor of driving his car across country by forcing him to take a cab to the airport. He hoped Christopher wouldn't mistake the gesture as acceptance of his intended marriage. Trev intended to fight that in every way he could.

Jennifer, meanwhile, walked out the front door of the

house and resolutely headed for the silver all-terrain vehicle parked beneath picturesque palm trees.

Christopher stood at the rear of the car, angrily jerking luggage from the trunk and tossing it onto the crushed-shell driveway. Yvonne, the slim, dark-haired young woman who had been sitting in the passenger seat, was now strolling toward the beach, smoking a cigarette.

Jennifer was glad to find Christopher alone. How exasperating he and Trev could be! Trev was too protective of him—as he was with everyone he loved, but especially Christopher. His concern only made Christopher resentful and headstrong. As often as she'd seen them argue, though, she sensed that this time, their anger was more detrimental. If Trev didn't soften his stand, Christopher and his bride might always hold a grudge.

And that would break Trev's heart. She couldn't allow that.

Highly aware of her status as a stranger in their lives, Jen approached Christopher without a clear idea of what to say, but knowing that some form of intervention was imperative.

Stopping beside him, she leaned sideways, into his line of vision, and wriggled her fingers in a little wave to alert him of her presence. He tossed aside the suitcase he was holding and turned to her in mild surprise.

"Hello," she said, wishing she could just break free from her assumed identity and open her heart to him. Since she couldn't, she kept her gaze as impersonal as she could and squarely faced him so he could easily read her lips. "I know that I should keep out of this, but Trev has told me so much about you, I feel as if I know you." A lie, of course. Trev hadn't said much at all about his family. "He loves you very much. He's afraid that you'll get hurt."

His eyes took on a stormy look, and his mouth thinned with annoyance.

"I know you think he doesn't like Yvonne, but that's not necessarily true. He just isn't sure she loves you."

Christopher wrenched his gaze away from her and abruptly turned to finish removing his bags from the trunk of Trev's car. He couldn't have told her more clearly to mind her own business.

She touched his shoulder, bringing his gaze back to her. "Please, Christopher, give him time. As soon as he knows that Yvonne loves you, he'll take her to his heart as one of the family. Then he'll be one of her staunchest supporters. You'll give him that chance, won't you?"

As if he couldn't hold back the words, even if he had to sign them to someone who wouldn't understand, he spelled out with quick, emphatic motions of his hands, *Doesn't Trev believe a woman can really love me?*

Jennifer's heart gave a pang. "He *knows* so. That's why it's killing him to think that Yvonne might not."

They stared at each other for a long, emotionally charged moment. Then a flicker of realization disrupted Christopher's gaze, and puzzlement mingled with surprise. *You understood me,* he signed.

Ignoring a prickle of unease, she said, "I understand a little sign language, but not much. And I haven't learned to do it well myself." Nervously she clasped her hands behind her back. It occurred to her that if he focused too intently on her hands, he might recognize them. He'd spent months teaching her signing techniques. "I've worked around deaf children, and learned to read the basics."

His gaze lit with the same approving warmth that had always touched her in years gone by. *You're a good person, Jen. I don't know what your relationship is with Trev, but I hope it will be a long one. I'm sure he needs you.*

Warm gratification and affection for him filled her. She wished she could hug him. She wished she could swear that she'd never leave Trev, and that if Christopher himself ever needed her, she'd be there for him. She couldn't promise either of those things.

Before she'd marshaled her feelings enough to reply, his gaze narrowed on her eyes. He then searched her face. A frisson of fear curled through her. Had he recognized her? Had her emotions given her away?

"Is something wrong?" she asked, her heart beating high in her throat.

His intensity slowly dissipated, and after another moment, he shook his head. *No. Nothing's wrong. You just remind me of someone.* With a gentle but sad smile, he added, *Someone both Trev and I loved.*

She had to turn away from him, then. She couldn't take the chance that her emotions might show too vividly again. But her sudden pivot toward the house brought no respite from watchful eyes.

She found herself staring directly into Trev's.

His gaze held her transfixed, and the air around her seemed depleted of oxygen. She couldn't quite draw a breath. How long had he been standing there? Had he heard their conversation? What was he thinking behind that intense, unreadable stare?

Abruptly breaking eye contact, he strode past her to Christopher.

Jennifer grasped the opportunity to escape to the house. She used the solitude to calm herself, gather her composure and devise answers to questions Trev might ask. If he'd heard what she said to Christopher, he might wonder why she'd pretended not to understand sign language earlier. He also might wonder why she'd been presumptuous enough to butt into his family's affairs.

Or, worse...*he might guess the truth.*

Anxiety gnawed at her stomach. Surely he wouldn't assume that much from one conversation. She'd been careful not to say anything she couldn't reasonably deduce from what he'd told her. Any perceptive, caring individual could have assured Christopher that Trev loved him and wanted only the best for him.

Besides, Trev was too open and direct to hide a suspicion as momentous as Diana's return from the dead. He would confront her immediately. When she thought of the situation in that light, every moment that passed helped calm her fears.

Trev soon returned to the house with Christopher and Yvonne. Surprisingly enough, they stayed for a fairly long visit, including dinner. The men grilled steaks on the back deck, while Jennifer and Yvonne prepared salad, rolls, sautéed mushrooms and steamed vegetables. Jennifer found the younger woman to be friendly, soft-spoken and clearly intimidated around Trev.

The meal they shared on the seaside deck in the balmy evening breeze went a long way toward lessening tension. Both Trev and Christopher seemed determined to maintain an amiable truce, and drew the women into conversations about light, impersonal topics.

By the time the meal was over, Jennifer felt sure that she'd read too much into Trev's stare earlier, when he'd come upon Christopher and her. He'd shown no further signs of tension and seemed to accept the explanation she'd repeated for his benefit—that she understood only a few basic words of sign language, and grasped very little of what Christopher said.

She also came to believe that Trev was wrong in his assessment of Yvonne. Wasn't it just like a man to overlook her adoring glances at Christopher? Then there was the fact that she'd been studying sign language for a long enough time to be proficient in it. The poor girl had probably been secretly in love with Christopher for years. Of course, Trev, as busy as he kept himself, wouldn't have noticed his shy next-door neighbor's crush on his brother.

Christopher and Yvonne left shortly after dinner, in the rental car, headed for the airport and their wedding trip to the Virgin Islands. Jennifer wished them happiness with heartfelt sincerity, her voice barely quavering despite her tightening throat. She'd never see either of them again.

Trev, meanwhile, didn't acknowledge their upcoming nuptials at all.

Jennifer felt like prodding him with a discreet kick in the shins. Managing to resist the impulse, she waited until the couple had driven off before rounding on him. "Go ahead and be stubborn about this, Trev Montgomery, and you'll be sorry. They were waiting for you to say something, anything, that would let them know you've changed your mind about their wedding, and you deliberately withheld it."

"Because I haven't changed my mind."

"You'd have to be blind not to see that she loves him. And if her interest in him began only last month, how and why does she know sign language so well?"

"It's a ploy to sucker him in."

She buffeted his muscle-hard shoulder in exasperation. "She had to study and practice for months, maybe years, to be that proficient. She was probably too shy to use it with him until she got it perfect. She *is* shy, you know. You scare her half to death."

"That's ridiculous."

"But it's true. And if you don't welcome her into your family, you will lose a brother!"

He crossed his arms, leaned against his car and frowned at her. "You divined all that from this one short visit?"

"It wasn't difficult."

"You think you know my brother better than I do."

"Oh, Trev!" she cried softly, her exasperation giving way to concern that she wouldn't get through to him. "Maybe it's easier for an outsider to see what's going on. You care so much about your brother, you're afraid to let him go."

He stared at her with inscrutable eyes for a tense moment. "Maybe you're right," he finally whispered. "Maybe I do have a hard time letting go of people I love."

The severity of his gaze, the gruffness of his whisper, made her think he was referring to something other than Christopher's marriage. Was he talking about Diana, and his memories of her? Or did he mean *her*, Jen—and the fact that tomorrow would be their last day together?

No, he couldn't have meant her. He'd never said a word to her about love. And if he were to broach the subject now, she wasn't sure she could keep from falling apart completely. The day had been too emotional; she could take no more talk about love or family or relationships. After tomorrow night, her life would be barren of all those things.

"I—I think I'll go in and read that play," she said, backing toward the house. "I've been dying to get started on it."

TREV NODDED and watched her flee to the house. He remained outside, in the gilt-edged shadows of twilight, his gut tied in knots. Who was she? *What* was she, besides the woman he wanted to keep as his own? Oh yes, he wanted her. And not only in a sexual way, although his desire for her never completely left him. He also wanted to make his home with her. His life with her. Forever.

Under the circumstances, that couldn't be a sane desire, could it?

But she filled a terrible void in his heart, and in his family. *Maybe it's easier for an outsider to see what's going on*, she'd said. She hadn't been an outsider, though. She'd been emotionally involved from the very start. Before he'd had a chance to sort out his own rampaging emotions, she'd smoothed things over with Christopher and expressed the very feelings that Trev hadn't been able to communicate.

And Christopher, who usually guarded his emotions closely, had opened himself to her—a perfect stranger.

Doesn't Trev believe a woman can really love me? Trev hadn't guessed that Christopher suspected such a thing. He'd tear his own heart out and stomp it flat before ever purposely giving his brother that impression. His brother was one of the finest, strongest, most decent people he knew, and Trev had no doubt that a lasting love awaited him somewhere. And Jen had known that. She'd answered his heart-wrenching question better than he himself could have.

She'd behaved exactly as Diana would have...with loving warmth and an uncanny ability to read him. That had been one of the many things he'd missed so damn much—having Diana open his eyes to subtleties in relationships; turn him around when he headed in the wrong direction; relieve his mind when fears piled up regarding the people he loved.

And today Jen had relieved his mind the same way. She'd convinced him of the possibility that Yvonne really might love Christopher. Why hadn't he been willing to give her the benefit of the doubt? More importantly, how had Jen understood the intimate dynamics of his family so quickly?

But that led to thoughts that were even more disturbing. Why had Caesar gone nuts over her? Why had she cried what looked like happy tears? Why had she acted as if she couldn't read sign language when she first met Christopher? She said she knew only the basics, but he doubted that. How, then, had she recognized Yvonne's proficiency?

Questions rose in his mind at such an alarming speed that soon he doubted everything. Except for one absolute fact: Jen was no prostitute. He knew that with a certainty beyond reason.

Needing a long walk and fresh air to clear his mind, he retrieved Caesar from the fenced-in area of the yard and led him down the beach, allowing the sleek black-and-tan shepherd to roam in gleeful exploration. The setting sun tinged the sky and water with brilliant shades of russet and gold, and a chill crept into the air.

Night would soon be upon him. His second night with Jen. He'd have her in his home tonight, and tomorrow night...but what then? Would she vanish into thin air, the way Diana had? That possibility pierced him like a knife. How could he lose the two women he wanted most in the world without even knowing why? Or was she, in fact, *one* woman—with a secret that would tear her away from him again? What kind of secret could possibly do that?

Had he lost his mind to suspect that Jen might actually *be* Diana? Probably.

Nevertheless, he thought back to everything Jen had said and done, and slowly, logical answers occurred to him for many questions that had been nagging. If she *was* Diana, she'd run from him in that hotel lobby because she'd panicked at the sight of him—the husband she'd deserted. She probably then made up the story of being a prostitute to explain her outrageous behavior. And she came to his room, made love to him, simply because she'd wanted to. The emotional turmoil he'd sensed in her must have sprung from whatever reason she'd left him. And her more recent fear of getting naked with him in the light was because he'd said he wanted to "see her" and "know her."

Was she worried that he'd recognize something about her? *Would* he?

It was then that he remembered the butterfly. A tiny, jewel-tone butterfly with wings spread in flight, tattooed on Diana's abdomen—just beneath her bikini line. If he saw Jen naked, would he find the butterfly?

Or had he fallen into a delusional obsession of the very worst kind, fueled by desperately wishful thinking?

He had to know.

9

NESTLED AGAINST the cushions of the living room sofa after a soothing, fragrant bath, Jennifer sipped a comforting cup of hot chocolate and lost herself in the story she'd written so long ago—a wonderful escape from emotions that had grown too intense. She soon found herself fighting the compulsion to edit and revise the prose. She had to actually grit her teeth to stop from picking up a pen.

To avoid temptation, she resolutely closed the manuscript and set it on the table beside her. Only then did she realize how dark it had grown outside. And Trev hadn't yet returned from his walk. She'd watched him lead Caesar down to the beach over an hour ago.

It frightened her to think of him out there in all that darkness. The dark didn't bother Trev, though, as it bothered her.

Was he angry with her over their argument? She should be hoping he *was*, and that he'd drive her back to her apartment and wash his hands of her. Wasn't that the result she'd been aiming for? Somehow she'd lost sight of that goal. Every moment she spent in his company, in his home, made the prospect of leaving him more excruciating.

But she would have to leave him, and break all contact. Her father's enemies were no less dangerous now than they'd been seven years ago. She couldn't endanger Trev by involving him in her life.

A stifling sense of despair filled her at the prospect of leaving. How could she bring herself to do it? And how could she spend another night sleeping apart from him? She longed to touch him, hold him, kiss him...while she still could.

You'll be risking too much, the voice of reason warned. *He might already be suspicious of you. Don't give him the chance to recognize—*

Footsteps thudded on the back deck, and she heard the door open.

"Jen?"

Despite her inner battle, the sound of his deep, familiar baritone warmed her. "In here, Trev."

He appeared in the doorway of the living room, broad-shouldered and ruggedly appealing in a soft denim shirt and jeans, his tawny hair tousled by the breeze. Although he no longer seemed angry, she sensed a peculiar tension radiating from him. "If you hear anything in the garage, don't be alarmed. Caesar's bedding down out there. He's too wet and sandy for the house tonight." His gaze flickered over her mauve silk robe, which concealed a matching nightgown. Unmistakable need sparked in his golden-dark gaze, inciting her own irrepressible desire. And yet, she sensed resistance in him. He didn't *want* to want her.

Why? But then, she'd given him so many reasons.

Needing to ease the tension, she gestured toward the leather portfolio on the table beside her. "I've finished reading the play."

He ambled nearer, bringing with him the scent of forest, wind and ocean. "So, what's your verdict? Who's the murderer?"

"Elementary, my dear Watson." After a pause for dramatic effect, she announced, "The murderer is Bertram Pickworth."

He wedged his large, tan fingers into the pockets of his jeans, leaned against the doorway and regarded her with suddenly veiled eyes, a look reminding her of his earlier stare—the one that had disturbed her. "No, it's definitely not Pickworth. It's either Marie Van Hagen or Ross Kincaid."

Jennifer blinked incredulously. "Don't be ridiculous. Marie was confronting her husband's lover at the time of the murder, and Ross Kincaid is the protagonist. The killer is definitely Pickworth."

He shook his head. "I don't think so." With a slight shrug, he then turned away. "I'm going to take a shower."

Jennifer shot up from the sofa in pursuit, as he sauntered toward his room. How could he be that blind when it came to solving mysteries? "Trev, you're not going to write the last act with Marie or Ross as the murderer, are you?"

"Ross, I think," he called over his shoulder.

"Ross! But that's ridiculous." Grabbing his arm, she forced him to a halt in the doorway of his bedroom. "If you make Ross the murderer, the play is ruined. Don't even bother finishing it, if you can't do better than that."

"Thanks for your opinion, Jen." He aimed a rather patronizing smile at her. "I'll take it into consideration."

"Come sit down, and I'll show you, in black and white, every clue that points to the murderer. And you'll see for yourself that neither Ross nor Marie could possibly—"

"Jen." He gripped her shoulders, surprising her into silence. "You're not *upset* about this, are you?"

She stared at him in sudden dismay. Yes, she was upset. It had taken her years to craft that story. The wrong ending would destroy it. The play would be a joke. She cringed at the very thought! But, of course, she couldn't admit that.

And his gaze, she now realized, was far too searching. As if her passion over the script had raised questions in his mind.

"No, of course I'm not upset." She pushed back a heavy wave of hair that had fallen into her face and struggled to regain her poise. "But you said you wanted the play to be produced to honor Diana's memory. If you write it with the wrong ending, it won't be produced at all."

"Then write the ending for me. Any way you think it should be."

Oh, the temptation of it! The tormenting, agonizing temptation! But her writing belonged to her old life, not her new. And if she showed any aptitude at all for mystery writing, he'd definitely have cause to suspect.

"I'm going to take a shower now." His gaze drifted over her face with renewed intensity. "Any chance you'd join me?"

"No, thanks," she whispered, shaken by her longing to end the emotional turmoil of the day with a night of hot, hard loving. Her defenses had worn too thin. She felt as if she were hanging on to her self-control by a mere thread. "I've already showered. I—I think I'm going to turn in early."

Clear, strong desire burned in his stare, and her heart lifted and leaped in response. But then he turned away without another word and strode into his bedroom. Moments later, she heard the shower running in the master bath.

Deviled by the urge to climb into his bed and wait for him, she strode directly to the guest bedroom and purposefully locked the door—as if the lock would prevent her from leaving the room, if her weaker half won the battle. She wanted to make love to Trev, sleep with him, hold him in her arms all night. Ease her heart and soul with his passion. But she couldn't take that risk.

He might look at her body too closely—and she didn't believe she could survive the trauma of having to face him as Diana, not to mention starting life over again under yet another alias. More troubling still was the danger he'd bring upon himself if he learned the truth and tried to "save" her. He was simply too protective for his own good.

Regardless of how much she wanted to go to him tonight, she *had* to resist the temptation.

Safely alone in the guest bedroom, she doffed her robe, kicked off her slippers and retrieved her contact lens kit from her suitcase. She then peered closely into the dresser mirror and removed her blue lenses. Her eyes felt more sensitive than ever tonight, after a full day of fighting back tears. Blinking in relief at the absence of the nonprescription lenses, she switched on the bedside lamp and turned off the overhead light, casting the room into a cozy golden glow.

How she wished Trev were with her!

To distract herself from thoughts of him, she turned on the small television in the corner. Lulled by the familiar murmur of sitcom dialogue and canned laughter, she turned toward the bed, intending to prop up on pillows and snuggle beneath the covers.

But before she reached the bed, the television went silent.

And the lights went out. All of them. Darkness, thick and black as a spider, pounced on her.

Terror struck through to her very heart. She couldn't even catch her breath enough to scream. *Breathe,* she told herself, staring wide-eyed into the frightening abyss. She could see nothing. *Nothing!* Panic churned within her, and her fingernails bit into her palms. Just as she felt faintness overtake her, her lungs kicked into action, and she began to pant.

"Trev!" she cried, groping the air as she searched for the door. "Trev, where are you?" Terror sounded in her voice, and with the part of her mind that hadn't shut down, she realized she couldn't afford it. She couldn't afford the terror, couldn't scream for Trev, or run to him in panic.

She couldn't admit being afraid of the dark. He would know, then. He would surely know. Diana had been terrified. It would be too coincidental if Jen was, too.

But she had to find him. In her blind search for the door, she tripped over her suitcase, fell against the wall, then desperately felt along the surface until she found the door and unlocked it. She wanted Trev. Wanted him *now*. But she couldn't let him know of her fear.

Somewhere in the terrifying distance, she heard a door open. His voice came from the far end of the hallway. "Jen?"

With fierce concentration, she forced her breathing to a slower pace—a struggle she wasn't sure she could win. Her eyes had begun to adjust to the dark, she realized, and she made out vague outlines of doorways and furniture within the bedrooms. The vagueness itself terrified her.

"Trev," she said with only a slight tremor as she braced her hand against the hallway wall, "what happened to the lights?"

"We must have thrown a breaker." A hazy image of white appeared, and as he drew nearer, she realized he wore nothing but a white towel slung low around his hips. "Are you all right?"

"Yes," she whispered, dizzy from the force of blood rushing to her head with every heavy thud of her heart. "Why wouldn't I be?"

One large, warm hand slid around her waist, while his iron-strong arm hooked around her shoulders. "I thought I heard you yell," he murmured, pulling her against him.

"Yell? Oh...I was just startled." Leaning gratefully into him, she buried her face against his bare shoulder. His bare, *dry* shoulder. She'd thought he'd been in the shower. Obviously, he hadn't stepped into it yet—

"Are you scared of the dark?" he whispered into her hair, distracting her from vague musings.

"No."

He held her tightly enfolded in his arms, his strong, solid body an infinite comfort. "Then why is your heart pounding so hard?"

"Probably because I—I tripped over my suitcase. The fall gave me a fright. But I'm fine."

He didn't reply for a while. When he did, he sounded doubtful. "You're sure you're okay?"

"Yes." But she remained in his arms, flush against his chest, savoring his nearness and warm, muscular body.

"Then I'll go see if I can find the circuit box. It may be in the garage." He made a move to pull away.

"No, wait." She tightened her hold around his lean, bare waist. She didn't want to let him go, didn't want to face the darkness alone yet. Not until she'd fortified herself a little more. "You're not dressed." She ran her hand up the broad, sinewy planes of his back. "You'll catch a chill if you go outside. The lights will probably come back on by themselves, anyway."

"They won't, Jen." A huskiness had entered his voice, and he brushed his slightly abrasive face against hers, his breath warming her skin, stirring her hair. "I saw through the bedroom window that the other houses have light. Ours is the only one without power. We've thrown a breaker."

"Do you have a lantern, or flashlight, or candles?"

"I don't think we've unpacked them yet."

The ramifications slowly occurred to her. Unless Trev went searching for the circuit box, he wouldn't be able to see her very clearly in the dark. Which meant, as long as she kept him in her arms, she had no reason not to spend some time in his bed. She couldn't stay too long, though.

She certainly couldn't allow herself to fall asleep.

"The dark's not necessarily a bad thing, is it?" he rasped against her ear. With a slow caress down her back and backside, he fitted her body to his, and she felt the heat and size of his arousal through the thin cotton towel. "I mean, we could probably find something to keep ourselves occupied."

Sensual longing heated her blood. With quickening breath, she smoothed her hands over the towel in a lingering path along his taut, rounded buttocks, then down to his bare upper thighs—all hot virile flesh, silky hair and hard muscle. "Yeah...I'm sure we'll find something."

Trev's heart revved; his temperature soared. Abandoning the newest question that had been needling him—had she been terrified of the dark?—he surrendered with a tortured groan, dug his fingers into her lustrous, unbound hair and kissed her. She tasted of chocolate, sweetness and all things utterly delectable. As the kiss slanted and surged, he filled his hands with her breasts, so soft and accessible beneath the loose, body-heated silk.

The nightgown had to come off. *Now.* He needed her naked against him. He'd been waiting too damn long. Impatiently he pushed the satiny straps from her shoulders and brushed the gown down the curves of her body. She tugged the towel from his hips. He yanked her panties in frenzied pulls down her sleek thighs and endless legs.

When he finally took her mouth in another voluptuous kiss, he cupped his hands around her bottom and lifted her. Her legs went around his hips, enfolding him in her feminine softness and warmth. With blinding, voracious need, he carried her to his bed.

She would be his. That's all that mattered for the moment. He'd put everything from his mind—all doubts, questions and suspicions—until they both lay sated and exhausted in each other's arms.

Then, God help him, he'd go looking for butterflies.

PASSION POSSESSED HIM for hours. He loved her in countless ways, with his body, hands and mouth, in countless positions, each one taking him deeper and higher, coaxing her into loud, earth-shaking orgasms, and soft, trembly, weeping ones—and the kind that launched both her and him into some distant heaven where their souls soared and danced and floated back to earth profoundly transformed.

He couldn't get enough of her. He knew he never would.

Even as he lay spent and silent beside her in the small hours of the morning, their fingers loosely entwined, their bodies salty with the sweat of hard loving, he wasn't ready to quit. Maybe because he was afraid that once they did, he'd never have her again.

He couldn't tolerate that thought. She was a fever in his blood, but a life-giving fever. She was also an ache in his heart, because as much as she'd opened her body to him, she still kept a secret part of herself closed. The deeper he kissed her, the longer her loved her, the more aware he became of it.

Nor could he forget the fact that she would make love to him only in the dark. He wanted her body, heart and soul. She gave them, but only on loan.

He had to know why.

In taut, unmoving silence, he waited until the sound of her breathing changed to the deeper, slower rhythm of sleep. She wouldn't sleep long, he knew. Her determination was too strong. Every time they'd stopped and rested, she'd murmured her intention of leaving his bed "to get some sleep." He couldn't think of a better place for them to sleep than in each other's arms, but he knew better than to argue. Instead, he'd drawn her back into the passion, distracted her with another round of lovemaking.

He believed he'd finally worn her out. For the moment.

The time had come. His pulse pounded in his ears as he reached between the bed and nightstand and drew out a small gas lantern. Setting it on the stand, he took matches from the drawer and lit the wick. A bright flame illuminated the immediate area with a soft white glow.

He glanced at her face. She hadn't batted an eyelash.

Slowly, cautiously, he shifted onto his side, pushing up on one arm to loom over her. His first look sent a rush of renewed heat to his head, chest and loins. She was just so damn beautiful. He had come to know her body by feel, scent and taste, but the luxury of sight added a poignant richness.

Holding his desire firmly in check, he focused on his mission and skimmed his gaze down her body, bracing himself for what he might find imprinted below her navel. Conflicting emotions gripped him in that millisecond before he knew—a visceral fear that he'd find the butterfly and learn that he'd been the victim of some terrible deceit; and a gut-wrenching hope that he *would* find the butterfly, which would mean Diana was alive and well...and with him. The opposing forces clashed so fiercely in his heart that when he reached his targeted area, the final discovery came as something of a shock.

There was no butterfly. *No butterfly*. Only then did he realize how sure he'd been that he'd find one. He simply couldn't fathom that she looked, sounded, acted and reacted in every situation so much like Diana, without, in fact, being Diana. Even now, he refused to take the absence of the butterfly as conclusive proof that she wasn't. If she'd gone to the extreme measure of surgically altering her face, he reasoned, she could have removed the butterfly, too.

Realizing how crazy he would sound if he shared his suspicions with anyone—and wondering, for the umpteenth time, if he *had* lost touch with sanity—he was seized by the need to resolve the question of her identity here and now. If she *was* Diana, he could surely find another way to identify her. He'd been so familiar with her body, right down to the last detail. But seven years had gone by, and time always wrought changes—and dimmed even the most treasured memories. Would he recognize his wife, if he were staring at her now?

Desperately determined, he scanned Jen's body in search of telling features. Though the hair on her head was a dark ash-blond, the tangle of curls between her thighs was dark. A rich, cocoa brown...like Diana's. He couldn't make much of that, though. Thousands of women lightened their hair, and he wasn't even sure he could deduce that she wasn't a natural blonde.

Her breasts were fuller and rounder than he remembered Diana's to be. But the years that took her from twenty to twenty-seven could have accounted for the extra fullness, as well as the more voluptuous flare of her hips.

His attention then shifted to her nipples. They were a deep, tawny rose color, and reminded him of sunbursts. Something in his gut began to tighten. *Sunbursts.* How could he have forgotten? He swore he'd taken those very sunbursts into his mouth more times than he could count.

Other details soon returned to him from the foggy recesses of his memory. Adrenaline surged, accelerating his pulse and sharpening his senses, as he shifted his scrutiny to her navel—a neat, perfect oval in the concave dip of her stomach. Sure enough, he found within that oval a delicate swirl resembling the tip of a rosebud. His stomach constricted like a fist. He'd dipped his tongue into that rosebud many years ago.

He suspected he knew what he'd find on her inner thigh, too—a light, almost imperceptible beauty mark in the shape of a crescent. Her current position frustrated his efforts. She lay with her thighs angled in a way that cast the area into shadow.

With his heart thudding so loudly he feared she'd wake from it, he grabbed the lantern from the bedside table and brought the light closer, edging farther down on the bed, his scrutiny of her body intense. Before he made it as far as her thighs, the concentrated circle of light swept over her abdomen.

And that's when he detected it, just below the tan line where her bikini bottoms would start. *The butterfly.* Or what was left of it. A small patch of colors, faded from jewel-bright to dream-hazy. Even when he strained his eyes, he couldn't identify a definite shape. But the colors were there.

Or were his eyes playing tricks, painting illusions across her skin—illusions born of obsession?

He needed better light, damn it. Bright electric light, to see all the elements of her body that he swore he recognized. Until he examined them more clearly, he couldn't allow himself to jump to conclusions.

Intending to hurry into the utility room and flip the switch in the circuit box to restore the power he'd deliberately cut earlier, Trev braced himself on his elbow beside her and reached to set the lantern on the nightstand. The movement jostled her.

With a languid intake of breath, a leisurely stretch of her elegant body and a small, dreamy smile, she lifted her long, dark lashes. Blinked herself awake. Turned her head and glanced at him.

And his heart slowed to a near halt.

He stared directly into eyes he could never forget, or mistake for anyone else's. Vivid green eyes—forest green—with dramatic rays of gold radiating through them like sunbeams.

Diana's eyes.

10

HE COULD DO NOTHING but stare. He had no voice, no words. The shock of knowing for sure was too great a blow to absorb that quickly. *She was Diana.* She was the woman he'd married, and lost, and mourned. His bride, his wife. His greatest joy, his greatest sorrow. *Diana.*

"Trev?" Her brows gathered in a small frown as she pushed herself up on her elbows beside him, her hair a silky, disheveled cascade down her naked back. "Is something—?"

Her words cut off, and he watched as awareness settled in. He believed it was his thunderstruck stare that chased away the last of her sleepiness. Her eyes widened, and her glance darted to the glowing lantern, then down at her nakedness in unmistakable alarm. With a soft cry, she yanked a corner of the sheet that lay bunched on the far side of the mattress and tugged the white linen around her for cover. "What—what are you doing? Where did you get the lantern? You said—I thought you didn't have—"

Again she stopped mid-sentence, her voice fading in the thick, tense silence. Clearly she read the depth of shock in his gaze. She sat perfectly still, her back stiff, the sheet clutched against her chest and draped across her body. Her stunningly familiar body.

Gazing into her green-gold eyes, he had no doubts left. His mind still reeled, though, in an attempt to grasp the momentous truth and all its implications.

Before he realized he'd moved at all, he took her face between his hands. With a tight, sick feeling of awe, he scrutinized the changes in her appearance, turning her face slowly from one side to the other. She tried to pull away. He wouldn't allow her to escape, but held on tightly, sweeping his thumbs over her cheeks, jaw and mouth. Her nose was different, too. Her chin...her eyelids...

"Why?" he asked in a drawn-out whisper. "Just tell me why."

"I—I don't know what you're talking about."

Anger flashed through his mind-clouding shock. "No more lies. The game is over. Tell me, Diana. Just tell me." *She'd deliberately left him. Hidden from him. Let him grieve...for seven years.*

"My name's not Diana," she cried, sounding agonized. "Now let me go."

As much as he wanted to shake her—shake the truth right out of her—he released her. She scooted away from him, dragging the sheet with her. Swinging her legs over the side of the bed, she grabbed his denim shirt from a chair and awkwardly donned it.

"What are you going to do," he thundered, "run to put in your blue contact lenses? Throw on some clothes to cover up the butterfly?"

She froze in the act of buttoning the oversize shirt. "There is no butterfly!"

"You tried to erase it, but the colors are still there. I recognized you without the tattoo, anyway. You forget how well I knew you, back when you were *my wife.*"

She stared at him in stricken silence.

He rose from the bed, shrugged into his black flannel robe and briskly belted it. "You owe me *at least* an explanation," he seethed, slowly rounding the bed toward her. "Don't even consider taking another step toward that door until you give me one."

Her bottom lip trembled; her throat worked. Her eyes

filled and shimmered brighter than a sunlit sea. "I'm so sorry, Trev."

And though he'd thought he couldn't possibly feel any worse, somehow he did. Her apology amounted to an admission of guilt, and made the unthinkable all too real. He couldn't avoid the truth now, even if he wanted to.

"Sorry?" he repeated. "You're *sorry*? Do you know what you put me through—me *and* my family? Not a day went by that I didn't imagine the horrors you might have faced. I spent every dime I had the first four years, trying to find you. My grandmother is still suffering from serious depression, thinking she caused your disappearance. And you're *sorry*, Diana? As in, 'Ooops...sorry 'bout that'?" He clenched his teeth and struggled to rein in his fury. Shouting at her would bring him no answers. "Your apology doesn't mean a damn thing. I want to understand. I want to know why you left me without a word. Why you changed your appearance, why you're living as someone else...why I've spent the last seven years *in hell*."

Intensive guilt and regret showed on her face. "There's so much you don't know."

"That goes without saying. And the one thing I *thought* I knew as gospel truth was obviously a lie." He pressed closer, angrily probing her gaze, as if she were hiding the real Diana somewhere within. "I thought you loved me."

"We barely knew each other," she choked out.

He drew back, reeling from the blow. After all she'd done, he should have known—but he still hadn't expected that kind of answer from her. He'd been waiting to hear her tell him that she *had* loved him...because he *swore* she had.

In a tight but even voice, she pressed relentlessly on. "Our marriage was based entirely on lies. I told you I was born in Chicago and grew up in Tennessee and Oklahoma, but that wasn't true. I was born in New York, and grew up in Louisiana."

He frowned at her in bewilderment. Why had she lied about something so irrelevant? He'd never cared where she was from—except when he'd tried to track her whereabouts. He supposed the deception explained why the detectives hadn't found clues to her background.

"I told you my father was an insurance salesman," she said, "and that when he died, I had no family left. I said I had to work my way through school. Those were all lies. I have a huge family—cousins, aunts and uncles. And I grew up wealthy—in a mansion—with servants, a driver, limousines, private jets, and all the money I could spend."

He supposed he should have guessed that much. She'd always had expensive tastes, and her elegance seemed deeply ingrained. "None of that makes a difference, except for the fact you lied. Explain *that* to me."

"My father wasn't a salesman, Trev," she said, ignoring his request. "He was a bookmaker. And I don't mean he made the kind of books you read. He took bets and laid odds for extremely wealthy people from all over the world. And he's very much alive."

He blinked at that. Interesting though it was, she hadn't answered his questions. "Your father's business has nothing to do with us, Diana."

"I only wish that were true. And my name's not Diana."

He let out a soft, fluent curse. "Don't start again. We both know who you are."

"No, I mean my name never was Diana Kelly. It was a false name, Trev, on a fraudulent birth certificate. I married you under an alias."

Now *that* grabbed his attention—like a boa constrictor wrapping around his chest and throat. "What the hell are you talking about?"

"I was running away from home, trying to start a new life, and break all ties—" Her voice caught. She bit her lip and struggled with emotion. After she'd quelled an apparent insurrection of tears, she murmured, "It's time that I tell you the truth. I made a promise to my mother on her deathbed that I would never tell anyone—anyone!—but I feel you need to know how serious the situation is." She swallowed hard, and in an uneven whisper, asked, "Have you ever heard of...Big Vick Palmieri?"

Trev frowned. "The mobster? The one who testified against some crime boss?"

She nodded, her eyes suddenly too large and round for her face. "He's my father."

A feeling of unreality settled over him. "Your...father?"

"You understand what that means, don't you, Trev? You've probably watched news stories about organized crime, or at least a few gangster movies. What happens when someone testifies against a crime boss?"

"Retaliation," he murmured. "Against the witness—and, sometimes, his family."

Jennifer didn't say a word, but allowed him time for the idea to fully evolve. She hated to burden him with the truth, and yet, he knew too much already, simply by recognizing her. In this case, too little knowledge was more dangerous than too much. She felt compelled to make him understand that they were dealing with a life-and-death situation.

"Are you saying someone threatened you?" he demanded, the fury in his stare no longer aimed at her.

"No one *had* to threaten me. I grew up knowing what happened to 'rats.' When I saw my father on the news and realized he was going to testify, I understood what I had to do."

"My God," he breathed, looking shell-shocked. "You should have told me. We could have faced it together, found some form of protection."

"There's only one form of protection that can possibly work for long," she said, upset but not surprised that he thought he could handle the problem on his own. "I'm not saying it's foolproof, because I don't believe any organization run by human beings is invulnerable. But my best chance of staying alive is in the Federal Witness Protection Program."

She watched as full comprehension dawned in him.

"All this time, you've been in hiding," he mused, his tone one of wonder. "You had surgery, took on a new name, a new job." He released a harsh breath and shook his head, as if the concept overwhelmed him. "God, Diana, why the hell didn't you tell me?" The anger was back, but now rang with familiar protectiveness. Her knight in shining armor was climbing upon his white steed again.

The thought scared her witless. As much as she wanted his forgiveness, his understanding...his love...she had to keep a barrier between them. For his own good. She knew what happened to the loved ones of men targeted by the mob. Even the innocent were killed. Trev, Babs, Veronica, Sammy, Christopher—all of them could be drawn into the danger and slaughtered as her five-year-old cousin had been.

No, she couldn't allow it. She had to put a stop to any softening Trev felt toward her. "I didn't tell you, Trev, because I didn't see the point."

"Didn't see the point?" He took hold of her shoulders and frowned at her. "Diana, you're my wife. I should have been with you, 'for better or for worse.' Weren't those the vows we took?"

"I took those vows under a false name. And I...I—" she had to force the words from a tightening throat "—I came to regret them."

He stared at her, stunned yet again.

"I was only a kid when I met you," she whispered, drawing out of his hold. "Alone and on the run. I knew there was trouble brewing at my father's home, and I didn't want to be a part of it. When you came along, I—I found a safe haven with you. A place to stay, and people to help me through the tough times. I'll always be grateful for that."

"Grateful?"

"We both know that our relationship wasn't based on love. We didn't know each other. All we had was sex. *Good* sex, but...just sex."

His jaw squared, and a coolness entered his gaze. "Is that how you saw it?"

"Please understand, Trev. If this danger hadn't come up, I might have stayed with you for another few months, maybe longer. I certainly wouldn't have left the way I did. But I knew, almost from the start, that our marriage wouldn't work." How she hated to tell him these hurtful lies!

He said not a word. Merely stared with unreadable eyes.

She forced herself to continue. "The U.S. Marshals Service could have handled the divorce proceedings for us, but I had enough to contend with—the sudden move, the identity change, the surgery. The danger. I assumed *you'd* eventually divorce *me*. You know, for abandonment."

"So you left, without a word."

Pain lanced through her at his coldness. "Actually, I did send you a letter," she murmured, needing to tell him at least that much, "but I guess you never received it."

His mouth formed a grim line. "I *did* receive a letter."

It was her turn to stare.

"I thought it was a hoax. It was so vague and impersonal, I didn't think it could possibly be from my...loving wife." Unmistakable bitterness underscored every quiet word. "It was typewritten, and signed with only a *D*. I showed it to the detective I hired, but he rejected it as a prank, too."

Her heart ached to think that Trev had believed in her love so staunchly, he'd discounted the very possibility that she'd left him. *Oh, Trev!* Struggling to maintain a tough front, she shrugged. "I didn't go into detail, or write the letter in long-hand, or even sign it, because I thought it might be intercepted by the wrong people. Anyway, I saw no reason to draw a link between you and me. No good could come from it." Afraid to dwell too long on the truth—that she'd been protecting him the only way she knew how—she said as lightly as she could, "Neither the FBI nor the U.S. Marshals Service has a record of our marriage, or my alias as Diana Kelly. Your name appears nowhere in their files."

He didn't look the least bit relieved by that information.

She suddenly grew worried that he didn't understand its importance. She considered that secrecy vital to keeping him and his family uninvolved in the danger. "You understand, Trev, that it's important to keep all of this strictly to ourselves, don't you? You can tell *no one* about your association with me—not even someone in the government. You never know how information could leak out. You'd endanger both of us. Ruthless criminals could use you and your family to get to me."

Still, he said nothing.

Desperation spiked in her. "In a very real way, Trev, there *is* no connection between us," she stressed, fighting off a fresh threat of tears. "Diana is dead. She's never coming back. In fact, she never existed."

"You're right." His voice was deep, gruff and cold. "Diana never existed. And I didn't know *you* at all."

Her throat clenched. Her eyes blurred. Abruptly she turned from him and stared through a darkened window. She had to get herself under control. Trev's future depended on her playing out the game. The hour was only four a.m., and the moon barely illuminated the darkness. She shivered at the thought of going outside alone.

But she'd have to.

"Go to bed...Jen—if that's what you want to be called." His tone was dry, his voice weary. "I don't even know your real name. But then, I guess I don't need to."

She bit her lip and remained silent. It was better that he didn't know it.

"I'll restore the power so you can keep a light on in your room."

She nodded, painfully noting his implied suggestion that she spend the rest of the night apart from him. It made perfect sense. She'd hurt him, and he no longer wanted her.

Her heart ached too much to think about it.

"Actually, I was thinking of warming a cup of milk to help me relax," she murmured. "And I thought I'd go say a few words to Caesar." On a strangled whisper, she added, "It's been a long time since I talked to him."

He lifted a shoulder in an uncaring shrug. "Whatever gets you through the night."

Never had she heard him speak in a voice so devoid of feeling. She struggled to keep hers steady. "Would you please turn the power back on?"

Wordlessly he turned to leave the bedroom, wearing only his black terry-cloth robe, his feet bare.

As she thought of him venturing outside into the chilly darkness to find the circuit box, she considered suggesting that he wear slippers and take the lantern, but a sudden suspicion stopped her. The fortuitous timing of the blackout, the lantern materializing at his bedside, the fact that the shower had been running but he hadn't been wet—all this registered in her mind with a sudden *click*.

"You cut the power on purpose, didn't you," she called out.

He stopped in the hallway, cast a cool glance over his shoulder, then continued on into the utility room without answering.

The utility room. That's where he'd been when the lights had gone out, not in the shower. And he hadn't been surprised at all by the blackout. She pictured him clearly with his hand on the breaker switch, waiting to hear her scream.

She supposed she couldn't blame him for his trickery, considering the gravity of the situation. His deception had been nothing compared to hers. And her deceptions were not yet over.

The moment he was out of sight, she grabbed his jeans from an armchair, searched the pockets and drew out his car keys. With a pang of regret for what she was about to do — and for the pain she'd already caused him—she slipped the keys into the pocket of the denim shirt she wore.

The overhead light suddenly blazed on, and the television sounded from the guest bedroom. As she strode down the hallway toward her room, Trev brushed past her without a word or glance. His aloofness cut her to the quick.

But she didn't dare dwell on her emotions. Within moments of reaching her room, she donned her jeans and a fresh blouse, threw a few necessities into her overnight bag, grabbed her purse and headed for the door. She wished she had time to say goodbye to Caesar. She wished she didn't have to leave at all.

But life, as she well knew, wasn't about wishes coming true.

Forcing herself to part from the golden light of Trev's home and venture out into the frightening darkness, she stepped onto the porch. She hesitated only briefly. Swallowing her fear—along with the burn of emotions held too long in check—she resolutely closed the door of the house and ran to his car, which he'd parked in the driveway. She heard Caesar bark behind the closed garage door as she started up the engine.

Shifting into gear, she guided the powerful vehicle down the crushed-shell driveway. In the rearview mirror, she saw Trev throw open his door and step out onto the porch steps.

Goodbye, her heart cried in soul-deep anguish. *Goodbye,* for the very last time.

She sped onward, then, into the black, chilly night, away from everything warm, everything wonderful. It was the least she could do for the man who meant more to her than life itself.

TREV WASN'T SURE what to do, if anything. He doubted that she'd have taken his car if she wasn't planning to come back. Their confrontation had been emotional, and she may have needed time away from him. But he'd found her suitcase on the floor in the guest bedroom, which made him believe she hadn't left for good.

As the minutes dragged by into an hour, though, he began to doubt his original reasoning. The last time she'd left him, she'd barely taken anything with her. And if she'd decided to vanish again, she could easily abandon his car on her way out of town.

Anxiety filled him. Had she left him again?

He had no car in which to pursue her, or any idea where she'd gone.

Tense with foreboding, he called the police and reported his car missing. "One of my friends may have borrowed it without telling me, so go easy on whoever's driving it." He didn't want her mistreated if they apprehended her—and of course, he wouldn't press charges. He suggested they look for the car at her apartment, and asked that they call him when they had.

They called him back within moments. No sign of his car at her apartment.

He dropped down onto the sofa in a daze of pain and confusion. She hadn't gone home. Where had she gone? Would he ever see her again? The things she'd told him had left him feeling as if his insides were torn to bloody shreds. He'd barely been able to look at her without anger and resentment choking him. Yet, if she didn't come back, if he couldn't at least draw their relationship to a proper close, he swore he'd never be whole again. A damn pathetic way to feel after what had just transpired between them.

He still couldn't quite grasp the truth. She'd never loved him. For seven years, he'd been grieving for a woman who hadn't given a damn about him or his family. She hadn't even told him her real name. He'd been married to her, and didn't know her name.

How could he have been so fooled by her? Not only once, which was bad enough, considering he'd married her and mourned her for the better part of a decade. But then he'd fallen in love with her again, in a span of five days. He couldn't even blame her for that, since she'd begged him to leave her alone.

And he still wanted to talk to her. *Needed* to talk to her, if only to say goodbye. Damn it all to hell, she could at least have said goodbye! But would he have let her go? He didn't know.

He rubbed his palms wearily over his face. He was lying to himself. He did know. He *wouldn't* have let her go. He'd have found a way to keep her here. More proof that he'd lost his mind. Why should he want to keep her with him? She didn't love him, didn't want him.

That thought hit a jarringly wrong note, and brought his face up out of his hands. The last part, at least, hadn't been true. She'd wanted him. The sexual chemistry between them had been as hot and combustible as ever. As he thought back over the past few days to the times they'd made love, the times they'd kissed, the times he'd simply held her...another certainty hit him: She'd felt more for him than "just sex."

He'd sensed her intensely emotional reaction to him from the very start, when he'd cornered her in the hotel stairwell. He'd sensed her tenderness when they made love in his room. The quality of her gazes had turned his heart inside-out, and her kisses had spoken more eloquently than anything she could say. Hadn't it been her emotional intensity that had kept him coming after her, holding on to her, even while she pretended to be an incorrigible prostitute?

She'd almost cried at least a dozen times while staying in his home—over Caesar, and Christopher, and the play she'd written. He believed she'd grown misty-eyed over the photographs of his family, too. And their wedding picture...she'd pressed it to her heart, as if she hadn't wanted to let it go.

He hadn't imagined those emotional reactions.

He hadn't imagined her love for him. He knew that as surely as he knew the sun rose in the morning. She'd succeeded in convincing him that she wasn't Diana because of the physical differences, the subtle change in her speech and the fact that an impersonation made no sense. But she *hadn't* succeeded in convincing him that she wasn't the woman meant for him—the woman who would love him for all time, as he would love her.

She was that woman.

And no, he didn't know her name. She'd purposely withheld that from him.

A realization then dawned with such clarity that he marveled he hadn't seen it immediately. She hadn't wanted him involved in the danger. *Ruthless criminals could use you and your family to get to me*, she'd told him. Growing up in a family like hers, she'd probably experienced the pain of underworld violence in some way or another, which made the threat far too real for her to ignore.

She was protecting him. She'd told him she never loved him, that she'd wanted out of their marriage. She'd known those were the only reasons he'd let her go.

Ah, but she didn't realize he knew her better than that. Now that the shock had worn off enough for him to think, he *knew* she loved him, and would never stop loving him.

And nothing would stop him from going after her.

Another concern blindsided him: how close *was* the danger? She'd spoken of mob retaliation and explained the extreme precautions she'd taken to avoid being found, but he knew nothing about organized crime or the Witness Protection Program. How safe was she? The Program had kept her alive for seven years, but not very well hidden. *He* had found her, though inadvertently. Could her enemies be closing in?

He shut his eyes and strove to calm himself. He would find her and stay with her, whether she liked it or not. He'd get a gun. Brush up on his aim. Take care of her. *How the hell do you think you'll find her? You're too late.*

She'd probably already left town to vanish again in the Witness Protection Program. She'd assume a new name, now that he'd breached her cover, and relocate to a new place.

Anguish burned in his chest, followed quickly by torturous self-blame. Why hadn't he seen through the lie when she'd first said she didn't love him? He supposed he'd been too stunned, too overwhelmed by the incredible facts, to think clearly. He'd been operating in a state that bordered on physical shock, as if he'd lost too much blood and couldn't form a cohesive thought. That floundering may have cost him everything that made life worth living.

He couldn't bear to lose her a second time.

With growing alarm, he called the police again and asked about their progress.

"Haven't located the car yet, Mr. Montgomery. We're working on it. We'll call as soon as we get news."

He gave them his cell phone number, then immediately called for a cab. Just because the police hadn't spotted his car at her apartment didn't mean she wasn't there. Maybe luck would be with him and he'd catch her before she left town. While he waited for the cab to arrive, he cued his home phone to his cell phone, just in case she called.

Please God, let her call. Let her come back to me.

His cell phone rang fifteen minutes later, as he rode in the back seat of a cab toward Jen's apartment. His heart beat in his throat as he answered. He wanted so damn much to hear her voice.

It was a police officer. "We found your car. The keys were still in it. Doesn't look like anything's been taken or vandalized. Your CD player is still intact, and a laptop computer is in the backseat. The car was left in the parking lot of that new luxury hotel. There's a convention going on there, and the lot is crowded. Nobody we questioned noticed who left the vehicle. Of course, that isn't too surprising at the crack of dawn. If you can come by the station, we'll have your car here for you."

Trev thanked him and directed the cabdriver to drop him by the police station. The fact that she'd left the car at the hotel puzzled him. Why had she gone there? Had she stopped by her apartment first—or not at all? Would she check in at the office today—or was she already flying off to some unknown destination?

He glanced at his watch. Almost eight o'clock. The office might already be open. As the cab pulled into the police station lot, Trev dialed her office number. "Jennifer Hannah, please."

"I'm sorry," said the receptionist, "but she was called away on a family emergency early this morning. I'll be happy to transfer you to Phyllis."

He hung up, tossed a large bill to the cabdriver and hurried into the station to reclaim his car. He then sped all the way to her apartment. Parking at a wild angle on the curb outside her quadruplex, he noticed that her car was still there, parked exactly where she'd left it two days ago. Maybe she hadn't left yet.

Hope hammered in his chest, throat and temples as he strode up the walkway and rapped on her door. No one answered. He knocked again. "Jen? It's me. Trev. Open up."

No reply.

"Jen!" He beat on the door again, louder this time. Perhaps she was simply being stubborn and ignoring him...while packing to leave town—

"Hey, stop making all that racket!" yelled a scowling older

woman from the doorway of a nearby apartment. "She's not there, so go away."

"How do you know she's not here?"

"That's none of your business."

He gritted his teeth, his patience wearing thin. "It *is* my business. I'm her husband. I have to talk to her."

"Her husband?" Her gray brows shot up in surprise, then converged over a frown. "She's not married."

"We've been separated. But I have to talk to her. It's an emergency. Did you see her leave this morning?"

She narrowed her eyes at him, and after an appraising moment said, "No, but I'm her landlady. She called me an hour ago. Said there's a family emergency out of state. Maybe it's the one you're talking about. She told me she'll be sending movers to pack up her stuff, and she'll mail me her key."

Sick, frantic anxiety squeezed him nearly breathless. She'd already left. Unless, by some miracle, he caught her at the airport. He had to try.

With an absent murmur of thanks to the woman, he returned to his car. As he reached for the door handle, a figure sauntered out from a nearby cluster of trees—a man wearing a baseball cap, sunglasses and a navy-blue jacket over jeans. A man as tall as Trev, and somewhat huskier.

"Excuse me, but, uh, I couldn't help overhearing." His low, raspy, nasal voice sounded northern. "You lookin' for Jennifer Hannah?"

"Yeah." Though every muscle in his body had tensed, Trev saw no sense in denying it. He'd been shouting her name and beating on her door only moments earlier. Maybe the guy was from the U.S. Marshals Service or the FBI, working to protect her.

Or...maybe not.

With his hands in the pockets of his windbreaker jacket, the man leaned closer, and in a confidential whisper, said, "So, you're her husband, huh?"

Trev didn't have time to answer, or to act. Something hard, metal and round dug into his back, near the tail of his spine. In utter disbelief, he realized it was a gun, probably still concealed within the guy's pocket.

"Let's you and me go somewhere and talk."

The cold, clear purpose in the man's seemingly friendly voice left Trev no doubt. He wouldn't think twice about pulling the trigger.

11

JENNIFER LEFT Trev's car at the hotel in Sunrise because she believed it would be safest in the crowded, well-lit parking lot until the police found it. She then called a cab to take her to the airport. She wouldn't return to her apartment. Trev might look for her there. After the horrible things she'd said to him, she knew he'd no longer want her, but she wouldn't risk the possibility that his protective instincts would get him further involved in her situation.

Besides, she couldn't face leaving him again.

From the airport, she called Dan Creighton, her security supervisory inspector. "I've been recognized, Dan. The woman I went to high school with approached me and asked if I was Carly. I told her I wasn't, but I'm not sure she believed me. She knows my father's history, and that Carly is probably living under an alias somewhere. I believe she's suspicious."

Dan instructed her to catch the first flight to D.C.

Three hours later, he and two other federal agents met her at the gate in Dulles International Airport. Dan, a tall, portly man in his late fifties with thinning reddish hair, a limp from a bullet he'd taken years ago, and a warm, fatherly way about him, hooked his arm around her in a comforting squeeze. He'd been her anchor through the storm, her only confidant for seven years, the one person in her life who knew the truth about her identity.

Though she felt an undeniable affection for him, she knew he believed in playing strictly by the rules of the Program.

You follow the rules, you live. You don't, you die. Simple as that.
He'd also made it clear that if she broke the rules, she could
be dropped from the Program and left to fend for herself.
That thought frightened her.

And now she *had* broken the most rigid rule—interacting
with a person from her past. She couldn't let Dan know, not
only for her own sake, but also to keep Trev safely uninvolved.

As Dan escorted her through the crowded airport, flanked
on either side by plain-clothed marshals, he told her that his
wife had sent home-baked cookies, which would be waiting
for her at the apartment. He then talked about his children as
he helped her into a windowless van, the kind she remembered from her first trip to a safe house and her initial ride to
the orientation center.

They were headed there again—the Witness Security Safe
Site and Orientation Center, the heavily guarded compound
somewhere in Virginia. Only when they were comfortably
ensconced in the backseat of the van did Dan talk business.
"Have you remembered this woman's name, Jennie?"

Jennifer shook her head. "No, I'm sorry. I've thought and
thought, but can't recall her name. I should have asked her,
but I was hoping to avoid conversation altogether."

"We'll try to get a yearbook from your high school years.
Until we can find her picture, we'll work from a sketch. A police artist will take a description from you. We want to inves-
tigate the situation and make sure there's nothing more at
work here than coincidence."

Jennifer murmured her thanks. She hated to lie to Dan
about her nonexistent schoolmate, but saw no other way to
explain her need for a new identity. She hoped they'd be unable to locate a yearbook.

Dan went on to assure her that he was arranging for a crew
to pack up her possessions in Sunrise. "We'll have your
things shipped to headquarters, and once you've rented an

apartment in St. Paul, they'll be forwarded to you. Except, of course, for anything that bears the name Jennifer Hannah. Can't have clues lying around that would connect you with the blown cover."

The thought of federal agents sifting through her personal items on a search-and-destroy mission should have disturbed her. At one time, it would have. Now she didn't much care. She felt frozen in ice, as if nothing could touch her. She suspected it was better this way.

Otherwise, the pain of leaving Trev would be unbearable. She wouldn't think about the past they'd shared or the future they wouldn't share. What could the future possibly hold for her but emptiness? Long, gray, lonely hours...*without Trev.* Or family, or friends. She had no alternative, though. She could allow herself no loved ones.

Dan stayed to see her settled into the neat, one-bedroom apartment within the compound. The living room opened onto a small concrete patio surrounded by high walls— rather like a prison yard, Jennifer imagined. Before leaving her for the day, Dan gave her information to study—the background story invented for the person she would become; videos of the city where she had supposedly grown up; and literature about St. Paul, where she would live. He also supplied a book of names to help in choosing a new alias.

She couldn't bring herself to begin the process of becoming someone else, though. The protective shell around her heart had begun to crack, and the pain of leaving Trev, of hurting him, racked her. Aimlessly she wandered about the apartment and stared outside at the walled patio, consumed by the desire to leave, to return to Trev, to pretend that life could go on in a normal fashion.

She knew better. The danger would always plague her. And though Trev used to love her, he no longer did. She'd killed his love with ruthless lies. *It's better for him that way.*

Now he can move on to a new love. That prospect brought her no comfort.

Later that afternoon, a sharp knock sounded at the door, and Jennifer admitted Dan into the apartment. She hadn't been expecting him. One look at his face told her something was wrong. Had he somehow discovered that she'd lied about the woman from her high school?

"We have a problem, Jennie. Come, sit down." With a guiding hand at her shoulder, he ushered her to the sofa, where they both sat. She'd never seen him looking so troubled. Foreboding filled her. "I hope you understand how important it is to be completely honest with me. I can't protect you if I don't have all the facts."

Her stomach constricted. "Yes, of course I know that, Dan."

His gaze drilled into hers. "Do you know a man by the name of...Trev Montgomery?"

Her heart rose and fell so sharply, she felt faint at the surge. "Trev Montgomery? Um, yes...I've met him." At Dan's persistent stare, she reluctantly went on, "He—he's a builder who recently moved to Sunrise. I met him Friday, at the new hotel." She could barely hear her own voice over the drumming in her ears. "Why do you ask?"

"It seems he was at your apartment this morning, looking for you."

"Well, he—he *had* mentioned the possibility of me helping him set up his office."

"He was taken at gunpoint."

Her world went silent—deathly silent—then spun around and lurched into sickening chaos. "*What?*" she cried, leaping to her feet. "Taken at gunpoint! Oh, no. Oh, no, no!" The trembling started in her legs and hands, and spread to every part of her. "Trev. Oh, my God, *Trev...*"

"Jennie." Dan stood and caught her by the shoulders. "Calm down. Let me finish."

But terror was pulsing through her in cold, relentless waves. *Gunpoint. Trev.* How had this happened? Who had taken him? What was he going through? Or was he—was he—

"He's being held," said Dan in a slow, deliberate voice that cut through the terrifying whirl of her thoughts, "by your father."

She stared at him, uncomprehending. "My father?" When the concept finally sank in, her eyes widened in disbelief. "He's being held at gunpoint by my *father?*"

"Vick believes him to be a hit man sent to find you."

"A *hit man!*"

"You've got to be extremely careful about people you meet, Jennie."

"But Trev isn't—"

"Whether he is or isn't, Vick has him, and is demanding to talk to you. Will you speak with him?"

Dizzy with alarm and thoroughly bewildered, she nodded emphatically. Dan leaned toward the phone on the living room table, lifted the receiver and keyed in numbers. "Vick? I'm putting you through on the speakerphone."

Within moments, her father's gruff, nasal voice boomed from the speaker. "Carly?"

"Yes, Daddy, I'm here," she cried, sinking down onto the sofa, her hands clasped against her breast. She'd seen her father only twice in seven years—and then, only for brief, furtive meetings in randomly chosen places. Had the stress of living in hiding finally pushed him beyond rational thought? "Do you have Trev? Is he okay? You didn't hurt him, did you?"

"Hey, slow down, girlie. Yeah, I've got him, and no, I haven't shot him. At least, not yet. I found him at your apartment, trying to wheedle information out of your landlady."

"He's not a hit man, Daddy! He's no threat to us at all. You've got to let him go."

"Not until I get the whole story on him."

"What were you doing at my apartment, anyway? You haven't visited, or answered my calls, or let me visit you for years. Why now, all of sudden, are you—"

"I told you, I don't want you hurt if someone fingers me. Better that you keep your distance. But when I heard from Dan that you recognized some gal from the neighborhood, I got worried. Seems too coincidental. Figured I'd go check out your place myself. See if I recognized anyone who might be trouble."

"With a *gun*? You brought a *gun*?"

"What, you think I'm crazy enough to go unarmed? You and me are human targets, babe. Of course, I got a gun. And it's a good thing, too. I caught this guy in the act of trying to track you down. Get this—he told your landlady he's your *husband*."

Jennifer's breath caught, and she glanced at Dan, who sat watching her closely. What should she do, what should she say? Damn Trev for not listening to her! She'd *told* him to keep their association secret. If only she could think above the thudding of her heart.

"He's sticking to the story, too. Says he wants to see you. I'm thinking I should send him back to his family in a box. Know what I mean?"

Her hand fanned across her mouth. She didn't know if her father was capable of killing someone or not. He'd grown up in a rough part of New York City where the dons of organized crime were worshiped as heroes. He was proud to say they'd considered him a real "stand-up guy" from the time he was twelve.

"Daddy, do you hear yourself?" she admonished, fighting against her rising fear. "You're threatening a man's *life*. You're not a murderer. You wouldn't—"

"I don't have much left in this world except you, Carly, and I'm not going to let someone whack you. This guy knows what you look like now. He also knows anything else you've told him. He's a threat. A loose end. The only reason I haven't finished him off is because he thought *I* was trying to whack you, which makes me think maybe *he* wasn't."

"Please let him go. He's not trying to kill me, and he's not going to tell anyone what I look like. He's...he's—"

"He's your husband, ain't he? He showed me this picture. Looks an awful lot like you in the bride dress, Princess."

Her vision blurred with sudden tears, and she couldn't speak.

"The photo is either real, or he doctored it—which would mean he's got some serious scheme in mind. Sending him back to his people full of holes might slow down the next yahoo they send after us."

"The photo's real," she confessed in a tight, agonized whisper. The surprise registering in Dan's gaze only made her more aware of what the admission meant for Trev's future. "I married him seven years ago. But it was under a false name, and the court has declared me dead, so—"

"I'm bringing him in," said her father.

"Bringing him in? You mean, *here?*"

"Of course, there. He's your husband. He's supposed to be taking care of you. We Palmicris don't believe in divorce, and no court is going to declare my little girl dead, just so this guy doesn't have to honor his vows. Dan, come get us. We'll be at the usual place."

"No, Daddy, no, you don't understand—"

The line went dead. She stared at the phone, feeling shaken and spiritually bruised.

"We're going to bring them in, Jennie," Dan said. "Before we allow Trev any contact with you, though, we'll run a background check to make sure he's not tied in with organized crime. Considering the fact that he hasn't whacked Vick yet, I'm assuming he's not."

"Of course he's not!"

"It's my job to make sure. You can fill me in on everything you know about him to speed the process along." Pulling a small recorder from his pocket, he quietly questioned her, drawing out all the facts about their marriage, including her alias as Diana Kelly. He then clicked off the recorder and rose from the sofa. "If you don't want to see Montgomery, that's your prerogative, but it's clear your cover's already blown with him."

"I do want to see him." She *had* to see him. She had to make sure he was okay. She also had to explain to him that as her acknowledged husband, his life might be in jeopardy. Unless they could somehow make it clear to the world that their ties had been permanently broken.

"There wasn't any woman in Sunrise from your high school, was there," Dan deduced.

Biting her lip, she shook her head.

His stare shone with patent disappointment in her. They'd been close allies. Her deception clearly hurt him on a personal level. "I don't understand why you lied—about any of it."

"Because I didn't want Trev's name in your files. He's a good, decent, hardworking man, and he doesn't deserve the kind of trouble that I've brought him. I'm sorry I lied to you, Dan—but don't you see? Once he's named as the husband of Carly Palmieri, the possibility exists that my father's enemies will learn about him...and go after him." When Dan failed to respond by comment or expression, she held out her hands in a plea for understanding. "If you were in my position, Dan, would you want your wife's name in those files?"

A flicker of emotion rippled through his gaze. She hoped it had been comprehension. He then let out a long, weary breath and tightened his lips. He didn't, however, answer her question or assure her that her fears held no merit. After a lengthy pause, he asked in a reluctant tone, "Did you initiate contact with Montgomery, or...identify yourself to him in any way?"

"No," she replied, aware that he was asking if she'd broken the most important rule of the Program. She couldn't forget that he was, first and foremost, a seriously dedicated U.S. Marshal entrusted with grave responsibility. "He recognized me. In the hotel lobby." She wouldn't tell him that she'd spent the night with him...and nights thereafter. She couldn't afford to be ejected from the Program. "I don't know what gave me away."

His reddish brows drew together in a frown.

"I swear to you, Dan, it's the truth." Despite all she hadn't told him, it was.

With a curt nod, he left her.

She spent the next two hours pacing. If only Trev hadn't gone to her apartment! It had been bad enough fearing for her father's life and her own. She couldn't stand fearing for Trev's, too.

The more she thought about the danger, the more vividly she recalled the horror—the thunder of gunshot on a hot afternoon. The faint, acrid smell of smoke lingering in the air. The screams. The blood, everywhere. Her uncle's body, spattered across the sidewalk. And her little cousin Petey, slumped in a heap over his new baseball mitt.

The horror wouldn't fade.

A knock at the door startled her. Anxiously she moved to the peephole and peered out. Dan stood there. Wondering if her father and Trev were with him, she swung open the door and came face-to-face with the tall, broad-shouldered, tawny-haired man beside him. The one with a nasty gash above his amber eye and a bruise discoloring his right cheekbone. *Trev*.

Her heart leaped; her anxiety skyrocketed. He'd been hurt. Fighting the urge to press forward into his arms, kiss his wounds, weep in gladness over his survival—and pummel him with her fists for getting himself caught up in the danger—she demanded curtly, "What happened to your face?"

"Let us in, Jen." The deep rumble of his voice sounded unnaturally hoarse. His face looked tense, beard-shadowed, overly tired, cut, bruised and heart-wrenchingly handsome. Her father, she noticed, wasn't with him.

She kept her chin high and her spine straight, while the two men filed past her into the apartment. Holding her tumultuous emotions tightly in check, she confronted Trev. "You didn't answer my question. How did you get hurt?"

"Just a little skirmish over the gun."

"Over the gun! You could have been killed!"

"Yeah," he agreed wryly. "That's why I took the gun."

"You *took* the gun? Away from my father?"

"Don't sound so amazed. He's in his sixties, at least, and not in the best of health. I'm not saying it wasn't a struggle, because it was, but—"

"He said he was holding you at gunpoint. How could that be, if you had the gun?"

"He called you from my back deck while drinking a beer and smoking a cigar. He'd returned the gun to his chest holster hours earlier. We'd just finished lunch."

Relief and anger surged through Jennifer in equal measures. "And you let him scare me like that?"

"I wasn't with him when he made the call. He used my cell phone, while I was booking us flights to D.C. But even if I'd heard him, I don't think Big Vick lets many people tell him what *not* to do or say."

She glared at him. Vick had tricked her into admitting she'd married Trev—while a U.S. Marshal listened in—and Trev didn't seem the least upset about it.

"Uh, Jennie..." Dan cleared his throat from beside her, reminding her of his presence. "I've got Vick in a suite upstairs. I have serious issues to discuss with him. We'd prefer that he didn't make a habit of taking people at gunpoint. You can probably see him tomorrow. As far as Mr. Montgomery goes, we've checked him out thoroughly, not only with a physical search, but also a background check. We've made sure that—"

"It wasn't necessary to check out Mr. Montgomery," she interjected, unable to curb the negative energy pumping through her. "He isn't a threat, and my father shouldn't have dragged him into this." She shifted her glare to Trev, though she continued to speak to Dan. "Not that Trev himself is blameless. He shouldn't have gone to my apartment or questioned my landlady or told anyone he was my husband. He should have stayed at home, kept his mouth shut and minded his own business!"

"And *you* shouldn't have stolen my car," Trev put in, his golden-dark gaze locked in battle with hers, "or left me without a goodbye...*again*."

"What difference would 'goodbye' make?" she cried. "We said all there was to say."

"No, *you* did all the talking."

"Oh-kay," Dan said, bringing his hands together in a conclusive clap. "It's perfectly clear to me that you two *are* married. Think I'll let you wage this war in private. Buzz me if you need me." After he'd strolled to the door and opened it, though, he paused, looking thoughtful. "At least I've found the answer to one mystery that's been puzzling me, Jennie."

She turned to him in silent question.

"I wondered why you haven't dated in the entire seven years I've known you."

Jennifer didn't comment, but continued staring at the doorway long after he'd left. Why, oh why, had he chosen *now* to say such a thing? She hadn't wanted Trev to know that, or to get the idea that she'd avoided other men because she'd wanted only him...or that she'd compared every man to him and grieved over the differences....

"I hope you didn't believe that was true," she finally mur-

mured. Without risking a glance at him, she locked the dead
bolt on the door, tossed her hair over one shoulder and
walked past Trev with deliberate nonchalance into the living
room, where she gazed out into the evening shadows of the
walled patio. "Just because I didn't tell Dan about my dates
doesn't mean I never went on any."

"Jen." Trev came up behind her, his hands strong and
warm on her arms, his breath stirring her hair, his virile scent
evoking poignant memories. "Don't try so hard to push me
away. It won't work. I'm going into the Program with you."

Her heart turned over, and she whirled around to gape at
him. "Into the Program with me?" She couldn't believe it.
Hadn't he listened when she'd said she never loved him?
Didn't he feel used and abused by her? Or maybe his decision had nothing to do with their personal relationship.
Maybe he realized the danger he'd been exposed to, and
thought he needed to go into hiding to survive.

Forcefully she shook her head. "No. No! I don't believe
that will be necessary. I...I've figured out a solution. You
have to start seeing someone, Trev. You know—dating." She
couldn't bear to look at him while suggesting he go to another woman, so she paced across the living room. "It would
be best if you actually remarried. That way, even if my father's enemies discover that we were once married, they'll
believe I'm gone from your life, and that you have no way of
contacting me or my father." She hoped he couldn't see how
much the suggestion cost her. "Yes, I—I'm sure that will
work." With an effort, she walked back toward him and
forced out through a constricted throat, "You've got to find
someone...to marry."

"Yeah, that's a great plan, Jen. There's only one problem."
He slid his hands around her jean-clad hips and slowly but
persistently pulled her to him, until she couldn't possibly
avoid his gaze. "I don't want anyone else. I want *you*," he
whispered fervently. "Do you hear me, Jen? I *want* you."

She met his heated stare with dazed astonishment and helpless longing. After all she'd said and done, he still wanted her! And God knew, she wanted him. She had to fight harder than ever to stem the desire. "Weren't you listening when I said I never loved you?"

"No, I wasn't listening. Because you said something very different with your eyes, and your kiss, and your body."

A groan tore from her throat, and she turned away, breaking from his hold, desperate to resist him. "You're not thinking straight. And you know nothing about the Program. If you entered it, you'd have to leave everyone behind—Babs, Veronica, Sammy, Christopher. You could never see them again."

"And that thought hurts like hell. But when all is said and done, they'll be fine without me. I won't be fine without you, Jen. Something vital in me died when you left, and I don't want to live that way again. My family will have each other, and *we'll* have each other—you and me. Don't tell me you don't want that. I know you do."

She pressed her lips together to stop their trembling. He was so damn persuasive. She had to make him see reason...before she lost hers altogether. But she'd already given her strongest argument, and he'd shot it down. Flailing for more ammunition, she said, "You'd have to leave your property and your business. All your plans for the new community. You'd have to start over, in some new field, doing heaven knows what for a living."

"I'm not afraid of starting over. I can always make a living. We'll face whatever comes, and make the best of it. Together."

Did he know he was offering her heaven, when she'd been consigned to hell? But she couldn't let him make such a sacrifice on her behalf, or put himself into danger by physically being with her. "If you go into the Program, Trev, you can

never have close friends, because you'll have too many secrets to hide. You can't be truthful with anyone. Ever."

"I'll be truthful with you—and you, with me. I'm still
waiting for that, you know—for you to be truthful with me.
As far as friends go, if I never have any, that's better than
never having—"

"No, no...shh." She pressed her fingers frantically across
his mouth to stop him from saying another word. Strong,
deep-seated fear rose in her, reminding her of the horror. "If
you go into the Program, it will have to be without me. I
won't be a party to you giving up everyone and everything
in your life for a woman you barely know. And no matter
what you say, you barely know me."

"Now *you're* not thinking straight."

"We knew each other a total of six months," she cried,
"and that was seven years ago. We're practically strangers."

"If that's so, then why did I recognize you despite the fact
that you've done everything you can to change your appearance?"

The emphatic question shook her. She'd wondered the
same thing.

"Your face is different, your clothes are different," he said.
"Your manner of speaking, the color of your hair and eyes.
You've succeeded in changing all of those things. But the
way you laugh, the way you make *me* laugh, the way you
tease, and blush, and kiss, and make love...and care so damn
much about me and my family—none of that has changed."

Held by the fire in those golden-brown eyes—a fire that
stirred her very soul—she fantasized for a moment, a brief,
beautiful moment, that she could let herself love him...give
him everything he wanted, always....

"Even while my logic told me I was wrong," he whispered, "I knew in my heart you belonged to me. I recognized
you, Jen, on the deepest level possible...as my woman. My
mate. My one and only. And I knew I had to hold on to you.

Just as I've known, since the day you disappeared, that if you were alive, you'd come back to me."

She blinked back scalding tears. "But I didn't. I tried to get away from you. I ran. I threatened to swear out a restraining order against you."

"You came to my room and made love to me. You stayed in my home, slept in my bed. And what made that possible was your move to Sunrise. Out of all the places in the world, Jen, why did you choose Sunrise?"

"Because I...I like it. It's beautiful, and serene, and quaint."

"And we'd planned to build our home there. Whether you admit it to yourself or not, deep down inside, you believed I'd move to Sunrise someday. And I did. Do you know why? Not because of the scenery, Jen. I can show you hundreds of scenic little coves along dozens of coastlines. I settled in Sunrise to feel close to you. To walk on the beach that we'd chosen as our own. To build the home that I'd promised to build for you." He shook his head, his expression fierce. "No, it wasn't a coincidence that we met again."

Transfixed by the heat of his stare, the passion of his words, she realized he was right. She hadn't admitted it, even to herself, but from the first day she'd lived in Sunrise, she *had* nursed a secret, burning fantasy, deep in her heart of hearts, that he'd return—and fall in love with her again.

Taking her face between his hands, he swore in an ardent whisper, "I love you, Jen."

Her heart stood still. She loved him so much! But that love could only destroy him. In desperation, she tore her gaze away from his. *Even the innocent suffer.*

"Don't be afraid to love me," he urged with a demanding stare. "I love you. I want to marry you, and live with you. I don't care where or how. And I'm not afraid."

Choking back a sob, she gave in to the horrific need and slid her arms tightly around him. "But I *am* afraid," she whispered against his ear. "Because I do love you. I'm scared that I won't find the strength to leave you again. And if you're with me, you could be injured or killed. I'd rather die than let that happen."

He groaned and cursed and kissed her throat, her cheek, her eyelids. Her mouth. Deeply, then. Possessively. The kiss ended in loud, labored breaths and hot-eyed stares. "And I'd rather die than let you go."

"No...no..." She frowned, cradled his jaw between her palms and feathered tender kisses across his face. "Don't say that! You've already been hurt. Almost shot. I couldn't bear it if—"

He cut her off with another passionate kiss, molding her body to his with long, hard caresses and needful groans. The heat grew to a startling intensity.

But just as they fell together onto the sofa with serious intent, the intercom buzzed.

"Don't answer it," he breathed.

"I have to, or they'll think something's wrong." And something *was* wrong. She was giving in to his kisses, his lovemaking, even knowing she'd have to leave him again. Now that she realized the depth of his love for her—his willingness to sacrifice everything—the pain was more excruciating than ever. Struggling to normalize her voice, she reached for the telephone and hit the intercom button. "Y-yes?"

"Jennie, we have another...development." The sobriety of Dan's tone left no doubt of his urgency. "We need to talk. I'll be right down."

Before she and Trev had the chance to do more than extricate themselves from each other's arms and straighten their hair and clothing, Dan arrived. Oddly enough, he carried a videotape and headed directly for the television. "Please, sit down," he urged, inserting the tape into the VCR.

Jennifer sank down onto the sofa in the warm curve of

Trev's arm, needing his warm, solid strength to help her weather this new "development." He was a comfort she wouldn't have for long. She loved him too much to allow him to stay with her. Her heart bled at that thought.

"I feel the best way to break this news to you, Jennie," said Dan, "is by letting your father explain it himself. He elected not to tell you in person, but insisted that I record this video."

"Record a video? He has something to say, but won't speak to me in person?"

Rather than replying, Dan turned on the television, clicked a button and started the video.

"Hello there, Princess." Vick Palmieri's swarthy face appeared on the screen and his gruff voice filled the room. "Yeah, yeah, I know. You're mad as hell that you have to watch this video instead of talking to me in person. Calm down and listen to what I'm telling you."

Jennifer watched her father shift his large, formidable frame into a more comfortable position in a leather armchair, then stare wordlessly for a moment into the camera. His face had been surgically altered, as hers had been, and he'd shaven his formerly silvering head completely bald. His eyes were blue now instead of black, and he looked much older than the last time she'd seen him. She wouldn't have recognized him on the street. Which, she realized, was a good thing.

"You should have told me about your husband. He's not a bad guy. He keeps decent beer in the house and fairly good cigars." A glint of humor lightened his gaze, and for a reason she couldn't quite grasp, Jennifer's throat began to tighten.

His humor soon faded. "When the feds first explained why you had to go into the Program with me, you said something I never forgot. You told me that I'd 'ripped your heart out.' At the time, I thought you were talking about your mother, and how I let her down. Now I know you meant the marriage you left behind.

"You should have told me, Carly. I didn't think I could feel any lower than I already did, but when I realized what I'd done to you..." He shook his head. "I gotta do what's right. I'm going home. I'm moving back to the neighborhood."

Jennifer gasped and tried to rise. Trev's arm tightened to keep her seated.

"Now, don't go thinking I'm doing this just because of you," her father said. "I ain't. I'm sick and tired of living around a bunch of strangers, with no one knowing or caring who I am or where I came from." Anger flashed in his face, and he thumped his chest with his forefinger. "I'm Vick Palmieri. I do what I think is right, and I'm not ashamed of that. I might have made mistakes. Plenty of 'em. But I'm not gonna die hiding like some yellow-bellied jellyfish. No more blue contact lenses, no more sissy clothes, no more aliases. When I get up from this chair, I'm changing back into *me*. My enemies want to whack me, they can try. I still have people on my side. The slime I put behind bars has more enemies than allies. I'm ready to take 'em on."

"Oh, my God," Jennifer murmured, her vision blurring with unshed tears. "He's going back into it."

"Hey, Princess," Vick called to her from the television screen, sounding stronger and more dynamic than he had since her uncle's murder, so many years ago. "I know you're gonna try to stop me. That's why I'm cutting out before you see this video. You gotta understand—I'm feeling better already. I can't keep living like a schmo. Big Vick's back, and that's nothing to cry over. And you—" he shook a threatening finger at her, his voice suddenly stern, his expression one she remembered from her childhood "—you go live with your husband. No more running away. Make lots of babies. Trev Montgomery, you take care of her and the grandchildren she gives me, or next time we meet up, I'll have to kill you." Someone who didn't know him might have missed the glint of lightheartedness in his eyes...and a deeper, underlying emotion that struck a vibrant chord in Jennifer.

The video faded to static. Dan shut off the VCR.

Jennifer sat with her knuckles pressed to her lips. He was on his way. Back to the old life. And possibly, his death. The emotions clutching her were every bit as surprising as the decision he'd reached. Because even though her heart ached at the danger he faced, she was glad for him.

Glad. The times she'd seen him in hiding, she'd known he was dying inside. She'd known that everything important had bled out of his life, and that death wasn't looking as grim to him as it once had. He'd never been a saint, but he was willing to pay for his mistakes...and he'd always lived by his own code of honor. If he died by that code of honor, so be it.

"Jen?" Trev nudged her chin with his thumb, drawing her attention. "Are you okay?"

Taking the question into solemn consideration, she thought about the expression she'd seen in her father's eyes by the end of that video. It was the look of a man breaking free from his shackles. Come what may, he'd set out on a journey for either liberty or death. He wasn't the kind of man who could settle for anything in between.

Slowly Jennifer nodded. She supposed she *was* okay.

"You understand what this means for you, don't you, Jennie?" Dan asked.

She glanced at him. "Actually, no. What does it mean?"

"As soon as Vick lets it be known that he's back, your part in this drama is over."

"Over?"

"More or less. I know about these men we're up against. I've studied everything about them for years—from rap sheets to wiretaps to informants' reports. His enemies want *him.* Big Vick himself. The only reason they'd take the time and trouble to hunt you down is to draw him out of hiding.

Once he's out, they'll have no interest in you. I wouldn't advise taking back the name Palmieri or visiting the old neighborhood anytime soon—vengeance may still seem sweet to the ones he crossed, if there's not too much effort involved. But with a little common sense, you can go about your business as you did before Vick testified."

"No," Trev said, drawing her closer to him. "That's not good enough." As much as he wanted her to be free, Dan's prognosis didn't sound like a guarantee. He couldn't stand the thought that Dan might have miscalculated. "Unless we know for sure that there's no threat to her—none whatsoever—she's staying in the Program."

Jen gazed at him in clear surprise, as if she might contradict him. He braced himself for the fight. He wouldn't back down on this point. Of course, she hadn't given him the right to speak for her, or even to participate in the decision-making process. She hadn't even given him any real hope of remaining in her life, other than the love she'd confessed to feeling for him. He intended to work on that with everything he had.

"Either way," Dan said to Jen, "whether you stay in the Program or not, I see no reason to change your name from Jennifer Hannah, or for you to move away from Sunrise. The only one who has breached your cover is Trev. As long as you intend to stay married to him, that shouldn't be a problem. Or maybe I should say, as long as you intend *to marry* him. As Jennifer Hannah, you're currently a single woman in the eyes of the law. If you decide you'd rather remain single—" Dan hesitated "—we'd have to rethink our strategy."

Trev and Jen glanced at each other, and tension gripped Trev with an iron fist as he tried to read her intentions. Would she stay with him?

"As far as my paperwork goes—" Dan leaned forward, his elbows on his knees, his hands clasped between them, his gaze on Jen. "There will be no mention of Trev Montgomery, or any previous marriage for Jennifer Hannah."

A beautiful smile slowly blossomed in her eyes.

Trev had a hard time looking away from her, when Dan shifted his focus to him.

"Which means there's no reason at all for you to go into the Program, Mr. Montgomery. You're not connected to the Palmieri case in any way."

Realizing the scope and importance of the favor Dan was granting him, Trev slowly nodded and gripped his hand in a deeply grateful handshake.

When they'd drawn back from the clasp, Dan crossed his arms, cocked his head and squinted at him. "For the sake of doing better next time, Trev, I'd like to know where we went wrong in disguising her. We had the best cosmetic surgeons in the business engineering the change in her appearance. How the hell did you recognize her?"

Jennifer tightened her fists in her lap as she waited for his reply. She hadn't wanted Dan to know about the days and nights they'd spent together—the intimacy they'd shared....

"She's my wife."

Dan stared at him for a long while. And though Jennifer half expected him to repeat the question, the U.S. Marshals security supervisory inspector nodded and sat back in his chair. "My hat's off to you, sir. She looks nothing like she did before. I don't believe anyone else will recognize her. Ever. Let me just say, Jennie, that if your fictional friend from high school had really existed, I'd have bet my last dime that she wouldn't have suspected a thing."

Jennifer smiled at the man who had proven to be her friend, her heart buoying up with irrepressible lightness. "Do me a favor, Dan. Don't book that bet with anyone named Vick."

Dan grinned, and before he left them for the night, squeezed her in a hearty hug. In an oddly earnest tone, he told her, "Things may look even brighter in a few weeks or so."

As she shut the door behind him and slid the dead bolt into place, she frowned and turned to Trev, wondering what Dan had meant by that cryptic comment.

Trev clearly mistook the cause of her knitted brows, and pulled her firmly into his arms with an answering frown. "I know, I know, I had no right to tell him that you were staying in the Program. And I have no right to hold you, either." He ran his large, strong hands down the curve of her back and pressed her into tight, provocative alignment against his hardening body. "Or to have you, every night and day for the rest of my life." He brushed his mouth in slow, light passes across hers, until she moaned with longing for deeper penetration, feeding the fire between them that never quite came under control. "But I want those rights, Jen," he whispered hoarsely. "Starting now."

She didn't argue. She melded into his kiss, stroked beneath his clothes, lured him in deeper, in every way she could. They soon lost sight of everything but the love that drove them together in a fever of sumptuous lovemaking.

It wasn't until morning, as she lay naked and languid against him, that Trev demanded confirmation of the answer he believed she'd given him. "You're not going to leave me, Jen. You're here in my arms to stay." Cautiously he peered into her face. "Aren't you?"

Her soft, loving smile transformed her from the sweetest, sexiest, most beautiful woman he'd ever seen into the very lifeblood of his heart and soul. "I'll never leave you, Trev," she swore, smoothing reverent fingers along the curve of his face. "I learned a lesson from my father yesterday—maybe the last he'll ever teach me. There are certain freedoms that make a person's life worth living. For me—" she gazed with glowing, heated sincerity "—it's the freedom to love you. I'm ready to fight for that in any way I have to."

His love for her pulsed and flowed in strong, hard currents. "Marry me, Jennifer Diana Carly Hannah Montgomery—or whatever name you end up with. Marry me."

She kissed him with the most beguiling tenderness, stirring him more deeply than he'd ever imagined possible. "Everyone will say you're in love with me," she murmured, "because I remind you of your first wife."

"They won't know how right they are."

Pursing her lips, she tilted her head and narrowed her gaze at him—her schoolteacher look that never failed to make him smile. "You aren't marrying me just to save money, are you?"

He raised a questioning brow.

"A hundred dollars a night," she mused, "times sixty years or more...."

He pulled her roughly to him, ready to start the next round. "Put it on my tab."

_____Epilogue_____

SHOUTS OF "Author, author!" gave way to wild applause, whistles and a standing ovation, as Jen led her writing partner from their front-row table to the stage of The Georgia Seaside Dinner Theater. Squeezing the older woman's delicate but capable hand, Jen beamed at Babs as they took their bows. In her long gauzy skirt, flowing blouse and turquoise necklaces, her brown eyes lit with a smile and her many silver earrings glittering in the stage lights, Trev's grandmother looked ages younger than Jen had ever seen her.

"We did it, Di," she crowed between the kisses she blew to the audience.

"It's _Jen_, Babs. The name's Jen."

"Oh. Yeah."

Jen suspected that most people took Babs's occasional slips as age-induced forgetfulness. Jen knew better, of course. The old gal was as sharp as a tack. With hands still joined and smiles beaming, they took another bow, gratified by the audience's response to the debut of their romantic comedy.

After the red velvet curtains had swept to a close, their favorite fans met them at the stage door with hugs, kisses and joyous grins—Veronica, Trev's soft-spoken sister who had recently entered med school; Sammy, as blond and high-spirited as ever at the age of seventeen; two young teenage girls from the school for the hearing impaired, both clearly enamored of Sammy, judging from the giggles and sign language flashing between them; and Phyllis, Jen's partner at the Helping Hand Staffing Services.

Jen still teased Phyllis about how she had mistaken Trev's name for "Montero" instead of "Montgomery" when he'd come to hire their services. Phyllis teased Jennifer about the kind of services she must have provided, considering she'd come back two weeks later married to the man.

The man himself towered at the fringe of their merry little group, his smiling, golden-brown gaze lingering on her. The mere connection of their gazes filled her with sensuous warmth. They would celebrate her success in their own way, later tonight, in the dreamy seaside house he'd built for her.

With a start of surprise, she noticed that Trev carried a huge bouquet of long-stemmed red roses. "Oh, Trev, they're beautiful," she murmured, as he made his way to her. "But you didn't have to buy me *more.* The bouquet at home is too extravagant already."

"This one's not from me. The hostess said it just arrived." He studied the two-dozen roses, then slanted her a dramatically stern glance. "I don't have a rival that I'm unaware of, do I?"

She smiled at him with so much love, she knew he had to see it blazing from her eyes. "Not one, in the whole world."

He shifted closer, the warmth in his smile intensifying, and she almost forgot about the roses. Almost. Her curiosity over who had sent them was simply too great to be ignored.

Evading his intensity with a deliberately teasing grin, she took the bouquet from his arms, carried it to their table and plucked a small envelope from the midst of the fragrant roses. The envelope was addressed to "Mrs. Montgomery." Inside the card was written in a bold, concise hand, *I'm sure your father would be proud. Best regards, Vick.*

Warmth crowded her chest and misted her eyes.

Before she had a chance to hand the card to Trev, Sammy loomed over her shoulder and read it out loud. "Hey, isn't

Vick that gangster friend of yours, Jen? The one they made the movie about?"

"Well, he's not a gangster *anymore*. I mean, that was the point of the movie, wasn't it? To show how he—"

But Sammy had turned away to address his two young admirers. "Did you see that movie about Big Vick Palmieri? Yeah, well, Jen knows him. The real guy, not just the actor. He sent us passes to go see the premiere of the movie in Hollywood. It was awesome—especially the scene where he goes walking into that warehouse. I thought he was *dead*, man."

Jen winced, unable to help it, even after all these years.

"But then he hits the ground, and the bullets start flying. It really *was* a setup by the feds, wasn't it, Jen? In real life, I mean. I heard about it on the news. They wiped out the rest of that crime family. What was their name again?"

"Uh, Sammy, the girls probably aren't all that interested in gangsters." Trev slid a supportive arm around Jen. "Besides, it looks like your grandmother can use help with those flowers. Why don't you go carry them to her car?"

As Sammy loped off toward his grandmother with the girls in close pursuit, Jen slid her arm around her husband's waist and hugged him. Though she knew she was being oversensitive, she cringed at reminders of the trap the federal agents had indeed set. No one had ever admitted it to her, of course, but they'd clearly allowed her father to use himself as bait to provoke his enemies into carelessness.

A team of federal agents had caught them in the act of drawing their guns and neatly finished them off.

Hollywood had come a-knocking. Big Vick retired in style. The last she'd heard, he was vacationing in Europe. He apparently didn't feel entirely free of the past, though, or he wouldn't have insisted on maintaining the secrecy of their relationship.

She supposed it was for the best. She felt safer as Jennifer

Hannah Montgomery. In fact, she felt as if "Jen" had always been her name.

"Uh-oh," Trev muttered beside her, his attention fixed on the stage. "I recognize that look in my grandmother's eyes. It's going to be an all-nighter."

Jen turned in time to see Babs call out from the stage, "Hey, everyone! Let's all meet at my beach cottage in thirty minutes. It's time to party!" A rowdy cheer went up, not only from their intimate group of family and friends, but also from the actors, technical crew, stage hands, waitresses, and everyone else lingering in the theater after the bulk of the crowd had left.

Babs, it seemed, had become a local favorite since renting a cottage nearby for the summer.

In the ensuing commotion, Jen looked around for Christopher and Yvonne. They'd been helpful critics during the three years she and Babs had worked on the play. Glancing around the massive dining room where waitresses and busboys cleared dishes from tables, Jen didn't see her two young in-laws anywhere.

"Trev, have you seen Christopher and Yvonne?"

"They were sitting right behind us when the curtain opened."

"You looking for Chris and Yvonne?" Sammy piped up from behind Jen.

Jen nodded.

Sammy jerked his thumb toward the darkened balcony. "Last time I saw 'em, they were headed up those stairs. Hey, isn't that them, in the last booth? Yeah, I think it is. I'll go tell them we're leaving."

He started toward the stairs.

Trev and Jen shot each other wide-eyed glances, then dove after Sammy. Trev grabbed his arm; Jen caught a fistful of his shirt. "Let's just give them time to, uh, finish their meal in private," Trev suggested.

"I'm sure they'll be down soon," added Jen.

Sammy shrugged and bounded off with the rest of their party, headed for Babs's place.

Trev and Jen met in a private huddle, trying to stifle their laughter—at least until the kids were out of earshot. Once locked together in the huddle, though, neither was in a particular rush to let go.

"Since our booth is taken," Trev whispered, drawing her body flush against his, "why don't you and I go find an elevator somewhere? I hear a lot of action takes place in elevators."

She kissed his neck, nipped at his ear, and asked in a throaty murmur, "Are you willing to hold the close button?"

He considered the prospect, then shook his head. "Nah. Hey...what about an air-hockey table?"

She slanted him a wicked glance. "Did you bring a cherry lollipop?"

He patted the pockets of his jeans. "Fresh out."

"Well, then. Looks like we'll just have to go home and...improvise."

Trev liked the suggestion. Plans sparked and simmered in his mind. As usual, though, he didn't stand a chance of resisting his incorrigible wife. Before they'd even reached the expressway, his plans took a slight turn—a hot, desperate one—into the first secluded spot along the highway.

ROMANTIC FANTASIES COME ALIVE WITH

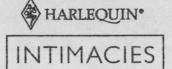

HARLEQUIN®

INTIMACIES

Harlequin is turning up the heat with this seductive collection!

Experience the passion as the heroes and heroines explore their deepest desires, their innermost secrets. Get lost in these tantalizing stories that will leave you wanting more!

Available in November at your favorite retail outlet:

OUT OF CONTROL by Candace Schuler
NIGHT RHYTHMS by Elda Minger
SCANDALIZED! by Lori Foster
PRIVATE FANTASIES by Janelle Denison

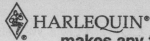

HARLEQUIN®
makes any time special—online...

shop eHarlequin

- ♥ Find all the new Harlequin releases at everyday great discounts.
- ♥ Try before you buy! Read an excerpt from the latest Harlequin novels.
- ♥ Write an online review and share your thoughts with others.

reading room

- ♥ Read our Internet exclusive daily and weekly online serials, or vote in our interactive novel.
- ♥ Talk to other readers about your favorite novels in our Reading Groups.
- ♥ Take our Choose-a-Book quiz to find the series that matches you!

authors' alcove

- ♥ Find out interesting tidbits and details about your favorite authors' lives, interests and writing habits.
- ♥ Ever dreamed of being an author? Enter our Writing Round Robin. The Winning Chapter will be published online! Or review our writing guidelines for submitting your novel.

HINTB1

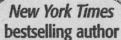

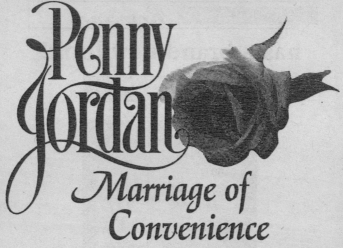

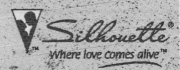

**All they wanted for
Christmas was…
each other!**

DECK
THE
HALLS by

MARGOT
EARLY

HEATHER
MacALLISTER

**It was the season for miracles.
And they definitely needed one….**

When biologist Jean Young joined David Blade and his son on their
boat, she never dreamed she'd end up surrounded by scandal—
or desperately in love with this unsmiling man who had too
many secrets and a little boy longing for a mother's kiss.

Bankruptcy lawyer Adam Markland had earned a reputation for
getting what he wanted—and he wanted smart, sexy Holly Hall.
Little did he guess it was his reputation as a cutthroat attorney
that was keeping her permanently out of his reach.

---

2 Complete Novels

---

at the **LOW PRICE** of $4.99 U.S./$5.99 CAN.!

Look for **DECK THE HALLS** on sale in November 2000.